COMING FROM AN OFF-KEY TIME

■ □ ■ □ ■

WRITINGS FROM AN UNBOUND EUROPE

GENERAL EDITOR
Andrew Wachtel

EDITORIAL BOARD
Clare Cavanagh
Michael Henry Heim
Roman Koropeckyj
Ilya Kutik

Coming from an Off-Key Time

A Novel

BOGDAN SUCEAVĂ

Translated from the Romanian
by Alistair Ian Blyth

NORTHWESTERN UNIVERSITY PRESS
EVANSTON, ILLINOIS

Northwestern University Press
www.nupress.northwestern.edu

This book is published with the support of the Translation and Publication Support
Programme of the Romanian Cultural Institute, Bucharest.

Printed in the United States of America

10   9   8   7   6   5   4   3   2   1

Library of Congress Cataloging-in-Publication Data

Suceavă, Bogdan, 1969–
    [Venea din timpul diez. English]
    Coming from an off-key time : a novel / Bogdan Suceavă ; translated from the
Romanian by Alistair Ian Blyth.
        p. cm. — (Writings from an unbound Europe)
    "First published in Romanian under the title Venea din timpul diez. Copyright
© 2004 by Editura Polirom."
    Includes bibliographical references.
    ISBN 978-0-8101-2684-8 (pbk. : alk. paper)
    1. Romania—History—1989—Fiction. I. Blyth, Alistair Ian. II. Title. III. Series:
Writings from an unbound Europe.
    PC840.429.U34V4613 2011
    859'.3—dc22
                                                                            2010028927

∞ The paper used in this publication meets the minimum requirements of the American
National Standard for Information Sciences—Permanence of Paper for Printed Library
Materials, ANSI Z39.48-1992.

Bucharest had remained faithful to its old custom of corruption; at every step we remembered that we were at the gates of the Orient. But nevertheless, the debauchery astonished me less than the insanity that dominated in every case; I confess that I had not expected to see such numerous and various species of folly flourishing, to meet such unbridled madness. As I was not to find almost anyone who, sooner or later, did not reveal some vice or other, anyone whom, unexpectedly, I did not have occasion to hear raving, in the end I lost hope of meeting, in the flesh and blood, any human being wholly sound of mind.

Mateiu Caragiale, *The Rakes of the Old Court*

■ □ ■ □ ■

CONTENTS

■ □ ■ □ ■

COMING FROM AN OFF-KEY TIME

■ □ ■ □ ■

CHAPTER ONE

THE STORYTELLER IS I. EVEN BACK THEN YOU KNEW THE END OF history and you saw, just as a bird peering down from the upper air sees the ants and the torrent coming at the anthill as the ants sun themselves, everything that was to come, from the moment of his entry into Bucharest to the last gasp of his prophecies. When he entered the city, no one expected him to cover himself in glory, and he did not come riding on a donkey, beneath olive branches, although the expectation that was floating in the air had long been foreordained to him. We were all expecting a miracle. Do you remember the 1990s, with all their mysteries and untold history? Behold the time has now come to write their true chronicle. For a long time it was said that on his arrival he had no face, that not until later did his visage coalesce in contact with the city air, or rather in contact with itself, an unheard-of coagulation of being. It was said that he had been born in the Transylvanian village of Weissdorf, which nowadays no longer exists or is marked on the maps, from a Saxon father and a Serbian mother, and that from the very moment she raised him in her arms the midwife had been astonished by the mark that covered his chest and which at first sight seemed merely an ugly deformity, a birthmark. And so they believed until the day when someone saw the babe with his chest bared and said, "Holy Virgin Mother of God, do you know what that mark is?"

The truth is that the peasants of that village which time forgot had never traveled far, and their minds did not dwell on things which lay beyond the bounds of the village. Seeing the child's bare chest and tracing the mark imprinted on the translucent skin, that old man, more widely traveled than the others, said, "The middle line here is Victory Avenue, then Gheorghiu-Dej Boulevard, Victory Square, the Titan District, this circle is the Ring Road, and this semicircle is Barracks Road, here is Herăstrău Lake, and these are the streets of the Linden Quarter."

When his chest wrinkled up, the map would shift, forming alternations, successions, slippages and expanses, corresponding not to a single time, but to a limitless series of images, whose beginning and end were obscure. Things could just as well be narrated from end to beginning, and this is what that peasant saw, although he was unschooled and lacking in any prophetic gift, for he said, fearfully, "I've never heard the like before. I don't know what kind of a birthmark this is, but it looks like what you'd never even imagine."

In fact, others said that it was not like that at all. It was impossible for a map of Bucharest to appear on the skin of a baby whose mother was Serbian and who had been born in the village of Valea Rea, below Nehoiu Mountain, to a family of sheep breeders who of old used to take their flocks as far as Stara Zagora and then back again every spring, but who today take them up to the Gemenea sheepfold, where the only white bears in the Carpathian Mountains had once been sighted. An old midwife is supposed to have delivered the child and to have recognized the birthmark when she washed him, a clump of blood and fortune and breath, saying, "This is the sign of the end of all times or the sign of all times together."

And she was also to say, prophesying from the very start something that an entire nation has been awaiting for centuries, "It is a map of the second Jerusalem, a sign begotten, not made, a sign from the Lord and which demands worship."

For which reason she spat on the babe thrice, to guard against the evil eye, lifted him into the air toward the dwellings of the four winds, and then proffered him to the sun.

It is not known whether the tale was concocted afterward, when his room was being trodden night after night by thousands of phantasms and he had begun to drape his mirrors with white cloths and to pray aloud. But that was another time.

Later, they said something else about him: that he had been the only man under the sun to be born twice. The two lives glimmered far from each other and simultaneously, but in neither was his body whole, or solid, but merely a mist, so that you would have been able to see through it, just as there are many transparent children throughout Wallachia. And the famed entrance into Bucharest, of which some rumors told, would have been no more than the meeting of the two lives, the intertwining of the two bodies, the weaving of two hearts into one, the superimposition of sign upon sign on two chests. This process cannot have been painless, and all we know—having read the documents, the records of some of the witnesses, the newspapers from the time, and according to the things we too recall—is that on the evening of November 4, 1992, an ambulance with vehicle registration number 17-B-1504 brought an emaciated, feverish young man to the emergency section of the Municipal Hospital, and that in the first moments no one paid him any mind. We have no X-rays which might have recorded what was happening to his body at that moment, nor any illusions that the first medical observations were correct or sufficiently attentive. They did not know what they were looking at. They had that unique, admirable, wonderful phenomenon beneath their eyes, and they did not know what they were looking at. It is human nature to suppose that every being with two hands, two eyes, and a chest is necessarily a man. However, the chemical reality is surpassed by the metachemical, by virtue of which each one of us is different, although the prejudice is widespread that we are all made up of the same stuff. His fever rose endlessly—and it was only when it reached 44°C that a nurse observed that his eyes were shining much too brightly and his lips were murmuring and his veins were boiling, as though a Transylvanian and a Wallachian destiny were being mingled, as though the heavens were boiling together with the loam. She heard him say something, and this is what she thought it was: "Follow me with angel cohorts, to the new birth, in time."

It made no sense, did it? It would have been no different from the delirium of any one of the raving madmen in the ward, had it not been for the crystal clarity of the diction, the correct and clear pronunciation, as though what must be said had not yet been said, and now the chosen moment had come, the hour when the air would whirl with words around him, restorative words, healing spells, binding formulas, most of which had never before been heard, spoken, thought.

"Hmm, yes," said Dr. Pamfilie, who happened to be on duty, "there is nothing out of the ordinary that is wrong with him; he has a fever typical of those they've been bringing in off the streets lately, the glue-sniffers who sleep in the sewers. Everything's normal. Give him an aspirin. Allow him to leave."

On his hospital discharge sheet the name Vespasian Moisa could be read, inscribed by a careless hand. It is the first document about him, because before it there is nothing. No birth certificate, no school report, no vaccination record, absolutely nothing.

It is here that the story of beginnings concludes, and also our documentation, for the facts now become as fine as Bible paper, as spiderwebs, as thoughts of love. We pick up the thread of history a month later, in Piteşti, at a lecture which professor of history Diaconescu, one of the town's worthies, was about to deliver to an almost empty auditorium. It was winter. At that time, the professor was nearing the final horizon of the theory that had been his life's work. He had first expounded it at a history conference in 1985, where he had garnered merely shrugs and smiles, then he had worked on it together with renowned physician Apolodor Arghir, constructing arguments for the details or rather technical components of the medical side of the theory. In the first instance, the professor had had no success of any kind when expounding his ideas, perhaps also because dictatorial oppression quelled in its swaddling clothes the energy of many superb ideas back then, the enthusiasm of many inventors and creators, as well as the elegant proofs of many savants, mathematicians, logicians, philosophers, and scientists. Professor Diaconescu drank coffee without sugar, was a vegetarian, wore sandals without socks in order to ensure continuous aeration of the foot (however hard it was for him, he remained true to this principle even in winter), and talked much about Sartre, one of his favorite philosophers. At the political level, he was an unconditional admirer of Gandhi. After the professor's lecture, the young man who presented himself as Vespasian Moisa asked him, "Have you thought of writing a book about all this?"

The professor felt awkward, sitting there, in front of an empty hall, in the presence of five or six members of the naturist club.

"My dear man," answered the professor with an absent smile, "neither literature nor theory can influence history."

He was very much in the right: all the pages to which he had put the finishing touches were invariably marred by a literary note. In essence, his theory had nothing literary about it, but the lyrical air that absolutely all his texts acquired gave them a confused character, which captivated for a moment, but no more than a moment, the reader or audience. And this is what it was all about. According to the classic theories of the 1950s and '60s, the Gaeto-Dacians are supposed to have arrived north of the Danube around the year 3000 B.C. In the 1970s, an idea began to be accredited according to which the Gaeto-Dacians had arrived together with the first waves of Indo-Europeans, probably a thousand years earlier. Professor Diaconescu was more categorical: he confidently put forward the year 5000 B.C., and elaborated vehement arguments using heterogeneous passages from ancient writers such as Dio Cassius, Herodotus, and Apuleius, as well as George Coşbuc, Octavian Goga, and others. Once this part of the theory had been thoroughly demonstrated, the professor argued that even back then the Gaeto-Dacians spoke the same Romanian as we speak today, which made the language more than seven thousand years old and transformed our everyday idiom into the oldest living tongue on the planet. Of course, as the professor argued polemically, there is a theory that Romanian is a descendent of Latin. It is a widespread theory, and in some cases it is even studied in school . . . Maybe, of course, but that aspect of succession ought to be a question much older than the year 5000 B.C., which is to say, it doesn't even concern us today. The essential fact is that the Romanian language is an extremely ancient idiom and that it must be read and interpreted in terms of a code. We can speak of a true understanding of the Romanian language only after deciphering the initial and highly secret meaning codified in the syllables and letters of every word. As the Romanian language has a phonetic orthography, decipherment does not depend on writing: an analogous truth would have been arrived at even if texts written in Slavonic script had been analyzed. The professor was convinced that, beyond the words of Romanian, there lies a code that not even the wisest initiates have ever deciphered. He liked to say that the Romanian language is the combination to the safe of the universe; it is a means of access at mankind's fingertips, for

CHAPTER ONE

discovery and understanding—as though God had slipped the house key under the mat.

The first person the professor convinced was his nephew, Emanuel. The truth is that Emanuel was a young man of sincere patriotic sentiments, in whom the theory of the antiquity of the Romanian language found fertile ground, just as a seed borne on the wind might find mellow and fruitful soil. Emanuel's education had been highly complex, including not only good marks at school, but also plentiful listening to the radio and watching television. Since the times when he had listened intensively to the propaganda spectacles of the Flame Cenacle on the radio, which were broadcast every Thursday evening and which he attended twenty-six times, not only in Pitești, but also in Titu, Costești, Găiești, Topoloveni, Leordeni, Bragadiru, Vedea, and various other venues, Emanuel had been left so sensitized that it verged on trauma. For him, the impression had been so profound that the magical slogan *The First of December Unites Us* would lave him in tears, and the lines *And nonetheless a love exists, / And nonetheless a curse exists,* even when hummed softly, would provoke in him brief erections, as fleeting as summer rains, concluding spasmodically, leaving him drained and breathless.

The professor expounded his partial conclusions to Emanuel in the spring of 1989. This took place in the professor's room one evening, in the spring of 1989, while through the open window streamed the noise-saturated air of the most congested road in north Pitești. "Let us imagine that the Romanian language were written using ideograms, no different from Japanese," said the professor, launching into his argument with disheveled hair and wagging finger. "Let us imagine that each ideogram corresponded to a syllable. Each syllable would have not only a phonetic value, but also a secondary signification, codified by the passage of millennia, one that might contain the hidden remedy for the restoration of the respective thing to its initial meaning, in the case of its deterioration over seven thousand years."

The professor had easily managed to decipher the fact that *so* or *sol* meant "sun," and it followed that the word *solitudine* (solitude) could be translated "one born under a solitary sun." *Ridiche* (radish) meant something odd: "pe mine mie redă-mă" ("render me unto myself"). His nephew Emanuel was enthused, although he kept asking all kinds of stupid details:

"How do we know that the Gaeto-Dacians had the word *solitu-dine*?"

"I have no doubt," said the professor, nodding, his eyes closed, as though in a trance. "The two languages are, at this level of vocabulary, identical. It is something that has been sensed since the late eighteenth century, since the time of Samuil Micu. The old man scented it, without a doubt!"

Then the professor added, "But what does all this mean?"

For it seemed to him that his theory was merely part of a much broader, much deeper whole.

The Romanian language must be milked of meanings, as he also used to say. The verbs must be liquefied, the root of the meanings unraveled, the steam of its boiling appraised, the space between its substantives wrung, for there the Lord God, He Who Is, fearful be His name, has placed the key to redemptive meanings. If you follow that key, you can collect the cures for which mankind has forever struggled. It is incredible how clear and how simple it all is. All ideas of genius were, he believed, simple, were natural; they could be communicated straightforwardly. For example, Einstein: everything is relative, damn it. That's not a complicated idea, is it? Emanuel nodded and agreed that no, it wasn't.

Dr. Apolodor Arghir was passionate about the idea that he might discover at least one of those golden cures. He wasn't a man to dream his whole life about finding a cure for cancer, leukemia, or diabetes, but a man with his feet on the ground, with down-to-earth thoughts and desires: a tall man, with a rotund face, with large, blue eyes, who walked with a slight stoop, thrusting before him a gleaming bald pate, wholly vindicated of hair. Dr. Arghir dreamed of discovering a definitive cure for baldness, which he had come to regard, in its totality, as toxic both for physician and patient. He had lost all interest in professional reviews, treatises, and conferences, and had begun more and more to believe in the traditional, natural medicine that had been practiced before Vasile Alecsandri frequented anatomy courses in Paris in the 1830s. It was during the period when Dr. Arghir was appointed communist party secretary at Piteşti Municipal Hospital, immediately after receiving official acceptance of his application to purchase a navy-blue Dacia motorcar with a walnut dashboard. The conference he organized at the Municipal Hospital on that occasion was entitled

New Research with a View to Curing Cancer and was open to healers from all over the world, regardless of their academic qualifications or the political regime of their country of origin. The conference was a grand affair, reported by Reuters and TASS. To the symposium also came witch doctor Ougadou Li Gamba Wazaba Mimou, whose son was studying dentistry in Bucharest on a grant from the Democratic Republic of Zaire, and who performed a dance to extirpate tumors which shocked and enthused the audience, inducing fainting fits and ecchymoses. He was accompanied to Pitești by a troupe of twelve bongo players, who shook the hospital building to its foundations. The scars can still be seen today.

For a time, until he met Professor Diaconescu, Dr. Arghir tried various experimental forms of treating the sick through music (his experience with the witch doctor from Zaire had set him seriously thinking). He ascribed these inclinations to his being related, through a common ancestor, whose documentary attestation he considered to have been recorded around the year 1770 in a document recovered with difficulty from a village in the Caucasus, to great musicians of Armenian origin, including Charles Aznavour. He had begun to think about whether the only cure for cancer could be Bach. His patients, many in desperate medical situations, signed the form agreeing to experimental treatment and began sessions of listening to music and drinking medicinal tea. It is said that Dr. Arghir gave up this project during the spring in which news of his irreducible infirmity spread through town: he was completely tone-deaf. He could no more treat people by music than a mole could explain the color harmonies in a Picasso portrait or the texture of a sunset seen from the beach at Costinești. The rumor became public following the confession of a music teacher, the doctor's mistress, who had for a long time tried, during moments of reclusion, to motivate her lover with Ravel's *Bolero*, without ever receiving anything but an ambiguous response. Inasmuch as she considered that it was not a case of a colorless, odorless, insipid impotence that was amplifying with the pitiless passing of time, she continued a series of experiments whose subject was dear Apolodor, ultimately reaching the conclusion that he had no musical ear. In that period, extremely inauspicious both for his sentimental life and for his research, Dr. Arghir became close to the professor when the rumors about his musical mistress reached the ears of his wife. They spent long afternoons together, talking and smoking, hairsplitting and analyzing potential analogies between the theory of the antiquity of the codified idiom and the immutable truths of medicine. They took their comparisons as far as the level of modern studies. In the end, they decided to analyze one of the fundamental mythological motifs of the Romanian people, a myth that might date back to around the year 5000 B.C. The mandrake myth, to be exact. In fact, this was to be the unexpected care for *chelie* (baldness), insofar as the syllable *che* when added to the syllables *li* and *e*, then transformed according to a law of decryption on which the two had worked for almost three years, produced the secret name of mandrake. Baldness, which is to say mandragora. A broth of mandrake, to which they added sodium hydroxide, dried goatskin, Coca Cola, and butter, had spectacular effects, transforming any baldy into a person with a respectable endowment of hair. Dr. Arghir's public appearances after treatment were so surprising that not even the Securitate officer who had written reports on him for more than ten years recognized him any longer. A black, frizzy, gleaming Afro now covered what had long been the most celebrated baldpate in the city.

The fact that the theory was true ought to have brought thousands of patients to the two discoverers' door. However, events took an unexpected turn. One evening, after the aforementioned lecture, Professor Diaconescu received a visit from Vespasian Moisa. In the professor's office, a discussion on religious and historical topics took place. After not so much as an hour, the professor telephoned the doctor and urgently summoned him. His voice quavered, it was the voice of one who had seen the world's abysses at close hand, the ultimate things of wisdom, beyond which all truths are equal and before which imposture and endeavor are all one. He was shocked. He was beyond the boundary; he was in the land of fable.

"Our theory," he told him on the telephone, "is indubitably true and is part of something much more elevated and much closer to the heavens."

It was harder to convince the doctor: it took almost three hours. Vespasian Moisa unfolded to him a suite of devastating arguments, which implied subtleties of anatomy and logic, and, springing from the sphere of ideas, the proof which oriental wisdom had pursued for centuries: the existence of the Lord God is proven by the structure of the human body. Near midnight, the professor and the doctor knelt before Vespasian Moisa and said, "You are our Teacher!"

This took place on February 26, 1993, and constitutes the first spectacular conversion to be recorded in the history of the Teacher. In strictly philosophical terms, Diaconescu and Arghir placed their theory in the service of a belief, of a heresy, of a theoretical construct as to whose validity history would decide. The two were the first of a long line of believers convinced beyond any doubt that Vespasian Moisa was a prophet of the Lord God. Their minds did not have an exaggeratedly religious makeup, they were not religious fanatics who could barely wait to be told things about which they were already convinced, in spite of all the excesses of their previous theories. In this sense, we must speak of a spectacular conversion.

Vespasian embraced them, lifted them to their feet, and is supposed to have spoken as follows: "You have discovered your whole truth in the parts of knowledge that have been given to you. But only a man born twice could see the whole, for the whole comes from God in Heaven. I have come. I have brought you this whole. I am here for you."

When Vespasian Moisa sent word to them to come to Bucharest, a few months later, at the beginning of the summer of 1993—for the hour to integrate the City had arrived—both professor Diaconescu and Dr. Arghir dropped everything, hospital and family, and came to Bucharest. And likewise did so many others, because Vespasian was bringing Life, Truth, Freedom. It is complicated to explain, but this is how it all began.

■ □ ■ □ ■

CHAPTER TWO

IN THOSE DAYS, IN THAT PLACE OF DIABOLICAL SPLENDOR KNOWN AS Ferentari, there lived a tall young man, long of hair and white of cheek, like a maiden. We all used to see him in the University Square subway station, where, on numerous occasions, he would busk a dazzling blend of Andean melodies and rock ballads, a motley repertoire in which the place of honor was reserved for the glorious songs of Phoenix. His favorite Phoenix number was "Andrii Popa," although at home, in secret, for the sake of its flow, he also listened to the music of Mozart. He adored Mozart. His friends called him the Troubadour, but his real name was Toni. He lived with his grandmother, a cynical and highly realistic old crone, who used to tell him all day long how much she regretted that the years of economic freedom had arrived so late. And she would urge him to go into town to make some money. Her business plans had the same huge potential as those of the great interwar magnates but seemed to have been all too swiftly crushed by the fiscal obligations of the late twentieth century. Toni didn't have the business acumen for things like that. As long as he had the minimum freedom to get up at ten o'clock in the morning and set off into town with his guitar on his back, he did not care about anything else. For a while, he used to meet with other alternative music fans at the edge of Cişmigiu Park, where he attempted to join one of the eternally evolving and perpetually forming rock bands of the time. Many passersby used to mistake them for a conclave of homosexuals, strangely attired in all kinds of leather articles with ethno inflexions. But they were nothing of the sort. It was in that period that he met Margot.

Back then, Margot wore sadness in the corners of her mouth and conveyed it to all those around her as radiance. She had no plans for the future. She did not even have any plans for the day after next. She wore tight black jeans and brightly colored blouses, always in contrast with her green eyes, which, when she was in love, turned blue. The story of the love between her and the Troubadour was the most beautiful ever to have been told. Once, they were caught by a patrol of gendarmes as they made love in a lake of moonbeams in the middle of Herăstrău Park, and fled hand in hand, laughing. They were fleeing not only from those two soldiers, who had been left petrified in amazement, but also from the whole world, a world that was distant and unfriendly, indifferent, conformist, and irreparably stupid, for which the best cure was to blot it out with a little love. Love laves all misfortunes, as a sarcastic ballad sung by the Troubadour back then used to go. They were their own world, as she whispered to him many times, and he put this into the last verse of the ballad. After meeting Margot, Toni began to sing exceptionally, to compose his own songs, to acquire a mature vocal style and (as some used to tell him) the aura of a genuine artist. "To hell with it," he would say, "let's just sing." That was something new at the time, because for a while the major underground trend had been, "Let's sing until the government falls." In spite of him putting a lot of soul into everything he did, in spite of his quality performances, and in spite of the fact that he could be heard by the whole of a Bucharest that was always just passing by, no one ever noticed him. Which is to say, none of those who could have discerned the difference ever noticed him. He seemed doomed to sparkle in anonymity, as if his gift had been so unique that only the initiated could have appreciated it. He would sit on the steps of a building on Magheru Boulevard, with his black hat upturned on the ground in front of him, with Margot beside him, and, *wing beating next to wing*, he would fill the air with harmonies. Around lunchtime, Margot would say to him, "To hell with them all, let's split."

"Let's lave the world with the cure," would come the reply.

Toward evening, he would sometimes sing with a band of street musicians in Roman Plaza. It was a different kind of music, whose instrumentation was provided by others, but which absolutely required his voice. Without his voice, the nineties in Bucharest would have been like the seventies without Garfunkel.

Margot was vacantly smoking a cigarette on the evening when Barbie first appeared. At the time she could not have imagined that any danger lay in wait for her. That danger came in the form of a girl who was doll-like, spindly, and lithe. A girl who lent her every word an insinuating tone. And when this girl was in love, her blue eyes became green. She used to wander around with a gigantic sketchpad under her arm, immortalizing street urchins, car crashes, and the mounds of uncollected garbage in the city center, which she drew as fish on dry land transformed into contemporary bipeds. She drew portraits of crippled mutants that vaguely resembled her friends or President Ion Iliescu, whom she liked to depict with a horn on his forehead and a penis dangling out of his mouth, as a way of depicting the virile chauvinism of the political discourse dominant at that time. Had you chatted with her, you would have discovered straightaway that she did not talk decorously. Which is to say, she was well bred and polite in her way, but she would not have been suitable, let us say, for the job of kindergarten teacher: the children would not have learned poems from her, but obscene ditties. As soon as she laid eyes on him, Barbie observed that Toni had a figure more handsome than Michelangelo's *David*. The sight of him struck her like lightning. He was diabolically handsome, so handsome that it was unfair to the rest of the world for a person to look like that. In the thick air of dusk, his outline seemed phosphorescent; he looked like the lucky combination to the night safe. Between two numbers and beneath the absent gaze of Margot, she went up to him and, without anyone overhearing, she asked him to pose for her in the nude.

Two days later, Margot burst into the studio that Barbie had knocked together in a house on the outskirts of Bucharest, where she lived alone, as if in the country, in the midst of a chaotic world of hens inherited from her grandma, recalcitrant turkeys and stray dogs that sought political asylum in a ramshackle shed. Margot had located her with difficulty, after having inquired all over the city: where the hell does that floozy who draws ordure live? Yes, it looks like she made off with Toni a few hours ago. I'm going to trample her brains into the dust. I'm going to rip her guts out and leave her corpse out to dry in the sun. I'm going to maim her with etching acid. How could she do a thing like this? I'll stuff her own plasticine down her throat until she chokes! Then she passed from the declamatory phase to the phase of silent fury, until she eventually found them.

She burst into the front room of that old house and found no one. The house was in the Levantine style, with do-it-yourself alterations. The thick curtains were swaying in the breeze. On the table, two glasses of red wine—probably left there the evening before. Margot went into the hall that ran through the middle of the house and then into the second room. She saw him waiting meekly, naked, in front of the easel, just as Barbie had posed him. The man had turned into modeling clay. Margot understood from a single glance that the Troubadour's free spirit was attached to puppet strings and that someone else was pulling them. Barbie turned around and gazed at her with the air of a slaveholder. Her gaze did not alter even when she espied the blade of a knife in Margot's left hand. She had completed her most successful charcoal study yet; it was a good moment to die happy. There followed a brief struggle, a scuffle during which the knife blade was held to the throat of now one, now the other.

But there was to be no death that day. Toni had the gift of reconciling souls. The truth is that we do not know how he caused the situation to turn out well. There are no rumors concerning what went on there. And without rumors, we do not know how to tell the tale. He talked to them. He explained to them. He sang to them. He melted their hearts, the hearts of intelligent and sensitive women. Later, it was said that this was the first night when all three of them slept in the same bed, in the purest embrace under the sun. They had sat talking for many hours and discovered that each of them was incomplete without the other two. They had come to understand their love, so that there was no more room for the slightest jealousy, as if it were a dodecahedron whose all twelve facets arose from clay, in the harmony of all fetal positions, to reconstitute a primordial triad, two times woman, one times troubadour, repeated until perfect completion.

Toni was not at all the type to belong to a single woman. A year later, it was said that he had lovers of all ages, professions, hair colors, and artistic orientations, in every corner of the city of Bucharest. He had learned the city inside out, and he visited them so often that he almost had no time left to sing. First thing in the morning, he would present them with a red carnation and lovemaking as serene and pellucid as Bohemian crystal, to each of them exactly as she desired, to each of them just like in her sweetest dream. For him, beauty had become his ruin, his madness, and his prison.

One who was genuinely in love with him was Magda Arsenie, the poetess whose verses had made such an impression on us in the eighties: *Come back, moon, into my hair / And open the secret eye of my love, / The lunar erotic of light,* as she wrote in her collection *When You, Love, Are the Hourglass.* She was crazy for him. We do not know when Magda met the Troubadour, but without doubt the almost twenty-year difference in age between them did not count for much. She had been very beautiful in her youth, and even at the age of forty she had lost none of her radiance. Almost as tall as he, she had a countenance ennobled by a Luciferian gaze. Her long-limbed frame allowed her a physical flexibility that Toni named *tigritude,* from a word coined by Wole Soyinka, but which in the original context meant something else. She looked like a ballerina aging beautifully. She was very different from the young women Toni had gone out with up until then. For some, it might have been a mystery: why had a young man with so many lovers become fascinated with an old poetess, when every night Barbie and Margot (who had moved in together and were now no longer embarrassed to kiss in public or to join every association for those with alternative sexual orientations) would be waiting for him on the outskirts of Bucharest?

It was at such a moment that Vespasian Moisa appeared in the Troubadour's life and spent some time talking with him. It was at two o'clock in the morning, and Toni was returning on foot from one corner of Bucharest toward another. Vespasian was sitting on the sidewalk in the lotus position. Toni bid him a good evening. Their discussion was simple, direct, radiant. It was as if Vespasian had completely transformed Toni, as if, in the place of the young man born to love, someone else had been brought in, to usurp his identity. More devastating than the spectacular religious conversions of olden days, for Toni the discovery of the Way of the Lord meant not so much an epiphany as much as a heart attack. It seemed to him that the heavens opened and received him in their huge, tender arms, arms more desirable than the embrace of love.

Thenceforth, things changed very much. For, Toni was familiar to very many young people in Bucharest. He was listened to, imitated, and he had a charm that was surpassed only by his charisma. When Toni came to tell all the devotees of ethno-rock, punk, Balkan jazz, reggae, and traditional rock that the only true prophet ever to have been born from the Romanian people was Vespasian Moisa, dozens and then hundreds of people who *had nothing else* began to seek him out. It was early summer. The hour of the City's integration had arrived.

■ □ ■ □ ■

CHAPTER THREE

ARGHIR THE PHYSICIAN BEGAN TO SPEAK, AS IF HE WERE EXPLAINING a theory that was not his own and his role were merely to translate a code of Vespasian Moisa's. He spoke to all the strangers, on the street and at the bus stop, in Roman Plaza and on Magheru Boulevard, to the hale and to the sick. He spoke to anyone at all, anywhere in Bucharest. In the beginning was the Word, there was code and light, vibrations filtered into code, and everything mixed together in the primordial silence until that moment of which we know nothing when the vibration decoded matter from the mute connections of the initial abyss. The history of this idea is as old as the world. For example, let us take the ancient treatise of Lao Zi, *Dao De Zhing.* The theme of the vibrations is present there from the very first passage, where it is said, *Beyond the road of experience flows the Road, / Greater and more subtle than the whole world.* The theme of the vibration also occurs in Parmenides, who viewed Being sometimes as a vibration, sometimes as a sphere or, depending on the case, a cube. The problem is also noted by Herodotus and broached, from a surprising angle, by Aristotle, in a secret, initiatory experiment, which in medieval times is supposed to have been recreated by Avicenna. The only version of the records of this experiment carried out by the magister of Afshana was lost in the twelfth century, during a free-for-all involving the Knights Templar. It was the original theme of the novel *The Name of the Rose,* as Umberto Eco recently declared in an interview for *L'Événement du Jeudi,* except that after a given point he decided to change the idea and used as a motif for the novel the loss of the second part of Aristotle's *Poetics*, an infinitely tamer work, and one that was not liable to cause any trouble with the Russians. When the story reached this point, the physician Arghir used to roll his eyes, wink, shrug, in other words he would give a signal, sometimes subtle, sometimes blatant, depending on the motley listeners before him. Oh, yes, the Russians also inevitably cropped up in the story. He would then go on, like this: in the modern world, the best-known adept of the theory was Sir Isaac Newton (January 4, 1643–March 31, 1727), whose work on vibrations was never published, but from whose research we have still gleaned an extraordinary benefit—we have understood the marvelous secret of gravity in the appropriate manner. Before Newton, things fell to earth miraculously, inexplicably, subject to the whim of a god that might at any time renounce his vocation and abandon things to float up in the air. How many men perished, burned at the stake, in the dark times of the Inquisition, Dr. Arghir would declaim, merely for having brought up the matter of levitation, far from having made connection between vibrations and the doubtful problem of gravitation, as would have been fit. But that's not the only subject salvaged by Newton, because it was also he who reexamined the celebrated dialogue of Galileo, whose fate had been sealed by the ill humors of a rascally pope. Closer to our own times, Albert Einstein's essays on vibrations have been explained for the understanding of the layman in a book that is a real page-turner and has gone through countless paperback editions. And before that there was Michelson's experiment, which attempted to answer the question of whether vibrations exist beyond the sphere of the perceptible. But all these admirable advances in science did nothing more than to mark out various points on the route to a great revealed truth, which the Church anticipated. For, nothing is more profound and at the same time more admirable than to believe before understanding, to believe before examining, to believe even if you don't understand one jot, merely because the priest, the only well-read person in the village, tells you so. This is how it has always been with us Romanians, Dr. Arghir would say, and he accompanied this observation with an inconsolable sigh from the depths of his lungs. When the story got this far, he would tell them to wait and see. For an instant, the listeners would not know whether he was joking or in earnest. And his arguments flowed like the waters of a river. They flowed like the Way of *Dao De Zhing*. The primordial code emitted waves, like unmistakable fingerprints, and in this way the code remained inscribed in all the things that exist. Our Lord Jesus Christ was a decoder, he would recount, quoting Vespasian Moisa, before an audience gathered from the streets, an audience so motley that the eyes which reflected him seemed like the holes in a carnival mask. Everything is a decoding, our path to the salvation of our souls runs through our power to decode and interpret—and no physicists' equations or geologists' research can aid us as much as our power to interpret the code of Holy Scripture. The initial language preserves its analogies in every other language, and every idiom spoken by people today represents a mirror of the initial code: a lexical core, a grammar, a medium called vocabulary, endowed with certain relations. Our Lord was a decoder, because the words of the Holy Gospels contain sufficient elements to decode from Greek the expressions initially uttered in Aramaic or Hebrew. What needs to be retained from the structure of the code in Greek must be invariable in nature, invariable in translation and in the language in which it was uttered. In other words, certain passages contain a message that can be decoded in any language in which they are expressed, and the decoding is identical. An analysis in the Romanian language, which is merely one mirror out of infinite possible mirrors, is equally as justified as an analysis in the original Hebrew. It is an alternative, arbitrary mirror no less valid than any other language. The problem is that we must look only at certain passages, at precisely the ones that remain unchanged in translation. Thus, in Romanian what needs to be carried out is the operation of decoding the initial message hidden in the inner germ of the language. Partial analyses have brought to light particular decodings. That the name of a plant corresponds to a cure, as recent research has revealed, is no wonder, just as it is no wonder that the planets were formed following an evolution of billions of years after the Big Bang. In the language of waves it must be expressed in the same way: there is a cure just as there is a coagulation of matter. The grammar of matter, this is what must be sought in the Bible, in the Old and the New Testament, and if we want to understand this world, we will require a church that is like a research institute, and research institutes will have to become churches. A militant church, which strives to solve problems, to research and study as if it were praying, a church that is organized like a Macedonian phalanx, like a Roman legion, like Hamburg University, like a mound erected over the footprints of the Lord God. It's no joking matter. The words *I am that I am* in the Bible mean exactly that: the primordial vibration has been perpetuated through language, and it is present here and now.

When his exposition reached this point, the physician Arghir would always pause, run his hand through his Afro hair, and regard those around him carefully. He wanted to see how many were praying and how many had understood.

Now, of course, it can be argued that the theory of contextual grammars has never been placed in parallel with the physics of elementary particles and that many analogies have not been sufficiently proven. What has been demonstrated is that there are many fragments of theory, but no one has taken the analogy as far as this and no one, in a single lifetime, has been prepared to undertake this task. Perhaps it is not a task for one man alone. Theology here reaches the edges of linguistic research and the theory of relativity. It is a question of teamwork. God is here. And then the physician would hand over to Vespasian, who would preach the story that the Romanian language is seven thousand years old, as old as Greek, Hebrew, and Aramaic.

"I am two men, not one," Vespasian Moisa used to say, and all those present could sense it. Some would lift their hands to their chests and begin to pray. Others would shut their brimming eyes.

"He is the Prophet!" said one of the listeners one evening.

"He is the Son and this is His second coming!" said another.

At the time they were talking under the arcade on one side of Roman Plaza, in view of all the passersby. They were talking about decoding vibration in terms of grammar, about the *Lives of the Church Fathers* and *The Gospels*. It was of all these things that Vespasian Moisa was speaking. At the time not even he knew very well who he was. He knew only that he had been born with a strange mark on his breast. His words were his way, and then his foundation, his house, his roof, under a towering sky grooved with illusory battlements, like a fortress. The Romanian language—a code as good as any other, because all were equivalent, and for this reason we say that it is up to the Chinese to understand the Han language, the French the French language, while our aim is to decode Romanian down to its very last outcomes, to the final decortication of its fundamental meanings, the equilibrium between word and matter, between word and vibration, which it has generated in the consciousness of a community. "Have you heard that mandrake in fact cures baldness?" "No. Who was it that discovered that?" someone in the crowd asked. "It's the first result of decoding, and it was discovered by studying the Romanian language." And Dr. Arghir showed them his cranial adornment, and no one could believe that a year before the man had been completely bald. But it was true. It was so true . . .

■ □ ■ □ ■

Back then, a middle-aged character, whose father had played in Maria Tănase's backing orchestra in the 1940s, was basking in a successful business. He had become the general manager of an international haulage company, with a fleet of dozens of heavy goods trucks. At the terminus of bus route no. 368 you could see a blue sign with huge letters, which read ROBOT IMPORT EXPORT CO. That was his firm. His name was Vasile Gheorghe, and he had bought a villa right in the center of town, in Lahovary (formerly Cosmonauts) Square. The villa right behind the statue of Lahovary, to be precise. He did not believe in God and had never had time for such nonsense. He did not care about such things. Business was his life. In his world, actions spoke louder than words and man held his destiny in his own hands. Money should be kept at home, not in the bank. Not prayer, but deeds—that was his creed. No little must have been the wonder of his acquaintances when the man started to mix with the group of rockers, guitarists, weird girls, drug addicts, physicians, and philosophers who had begun to gather under the arcade in the nearby Roman Plaza every evening at six to listen to Vespasian Moisa. One evening, as if struck by a bolt from the blue, Vasile Gheorghe fell to his knees and, making the sign of the cross, told him, "I'm giving you my house!"

It was no joke: it was yet another of the spectacular conversions that the presence of Vespasian Moisa brought about. Vasile Gheorghe clung to the Teacher's arm and begged him to come home with him, together with all those who were praying there, and to stay with him forever.

It was a large house, with ten bedrooms, an inner courtyard, a habitable attic, and a dining room as big as a conference hall. The house had been the property of a famous lawyer in the twenties, who had died in prison in the communist fifties, choking on his own vomit in a six-feet-by-six-feet solitary confinement cell. A street in Bucharest was now named after him, in another part of the city. For a while it had been an annex of the Department of Pharmacology and Dentistry, then the headquarters of the Motor Bus Chess Club and, on the ground floor, the Willpower Tennis Club, only to end up in the eighties on the list of buildings scheduled for demolition. Escaping destruction as if by miracle, the villa had been renovated by Vasile Gheorghe, who restored its former brilliance, as well as adding a late Meiji dynasty pagoda, meant to symbolize democracy. To the top of the building he added a series of battlements, which made it architecturally unique, if not downright unreal, for that area of Bucharest. To him it seemed a fairy-tale house. He moved his family, wife, two children, parents and parents-in-law, into the villa and set up a business office for himself in one of the bedrooms, endowed with a satellite telephone, although for the time being he only had business dealings inside Romania.

Things went well for a while, until his conversion, when his father left, so as not to have to see his son turned into a loony, which is what he shouted at him from the street on that very evening. It was a genuine religious shock, such as had been experienced by others who had talked to Vespasian Moisa that spring. It was like the reflection of lights in the focus of a gigantic parabolic mirror, as if the rays of an unseen force had, out of the blue, inflamed those who were contaminated with belief. On the evening when Vasile Gheorghe discovered the Teacher, he took him by the hand and told him, "Come, come with all your friends to my house." And so it was that he arrived for supper accompanied by some twenty rockers, vagrants, and lumpen proletariat laborers, at the head of whom were Toni, Dr. Apolodor Arghir, Barbie and some guitarists from a group in which Toni had played for a while, a homeless boxer, two geology students, and a bespectacled man of no fixed profession.

"Who are they?" asked his wife.

"They are my brothers in the Lord," said Vasile Gheorghe. "My house is their house. My table is their table."

And they sat down to their meal and the Teacher blessed the bread, fish, and red wine. They ate in silence. Some sat at the table, others on the carpet. On the first night, they all slept together, after listening to Vespasian Moisa until very late. He told a story about quantum physics and quasars, about *The Lives of the Church Fathers* and levitation, about the miracles of medieval Moldavia and the Holy Mountain of Athos, about the electromagnetic implications of gauge theory, and about how we can deduce what happened during the Big Bang by reading within ourselves. Listening to him speak, Vasile Gheorghe's wife said nothing, but at midnight she began to sob in her husband's arms.

"What's wrong?" he asked her, standing on a marble step in the dining room. "Is it not so that this man is the Truth? Is it not so?"

"I don't understand a thing," said the woman and went on weeping.

■ □ ■ □ ■

CHAPTER FOUR

MANY PEOPLE BEGAN TO CONVERT TO THE FAITH OF VESPASIAN MOISA, to call him Teacher and to come to hear him speak in the courtyard of the villa in Lahovary Square. Back then they had begun to say of him that he was the only possessor of the true Christian faith, which is to say the Orthodox tradition. They said that the great and enormous truth was not in the hands of the priests and theologians, but in the hands of the Teacher. Vespasian Moisa, the Teacher, gathered many strange characters around him. All were drawn to the new faith by a word, by a glance, by a thought, and ended up converted by a wave of light—as if they had been hidden in a secret world and emerged into the open only when inspired by the words of Vespasian, as if only he had ever spoken to them meaningfully. In the life of each of them, the Teacher seemed to appear at exactly the instant before they would have been lost forever, and so the people around him gave the appearance of being the antechamber of a complex circus, of an extent and complexity not seen in Romania since the entry of the tsar's army into Bucharest, whenever that wonder will have taken place.

Thus, in the company of the Teacher could be seen a man who, so they said, had a penis of normal length but so thick that he had spent his adult life alone. It was rumored that his erect member resembled a brick wrapped in the left biceps of Muhammad Ali. He had become national karate champion shortly after the revolution and he was by no means stupid: his theory was esthetic in nature, and he discussed it with the Teacher. In his thesis he elaborated various modern applications for the proportions of Phidias's caryatids. He talked about this constantly, and, at the time of his conversion, the Teacher allowed him to talk for a long time on the terrace of the villa, where no one could hear them and where confessional scenes took place, as sometimes happens in the presence of great spiritual guides. He had discovered unexpected similarities between various geometric properties of the Acropolis and today's everyday consumer goods: all the televisions in the world, he used to say, contain an opening onto the horizons of the Erechtheion. He journeyed accompanied by very many illusions, wearing an aureole that was solitary rather than erotic. His conversion to the creed of Vespasian Moisa's Orthodox order was extremely natural: he had become lost in a sea of humanity to which he was not at all adapted. Women horrified him, and he never told the Teacher why, although so many rumors floated around him. The closeness of a woman would give him goose bumps, and he would always turn his head away in disdain. The Teacher knew, however. This was one of the first cases of souls that were saved, the case of a man who, without faith in Vespasian Moisa, would have ended up a serial killer, if not worse. The Teacher converted all his frustrations into positive energies. And he made the Teacher an oath to pray ceaselessly on the lawn in the courtyard of the villa.

It was also around then that Julius appeared, in the summer of 1993, having come to hear the Teacher after one of those dreary parties at which there are more boys than there are girls. Slightly stooped, with a rebellious mustache ill-suited to his boyish and overserious face, he had but one interest in life, a passion that formerly would have come under the heading of literary history: Julius collected Nichita's kisses. You can think of the Nichita Stănescu in the high-school textbooks, in the university lectures, or in the essay of some critic, but that is not the real Nichita. The only way to get to the real Nichita, Julius used to say, was by following the trail of his kisses, for each touch of his lips left the stigma of a poem behind it in the world. According to his research, the poem "Autumn Feeling" seemed to have been deposited on the eyelids of a blonde lady who lived in an old house, with a maple in the yard, a house over which no bird ever flew. Each kiss had its own rhythm and meter and revealed the spectacular, always surprising ideas of a poet who wagered not only on flight into the upper air but also on inner flight. Julius's faith in the Teacher was so great that once he kissed his heel and said, "Tread softly. The ground of Bucharest aches."

His theory was that each footstep crushes a poem, just as each inspired word of the Teacher brought a new conversion. It all happened naturally, for those people seemed always to have been expecting the Teacher. And now he had come and taken his place in their hearts. Perhaps their words sounded mawkish, but after a time they had all begun to speak only of the heart. Julius was transfigured by his discovery of Orthodoxy, or rather the version of Orthodoxy preached by Vespasian Moisa. Nichita Stănescu ought to be canonized, he believed, and all of us ought to pray toward Ploieşti, the same as the Mohammedans prostrate themselves toward Mecca. It was also Julius who discovered, while collecting eyewitness testimonies with a view to the poet's canonization, how Nichita used to exchange greetings. This is what he is supposed to say: "I send you my kiss," which, for Julius, had become a supreme proof that kisses are both the starting point of the work and its terminus.

It was also at this time that Maximilian, the man who could hear ultrasound, converted to the faith of the Teacher. He had built himself an alarm clock that only he could hear—an alarm clock that could wake all the bats in Floreasca Park, near the Ceauşescus' villa, the same bats that the Securitate had tried to drive away with ultrasound in 1987. It was a cassette player that was triggered at six o'clock sharp and played a tape of the "Ode to Joy" transposed into an audio range beyond the horizon of this world. It could detect a duodenal ulcer by the noise level of someone's intestines, in sound ranges imperceptible to ordinary people, an invention that was never accredited by the Ministry of Health because its promoter had not had any specialist education. Maximilian and Dr. Apolodor Arghir were to talk for long hours and agree upon all the scientific aspects. "The lad is very good!" the doctor said of him. They began to work together on deciphering the language of the Dacians and its medical applications. Later, when Diaconescu and Arghir discussed the matter and realized that their public success might create enemies for Vespasian, they begged Maximilian to stay close by the Teacher's side as much as possible and to hear all. They were afraid of an attack, although they could not have said by whom.

Back then, somewhere on Floreasca Avenue there was an old photographer, the greatest living master in black-and-white portraiture. He was not only a creator of images, but also a healer, a witch doctor who had learned to use the energy of the aura in order to modify the luminous being of his fellow man. He could feel in the palms of his hands the outline of the rays and the wild intensity of each subject. And he soothed them, reduced their blood pressure, and calmed their pulse by a mere touch of the hand. He used all these abilities to create revealing portraits: all the subjects who appeared in his works attained the greatest profundity they had ever been capable of, even if thitherto they had never achieved much to speak of. In his portraits children who were dullards looked like budding Mozarts, and lunatic carpenters acquired the steep brow of Mihai Eminescu, as he appears in the Prague photograph. In contrast to other photographers, he worked not with sunlight, artificial lighting, or flashguns, but with the subject's inner light, which he perceived with his right eye, which turned inward rather than outward.

But not one of these conversions was as useful to Vespasian Moisa's religious order as that of the old man whose nickname was Saint Peter, whom I first saw in Roman Plaza in the summer of 1988. He was wearing a shabby coat with baggy, torn pockets full of books, and had grubby carrier bags full of dog-eared old tomes, marvelous treatises, instruction manuals, and apocryphal editions of the *Philokalia*. Let us imagine the most innocuous person in the world, an old man who nourished himself with nothing but bread and water (he used to begin the loaf first thing in the morning, and by evening he would have munched three quarters, and this was all he ate) and spent all his time at mathematics or architecture lectures. He lived somewhere near the intersection of Polonă Street and Mihai Eminescu Street, in a hideaway known to no one, where the initiates said that, in something resembling an air-raid shelter, there could be found the largest library in Bucharest, vastly superior in terms of its number of volumes to the Library of the Romanian Academy, which, according to the statistics of the Library of Congress, is supposed to be the ninth largest in the world. It was said that he had read everything and that when there was no more room for him to sleep in his cellar because there were too many books, he spent his nights on the streets, in various nooks. He was wont to appear out of the blue in various unexpected places. It was said that he talked in a way that people could not understand,

CHAPTER FOUR

with numerous literary references, quoting entire passages from long-forgotten books. He had dreamed up his own system for indexing, classifying, arranging, and retrieving volumes, so that he never got lost in his infernal database. That cellar was a unique place, branching off into the sewers in numerous recesses. Every niche was filled with files, books without covers, photocopies, forgotten editions, all of them by obscure authors, authors of whom no one had ever heard, as if his library had taken shape as a plausible alternative to the entire known universe. That space was a laboratory and reading room, a place for meditation and prayer, the walls covered with icons in the spots where there were no shelves. His theory was in principle based on a commonsense consequence of one of Lorentz's equations, which led him, analyzing it in a highly personal manner, to conclude the existence of angelic matter. At the urging of Vespasian, Saint Peter discussed this theory with Maximilian for hours at a time, and from the latter he learned the manner in which an apparatus to detect all the audible ranges of the perceptible should be constructed. Above all, from Maximilian he was to learn what it was he had to discover, because he did not know what the unheard voices he was seeking might sound like.

On the evening of December 12, 1992, shortly before he joined the retinue of unique characters surrounding the Teacher, Saint Peter was standing pressed up against the wall of block no. 23, Victory Avenue, the building with the headquarters of the Express Trust. It was on that evening that he was to inaugurate his series of experiments designed to demonstrate the existence of angelic matter. It was well known throughout Bucharest that the foundations of the block in question had been severely damaged by the earthquakes of recent years. It was therefore going to collapse at some point. This collapse should not be imagined other than as the setting into motion of an object that had come to rest, a motion preceded by a chain of musical vibrations that anticipated the final disaster. At first, on that evening it seemed to him he could not hear anything. Subsequently, it seemed he had found a better means of capturing vibrations, or to be more precise of adjusting the filter for the Absolute Capture of Vibrations, the miraculous instrument that allowed him to achieve the advances of which we have all heard and which ultimately mean that one can listen to what the angels are saying. Based on that secret procedure, he predicted that on June 29, 2008, the building in question would all of a sudden collapse, not because of an earth tremor, but because its inner music would on that date reach its apogee. And he decided to write a treatise entitled *On Angels* or something like that, although the manuscript has not come to light even to this day.

A fundamental concern in the seventeenth century, the Capture of Vibrations has a long history. Imagine if you will that we can hear two separate drums, without seeing them. The question is whether it is possible to determine the shape of a drum by resorting only to an analysis of its sound. Can you hear the shape of a drum? In fact, matter leaves perceptible traces throughout space, the same as a slow-witted thief leaves fingerprints. And what you want to do is to guess the shape of the matter that left them by reading these traces. What kind of vibrations does angelic matter produce? Saint Peter, in search of lost angels, did not know what to expect. For, the Reading of the Vibrations would bring with it a better description of the Big Bang, which was mother to both the angels and us. But it was in this context that his theory encountered the theory that Professor Diaconescu had given to the Teacher as a present.

For weeks in a row the old man could be seen in University Square, carrying in his arms a kind of gramophone with a membrane stretched over its funnel. It was powered by a car battery, which he pulled behind him on a cart meant for gas canisters. Thousands of wires sprouted from the apparatus, some of them connected to the huge earphones, like those of a tank driver, which he wore over his disheveled hair. His large, blue, myopic eyes stared into space, and his ears could not hear what we, the others, said to him, as if he had left words behind on the normal wavelength and moved definitively and improbably onto other immaterial frequencies. One of the first applications of the apparatus was the anticipation, with nanosecond precision, of the movements of the no. 40 tram along Bassarabia Boulevard. He was convinced that cosmic anomalies could be picked up at the level of the vibrations in the middle of Bucharest. Saint Peter sincerely regretted the fact that the marvelously vibrating statue of Lenin had been removed from its plinth in front of the House of the Spark. The statue would have allowed spectacular predictions at the historical level. Amplified by Saint Peter's filter, the things it might have said would have been so clear that it would have been as if the living Lenin himself had climbed up onto the plinth to shout out prophecies. Each statue in Herăstrău Park vibrated its shape, and, as the countenance is the mirror of the soul, in the amplifier he picked up in the vicinity of the busts classical verses whispered in German, together with foulmouthed grumbles, colorful curses in Aromanian, a terrifying phthisical cough that went very harmoniously with the poetry, Italian terza rima, and delicately rolled R's with a Normandy accent. Everything vibrated its form. The titanic House of the People vibrated the grave of a forgotten Bucharest, the buried sensuousness of the picturesque Uranus Quarter on which it had been erected. The Vernescu Palace, the Continental Hotel, and the Princess Bălaşa Church each had a unique vibration, more often than not in complete disaccord with the present state of the building, as if their walls had fallen away from their own reality. The only things that were absolutely silent, thanks to their shape, were the crosses above graves. As if there were nothing more to be said, nothing more to add. But Saint Peter interpreted the data differently: for him, the absence of oscillations did not mean anything other than the transgression of matter into the angelic. Once we are dead, we all become angelic matter, and the soul leaves the earth for a destination unknown, at a speed greater than that of light.

Otherwise, everything is vibration. The old man used to laugh as he listened from a distance, in outlying districts of Bucharest, to the distinct vibrations of love. He had perfected his apparatus and enhanced its accuracy to such a degree that he needed only to close his eyes, like a shaman, and he could see with the clarity of a magic mirror the bodies of the lovers, the caresses, the physical closeness, the sighs. The ultimate intimacy of matter's signs. All of a sudden, surprisingly, in his earphones he heard a different kind of voice. It was like a song, like the rumor of a faraway choir, speaking as a single voice in the guise of ultrasound. "I know you are seeking me," the voice said. It had a very familiar timbre, as if it were the voice of Placido Domingo.

■ ◻ ■ ◻ ■

Maximilian flung open the door and cast himself into the middle of the room where the brothers were praying. Behind him came Saint Peter, barely able to walk, suffocated with emotion.

"We have spoken with the angels," he said. "We had a direct link. We were in University Square, and the angels spoke to us. The one who spoke to us was called Michael the Lesser, a different one than the Archangel Michael, and he revealed to us the truth. The Teacher is the second incarnation of Jesus. He is His second coming. This is the Answer."

He hurriedly made the sign of the cross. He was panting, gasping for air. Standing in the middle of the room, Dr. Arghir ran his fingers through his hair.

In the other corner of the room, the Teacher was sitting on an imitation Brîncoveanu period throne, of which Vasile Gheorghe had been very proud back when he cared about earthly things. Vespasian remained motionless for an instant, and all those in the room saw his countenance transfigured, illumined from within. Not saying a word, he then rose to his feet and made toward the door. He went out, vanishing into the night. Lately he had been wont to wander through Bucharest, returning at the second crowing of the cock, followed by an inexplicable train of new converts.

It was on one of those nights that the man of whom I heard it said in the eighties that he was the only true prophet ever to have been born in Romania came to see Vespasian. He no longer had a name. He had sold it once during a time of passing famine. Born in a village in Moldavia, he had the gift of foresight and could prophesy the future with the same precision as archaeologists reading the past in pottery shards. They told the Teacher that he was the seventh son of a seventh son, as the old folk ballad goes, which in these times of debauchery and perdition has been translated into English and made into a rock song. He told the Teacher that he had been expecting Him, that he had heard in the fish market in Galatzi that He had arrived, and he had come to bow before Him and acknowledge Him. He had come to Him here in Bucharest, he knelt down before Him, and told Him that he knew who He was. Then he told Him the truth about the foretokening that had come to him every night: Caiaphas will crucify Him with the help of Satan, a crucifixion like that of two thousand years ago. The crucifixion will not be complete, but will end with the body being rent in twain, with death in this world, a death by diffusion into the ether. Vespasian Moisa laughed and then kissed him. He laughed as if that man were telling him a joke. How about that? Diffusion, eh?

"We live in a world of love," he told him. "We live in a democracy. There's nothing to fear."

The other shook his head. "I knew you would not believe me," he told him with his eyes, "I knew you would not believe me, but heed me and guard Yourself, leave Bucharest, for this is the Babylon of our age, and it will enslave You and crucify You."

Then Vespasian Moisa unfastened his shirt and showed him the mark on his chest. And he questioned him, thus: "Where shall I go, when this City is inscribed on me? Were I to leave, it would be as if I were taking Bucharest with me, and I would drag it behind me."

The other said, "Do you think that this sign means you are doomed? It does not mean that, for you still have time to choose. If you choose to stay in Bucharest, I will not follow You, because I do not want to witness Your fall. You are the Son of the Lord, but I do not want to see something like that! In our times, heroism does not count for much . . . Leave, because you will be given many signs that will tell You to leave!"

Vespasian sighed deeply. Beside him, with a heavy heart, Dr. Arghir listened to all they said to each other.

"Do not be afraid," said Vespasian, "better you come and let me show you something."

At that time, a pipe had burst in Lahovary Square, to be exact the hot water mains for the entire Floreasca neighborhood. The city's underground pipe network was like an organism with a burst aorta. The geyser flung into the sky a column of water, and from the puddle steam was ascending into the vernal sky. In the square, holding his gramophone, Saint Peter could no longer hear the angels because of the gushing water. The passing no. 368 buses bathed their muddy tires in a steaming lake, to which the passersby were indifferent. On the first-floor balcony, Vespasian Moisa took the man who had come from afar by the hand and showed him the water. Then he closed his eyes, furrowed his brow, and leaned over the balustrade. The prophet looked at him and saw his wrinkled brow, saw his concentrated but relaxed face, and heard his own heart beating in the silence of the evening. And the water in the street below began to give off even more steam and to ripple, then to gush upward. When the jet reached the height of a man, from the crest sprouted shoulders and a head, then a torso and thighs. It was a full, albeit bizarre, body, for it was impossible to say whether it was male or female. His eyes closed and his arms outstretched, Vespasian Moisa held it there for a while, then he sliced his hand through the air, as if he were conductor Sergiu Celibidache concluding a Mahler symphony, and the column of water withdrew back into the clay, with a final gurgle, a C-flat in the lowest key of the flow, and the pipe sealed back up inside the earth, an iron belly welding itself shut.

"The soul of the water rose up toward the sky," said Vespasian Moisa to the prophet who had brought him the tidings. "Do you or don't you want to see something like that?"

Then the prophet knelt at his feet and allowed himself to be baptized with the new name of Matei. And he swore eternal obedience to Vespasian Moisa, even if it meant his staying only in Bucharest forever and ever.

And those who were there with Him on the balcony, the Prophet and His apostles, and the people from the square, who were praying in the courtyard of the villa, and those in a passing bus, and those who were sweeping the road, and those who chanced to be passing, one and all, they fell to their knees and acknowledged the Son of the Lord and made obeisance to Him, and some of them saw His countenance illuminated. And yet others passed by in the street and saw nothing.

CHAPTER FOUR

■ □ ■ □ ■

CHAPTER FIVE

COLONEL FOCȘĂNEANU WAS LEANING BACK IN HIS CHAIR IN HIS OFFICE on the second floor of the central headquarters of the Romanian Intelligence Service, reading the reports from the section for surveillance of cults. The colonel was short, brown-haired, and had sly, squirrel eyes and small, feminine hands. He had remained motionless for an hour, until the moment when he felt the need to loosen his tie a little. He said to himself, "God, they'll inherit the earth! Just look at them: they could destabilize the country." He did not have sufficient data to be able to gauge exactly, but the flair he had honed in two decades of secret police work made him feel it. He thought for a while, then picked up the closed circuit telephone and ordered Captain Pleșoianu to come to his office.

This captain had eyebrows that merged above his nose and an expression so neutral that we might say he was faceless. An athletic frame, without belly fat, without tallness, without consistency, a blend of fibers and air, with an accent that recalled his native Bukowina and a gaze different to that of Bucharest folk. When you saw him for the first time, you would remark his overly high forehead, which gave him a permanently surprised look. He had been transferred to the Romanian Intelligence Service after the events of December 1989, when he had distinguished himself in a near-fatal beating administered to disruptive elements gathered in Victory Square on the evening of December 21. Colonel Focșăneanu had some doubts regarding Pleșoianu's intelligence, but he knew that what was to follow was not a mission that required an intelligent man. He had thought long on the matter. In any case, he didn't even have anyone else. When the captain reported for duty, the colonel revealed to him that he was about to throw into battle the Romanian Intelligence Service's secret weapon: a spy who could infiltrate anywhere. It was not a technology, but a living creature, an individual perfectly trained to gather information and evaluate the target's strategy.

"Understood, sir," said the captain, gazing fixedly at the map of Romania on the wall in front of him.

"Things are rather more complicated than that," the colonel went on. "No one must find out that we have this investigating officer at our disposal. It's top secret. The data have to be collected with the utmost care, and the planting of the undercover officer has to be in conditions of absolute secrecy."

"You can count on me, of course."

What the captain had to do was to go to Cosmonauts Square, or Lahovary Square as it had been known since 1989, and plant a bag behind the garden fence of a certain villa. He had orders not to look in the bag and to make sure he was not seen. The yard of the villa is always full of people, but no one must notice anything. He mustn't toss the bag over the fence too violently, just anyhow or anywhere. He mustn't let it get knocked about. This was why it wasn't exactly an easy mission. Bruisers to throw a bag around are a dime a dozen, but someone to plant it intelligently, leaving it at exactly the right strategic spot, well, that was something else entirely. If possible, the captain should try to get inside the villa on some pretext or another. It would be much better to place the bag gently inside the yard. It was true that his long-term mission was to infiltrate Vespasian Moisa's cult and destabilize it from within, but for a start he was to concentrate on intelligence gathering. For his mission, the colonel ordered the captain to dress in the habitual blue uniform of the Bucharest Sector 2 Department of Telephone Maintenance. He should look like a repairman. It was true that he had the high forehead of an intellectual, but he would have to make a special effort, especially with regard to his facial expression.

At precisely the same hour of the evening, in another part of Bucharest, Vespasian Moisa was suffering abdominal pains. In that part of the map on his chest was a point that corresponded to the Ferentari District. In Ferentari, in a forty-year-old apartment, there lived a child of ten and his grandmother, Maria Vîrsan. At the time, no one had any way of knowing that Vespasian's every pain was caused by something, most likely from moral reasons. When the physician Arghir stooped over him and saw him convulsed once more by spasms and fever, and when he heard him muttering, he thought that something must be taking place, but he could not be sure that the cause of the ailment was external. Thus, in Ferentari, Maria Vîrsan was teaching her grandson the basic lesson for survival in Bucharest: if something happens on the street, you should be either the first person to run from that place or the first person to run to that place. If you don't know that, you risk getting trampled underfoot or shot. Of course, the discussion could have been more nuanced, but the child needed some rules that he could grasp quickly. That evening, the boy and his grandmother took trolleybus no. 90 and rode to Popa Nan Street, where, at the back of a warehouse, part of the wall had caved in. The grandmother had seen it that morning. She knew very well what was to be done, for whenever a wall collapsed, the boundaries of the world changed. *In every hollow could be found a god.* For a while that summer sunflower-seed oil was five hundred times more expensive than gas. Maria Vîrsan lived in Ferentari, not far from the place where the Troubadour lived before meeting the Teacher. It was thus that the child went with his grandmother and saw for the first time old villas with verandas and oriels, in the historic part of Bucharest, where there must always have been a human settlement. And his grandmother told him where to enter, through the breach in the wall, into the warehouse storeroom. She showed him where to pass the bottles of oil through to the outside. And because he was an obedient child, he did as his grandmother told him, under cover of darkness. It wasn't even hard. The bottles began to fly out of the warehouse of their own volition. Grandmother caught them on the other side and put them in the sack, laying them carefully so that they wouldn't break. After a while she said, "That's enough! We've got more than we can carry."

Not far from the wall there was an abandoned refrigeration unit. It was a cooling locker turned on its side. Grandmother turned around and said, "They're heavy. We'll have to divide them up between the sacks. Put these in that sack."

The boy leaned one of the sacks up against the large, formerly white, now peeling box of the refrigeration unit.

"Hey," a voice within could be heard. "And here I was trying not to see it . . ."

For an instant, Maria Vîrsan thought that all was lost. She had never been caught, but she well sensed how things could take a different turn.

From the white box emerged an old man with ragged clothes, a ski hat, a wild beard, and feverishly gleaming eyes. Behind him tumbled some books. The old man was clutching to his chest a gigantic gramophone, and over his ears he had a pair of headphones, with which he was capturing vibrations.

"You know, it's not very nice what you have been doing here, is it?" said he.

Maria Vîrsan heaved a sigh of relief. It could be seen from a mile away that this man had nothing to do with the long arm of the law.

"Would you like some sunflower-seed oil?" she asked him.

He shook his head. "Wouldn't dream of it."

"What do you want, then?"

"I want you to repent for your deeds and for the sin of having stolen the nation's property."

Maria Vîrsan was a serious-minded woman, and this was why she took a step backward. No one had ever spoken to her so brazenly ever before.

"That's stupid."

"Not at all," said the old man, taking a deep breath. "The end of the world is nigh. It is time to repent and to give back what is not yours."

Maria Vîrsan genuinely believed in what she was doing. Which is to say she did not do it merely because she needed to, but because she was genuinely convinced that this was what had to be done, that swift and decisive action had to be taken whenever the sacred right of property became hazy. This is why she felt a need to argue the toss. But instead of what she meant to say, something else came from her mouth.

"What the hell, do you really think that I'm going to waste my time with you, here, at night, that I'm going to pour the oil down the drain so that I can hear you coming on holier than thou?"

"You err," said the old man, stepping away from the refrigeration unit. "You err because you are proud and because it seems to you that you know the straight path. It seems to you that what your rumbling belly says is the straight path. You worship Mammon, not God."

"Gran, shall I hit him?"

"Stay where you are," said the woman. Then, to the old man, "Don't you have anyone else to do your moralizing with? Or is this what you do when someone wakes you up?"

"It is not a question only of morals here. It is a question of souls. When a soul is lost, which is to say when it becomes debased, its vibration reaches the lower limit. It is as if a tenor were to become a bass overnight. An entire world is thrown out of symmetry because of a single soul."

"Look, do you know what, we've got business to take care of. We have to leave," said Maria Vîrsan. "We've got to find a taxi, or something, to take us home, because we've got too much to carry."

"Let me give you a single argument," said the old man.

He had a very affected manner of speaking, one that was old-fashioned and somehow higher than the words, as if he had learned Romanian as a foreign language or he had taken a blow to the head. There was something different about him.

"If you read, for example, *Holy Poverty* by Frans Sillanpää, an author unjustly forgotten, although in his day he won the Nobel Prize, whose style, somewhat akin to that of Dostoevsky, seems not to ensure him any wider accessibility after all these decades, you will see what connotation honor might acquire, even in times of economic depression. There, in the face of death, in front of a firing squad, a character comes to find amusement at the expense of the ritual of serial murder, even if he is the next to be executed. To be more precise, he is amused at serial executions. Today, we might come to find amusement at the expense of serial losses of soul. Mortal sins, the breaking of the Ten Commandments, murder after murder, can all these not be seen at every step? Let us say that you have not understood. What did you wish to be told? For the Lord God to leave Moses a special commandment: *Thou shalt not steal the state's cooking oil?*"

Here his voice became thunderous. Nearby windows began to shudder, and the woman thought he was going to wake the whole neighborhood. She put her finger to her lips as a sign for him to quiet down.

Then, all of a sudden, Maria Vîrsan had a vision. It seemed to her that this old man was a demon or something of the sort, something supernatural, something outside the framework of reality, something that might change many things if it put its mind to it. She took her grandson by the hand and urged him to walk away. She whispered something to him.

"Don't go," the old man said behind them, "for if you go, you shall lose your souls."

When they reached the corner of the street, the pair did not even look back. In their minds they could divine that figure which had uttered such aberrations withdrawing back into the refrigeration unit, enveloped once more in night. Maria Vîrsan made a broad sign of the cross and said, "God forbid!" with a conviction which, for an instant, replaced all her other convictions.

■ □ ■ □ ■

That June evening, Colonel Focşăneanu sat leaning his elbows on the windowsill of a café. Wearing a raincoat and sunglasses, he looked the part of a secret agent. The sun cast a russet light along the length of Victory Avenue. At that very moment, from the other side of the road, weaving among the cars, a tabby tomcat approached the window of the café. After rubbing his back against a green post, freshly painted by municipal workmen, the tomcat said, "I have the honor, Colonel, sir. I am ready to present to you the surveillance report."

"Fire away, I'm listening," said the colonel, sipping his coffee.

"They spend the whole day at prayer, doing breathing exercises. They don't talk about politics. They're neither Christian Democrat nor excessively Liberal in their convictions. On the other hand, they don't have any Social Democrat potential."

The colonel tapped his cigarette ash outside the window. The tomcat stepped to one side, watching the scattering ash with his green eyes.

"Are there any Hungarians among them?"

"I haven't seen any," said the tomcat.

CHAPTER FIVE

41

"Aha," said the colonel. "Go on."

"Vespasian Moisa talks to them, sometimes. They ask him questions, and he answers in parables. There are all kinds of fables which the disciples then debate. I haven't seen any miracles. I haven't seen any weapons. They haven't discussed the Hungarian nationalist question regarding Transylvania, and I haven't noticed any links with Hungarian protestant churches. They haven't talked about any plan for the federalization of Romania."

"Hmm," said Colonel Focşăneanu absently. "What the hell are they, then?"

"Are your orders for me to continue the investigation?" asked the tomcat.

"Go back and sit on the stove or the bookshelf, and stay there until I give you further instructions. We have to find out. It's just not possible for there to be a religious cult of such a size, active in the very heart of the capital, and for us not to know what it is they're up to. Religious sect or madmen, we have to clarify it."

"Understood."

The colonel lowered his sunglasses and looked the tomcat in the eyes. "How would you classify them, Lieutenant? What kind of movement do they represent?"

The tomcat pretended to be washing under his tail for a moment and then answered, "I don't know. Probably a kind of reformist Orthodox order. I don't think we've dealt with anything similar in recent times. But I can't say for sure."

"Do you think it would be useful if we consulted an expert in religious matters?"

"Maybe we should find out more in the meantime," said the tomcat.

The colonel took a drag on his cigarette and gazed around him.

"Very well, that is what we'll do. It's too early to make predictions. Better you tell me: has Pleşoianu been behaving himself? Did he knock around the bag or handle it with care?"

"With care, Colonel, thank you for your concern."

The tomcat made to leave.

"Listen," said the colonel.

"At your orders," said the tomcat, his whiskers fluttering in the breeze.

"You were late this evening. See that it doesn't happen again."

The tomcat vanished. He was weary, having run quite a way that evening. Crossing Magheru Boulevard was becoming ever more difficult, given the increasing number of cars lately. Moreover, he had to cross the street without giving any hint that he knew anything about traffic regulations, so as not to blow his cover. And on Magheru Boulevard life and death are both just a matter of luck.

■　□　■　□　■

At that time, Colonel Focşăneanu felt that he knew more than anyone else. He had up-to-date information about all the sects and all the groups of various religious orientations in Romania. Never had a Romanian intelligence agency been so up-to-date. The day before, at around ten o'clock, Captain Pleşoianu had presented himself at the target for surveillance in Lahovary Square and said that his name was Mihai Cosma. Then he claimed to be interested in the religious developments around Vespasian Moisa and sat down on the carpet to listen to a lecture. He realized from what was being said that he was in an introductory session for new recruits. He was therefore to be subjected to an indoctrination session. One of his courses at military school had presented this to him very well. It was nothing new, or, in any case, nothing unexpected. Merely thinking about the detailed report he was going to present to Colonel Focşăneanu, he could feel his heart leap from patriotism and pride.

Without understanding very much from the substance of the lecture, because he was an atheist and had no time for such nonsense, Captain Pleşoianu saw that Vespasian Moisa was reading to them from the Bible and interpreting a psalm. From the corner of his eye he spied on the others in the room and wondered if any of them would be capable of handling a gun. Or whether they might at least be capable of some act of civil disobedience. His orders clearly stated that his mission was to "conduct surveillance, gather information, and contribute to the destabilization of the mystical-nationalist sect of Vespasian Moisa." That was his mission. So, here they are. What's so subversive about them? People like this don't seem very dangerous at all. Maybe Maximilian, with his eternally vexed air. Or Saint Peter, who seems to have lost all contact with the real world. It's obvious that he spent last night sleeping in the trash. Which of them could be dangerous? Let's be serious.

Maybe the physician Arghir. He looks like the only one who knows what he's doing. He keeps track of all the money and takes care of meals for the community. He gives orders and is obeyed. The owner of the house seems like a complete nutcase, and his wife's a hysteric.

Vespasian gave the floor to the doctor, who stepped up to the microphone that had now been installed in the dining room. He told them that Orthodoxy had been enriched in our times by a new light shed upon the old holy texts. The captain heard about a book called the *Philokalia,* which was supposed to be important. He heard that the doctor was best able to explain it, because its applications in medicine were miraculous. It was the doctor's turn to continue the session with the fresh initiates. Vespasian sat down in an armchair on the right of the room. He raised his hand to his brow and began to gaze at the floor. His motionless face was inscrutable. It was as if he were wearing a mask, like one of those in Japanese theater. I must remember to mention that motionless, unreal face in the report, the captain told himself.

Now, Arghir was telling them once again about the theory of vibrations and its connection to some code or other. The captain, disguised as a character with the commonplace name Mihai Cosma, was listening. It seems that Romanian is the chosen Language, in which the Lord God codified the cure to all illnesses. Stuff and nonsense, thought the captain. How stupid of Focşaneanu for making me infiltrate this lot! You'd think he knew exactly what boredom was in store for me. What did I ever do to him to make him send me here? Then something changed. Look, the doctor was saying, I was completely bald, and this leonine mane is the direct result of applying to my scalp the treatment I obtained by decoding the Romanian language.

All of a sudden, the captain felt like he was suffocating. He couldn't breathe, and he unfastened one of the buttons of his regulation issue undercover shirt. His most secretly guarded obsession, which preoccupied him so much that it had even invaded his dreams, was the progressive thinning of his hair, a phenomenon that had recently begun to accelerate. It preoccupied him, worried him, obsessed him. In the morning, when he showered, the bathtub would fill up with long strands of hair from the area around his forehead, but also shorter strands, from his nape. It was a natural process, he was told by the specialist dermatologist to whom his unit's doctor had sent him. But the captain was genuinely in despair, because he did not want to lose his hair before getting married. For him, there was an insoluble connection between the two. And so the sermon hit him with full force. For him, the fact that his hair was thinning was something more concrete than the Apocalypse. Therefore, the only thing in the world that would have been capable of exciting him was the decoding of the cures concealed in matter, exemplified by the issue of baldness. Let the preachers frighten others with the Apocalypse. It's baldness that's nigh.

It was no joke.

Baldness is irreversible.

The code at the terminus of matter, at the ends of the earth. The code that can be recovered if you know how to read it. The ends of the earth are here, and these common illnesses are the greatest challenge we face, because we see them at every moment. Thus spoke Arghir, and he was very serious, with that gigantic Afro of his perched on his huge head.

The captain rose to his feet.

"I'd like to try it," said he, and ran his fingers through his hair.

"Of course," said Arghir approvingly, "of course, that will be no problem at all. I'll give you the same solution as the one I used."

"No," said Vespasian, and for a moment those present thought they did not understand.

Mihai Cosma remained standing, puzzled.

"Take off your wolf's clothing," pronounced Vespasian, "and step into our midst naked, as your mother made you. And say the Lord's Prayer thrice, to cleanse yourself of what you are not. For you are not a lie. Come hither and rid yourself of the lie."

They saw Mihai Cosma overcome by chills and trembling, struggling to breathe, writhing like a fish out of water, while the Teacher stretched out both his hands toward him, as if he were transmitting to him a fluid. He shook his head and looked at Vespasian as if he were begging his forgiveness, but he said nothing, and perhaps he could no longer speak, because his throat had begun to swell. He clutched his throat with his hands and fell to the carpet. The others drew to one side, making way for Vespasian, who approached the man into whom they all believed a devil had entered. And he began to writhe.

"Render me unto myself," said the Teacher.

The captain looked at him and saw the same motionless face, and it seemed to him that the voice of him they called the Son of the Lord came not from his mouth but from somewhere overhead, from the sphere of the Heavenly Father, the One who breathed the spirit of life above us and then we found ourselves in the world and began to walk on this earth. It was in this way that he heard him, as if in a dream, coming from far away, from the heavens, and descending like a rain on his tortured body.

And all of a sudden he felt the air: he felt a breeze, below, like the draft under a door. Thinking his cover had been blown, he said, "Forgive me, forgive me. You have read what I am. Forgive me."

Seeing him from down there on the floor, it seemed to him that the Teacher had wings and rested above him, and that the air was coming from him.

"From this day hence your name shall be Pavel," decreed Vespasian Moisa, raising two fingers toward the ceiling.

"But that really is the name on my identity card," admitted the captain, his face drawn.

Then it seemed to him that as he uttered these words, the tomcat on the stove shook his head and made a sign for him to stop. It was as if he were saying, "Don't give yourself away, you moron." In fact, it even seemed to him that the tomcat was rather insistent in his demand, because he was waving his paws in desperation. But he closed his eyes, and when he opened them once more the tomcat was gone. And all of a sudden the captain's heart was invaded by infinite goodness, and he felt that he sincerely loved those people, that they were his brothers, that they would forgive him and love him, that they would give him hair lotion, if he told them the truth.

Two days later, instead of a detailed report about what had been said at the sect's indoctrination sessions, Colonel Focşăneanu received through the normal post (what nerve!) Captain Pleşoianu's resignation, accompanied by a request to renounce his military seniority, accumulated pension, and any other military honors. It was unbelievable. Wasn't that why he had become an officer? How could he have given up all those entitlements without a second's thought? Reading that piece of paper, the colonel felt a need to drink copious amounts of water. Then, through gritted teeth, in a strangled voice, he said, "What the devil does he do to them all?"

■ □ ■ □ ■

The next day, on Sunday morning, Vespasian went out onto the balcony and spoke to them for no more than a minute. In the courtyard of the villa there were almost one hundred people. All of them, in an orderly line, like on a nursery school trip, set off to church to pray. On the way, Vespasian made a signal and they began to sing a hymn. Since there were among them a few genuine musicians, the sound of pleasant music bathed them all. And it was beautiful. It was the most beautiful morning in the world. Many of them were overwhelmed by an elevated feeling, something unmatched by anything they had ever experienced before. But had you asked them to describe that feeling, they would not have succeeded.

From one side, an elderly woman wearing a black headscarf came up to them with a plate of boiled wheat and honey, and said, "Take it, for the sake of his soul!"

Later, many told of how that miraculous boiled wheat was sufficient for all of them to break their fast, many as they were, and that every morning miraculous offerings of that kind would appear. Some put these miracles down to Vespasian Moisa, but he was not the cause, at least not always.

"How beautifully you sing!" the woman told them.

The truth is that some of them were very good, even if their entire musical career had unfolded on the street. And so that ethno-rock fluid that resembled a funeral procession circulated down the road, without any kind of official permit, accompanied by a few astonished traffic policemen, who made no attempt to intervene. And they reached the courtyard of a forgotten church, where an old priest, used to officiating Mass mostly alone, was left with the feeling that the heavens had opened.

■ □ ■ □ ■

CHAPTER SIX

AS NIGHT FALLS, ROMANIA BEGINS TO BE RULED BY SOMEONE OTHER than the government in Victory Square. No one takes seriously that red placard on the first floor of an unfinished block inscribed in white letters with the word GOVERNMENT. How's that, the passerby might ask himself, how could the government be here? The government building is on the other side of the square. This is just an unfinished block. The pipes, connected to the city's mains before the revolution, have burst in the walls, spitting amid the blocks from the time of the construction of socialism cataracts of potable rust. The water seeps into the sandy cement of the subway ceiling, emptying ordure from the hidden guts of the clay. Stridently made-up women walk the boulevard in front of that very spot, spitting on the steps of the block where the troubadours had sung up until dusk. It is another world, one that is inchoate and naked, sprouting from the glory of the ruins. After the hour of twilight, the silhouettes of the unfinished blocks close off the horizon, blot out the moon and stars, erase the outlines of the world, and project a sea of darkness.

On the fourth floor of that block, opposite the Government Palace, a fire was burning on that Sunday evening. Around it could be seen a dozen silhouettes, dressed in long raincoats of indeterminate color.

"We are the real government of Romania!" said Darius to those present that evening.

He sincerely believed it. And with his brothers in conviction he was planning to conquer Bucharest, to wrest it from the influence of the so-called secular administration.

They had become a movement with important connections, with more than a hundred members, with their own code and pragmatic objectives. They regarded themselves as pragmatic, and this distinguished them from all the other undesirables who imagined they were destined by God to save Romania. They really would save it, because everything they did was ruled by pragmatism and action. That evening, what took place was merely a meeting of their general staff, those chosen from among the chosen.

Darius's theory had come into being in the year when the Romanian Orthodox Patriarchate published a large volume entitled *The Lives of the Romanian Saints*. A careful study of this volume had proved to Darius that Saint Stephen the Great had in his turn been a pragmatist, perhaps the most pragmatic Romanian of all times. Every time he ordered a beheading, which his contemporaries reckoned to be a manifestation of his drunken rage or perhaps an outburst of foolhardiness, it was in reality an operation of political cleansing behind which there was a purpose. Let us not view things superficially. The Moldavia of the fifteenth century benefitted from a number of such purges, just as the whole of the fifteenth century can be shown, on careful analysis, to have been surprisingly pragmatic in this respect.

"Our destiny," Darius Georgescu told his followers, "is to live like Stephen, to behave like Stephen, to conquer like Stephen. When our way of life comes to extend to the whole of Romanian society, the Romanian people will have been redeemed. We must suggest to the Romanian people that they should live like the Prince and Saint of Moldavia of old. For many centuries it was useful for men to think to imitate the life of Christ. But for us, in the present day, as Romanians, it is crucial that we go back to our peerless saint."

It is true that there were many theories about the redemption of nations. Darius almost always added to his sermons an important polemical dimension. He was not a Christian because he was inspired by Jesus Christ, but because Stephen had been the Athlete of Christendom. This was what he believed in, the sustained effort of the nation in a clear, well-defined direction. And if the Christian monks live according to the model of Christ, ought not the primary duty of a good and true Romanian to be to live like the nation's most illustrious prince? Darius preached as follows:

"Some have said that the absolute man of Romanian culture was the poet Eminescu. Pah! Nonsense. Not a bit of it! How can you take as your model an obscure journalist who died insane? Wouldn't that be pure madness in itself? Only someone who wished to see this nation slumbering would take such a model. The absolute man of Romanianness was Stephen the Great, and it is precisely his model we should follow. What he did we too should do in every hour. Just as the hermit monks practice ceaseless prayer, so we too should ceaselessly live like Stephen the Great. All that he did let us do also. If he could move a church over a mountain in one night, then we too should be able to do it. If he could defeat the Turks, Hungarians, Polacks, Mongols, and the Wallachians of Bucharest, then we too should be able to do it. And let us thank our God, the God of the Romanians, that He will have helped us to victory. For the message that comes to us from the past is very clear: we need only open the history book and read. That is our Gospel. We ought to conduct Mass using the history book, to pray from it, to take communion with it."

His words were accompanied by guttural noises of approval.

"Here is the commandment that I have for you on this holy Sunday, or rather for next Sunday."

A few of them pulled out their diaries to take notes. The others regarded him with determination. There was no room among them for joking or errors. Everything had to be perfectly coordinated.

"We shall all go, all those who believe in Stephen, to the Armenian Church and pray together. We shall take each in turn and honor with our righteous prayers all the right-believing churches in the capital. We shall pray for all the land to follow us and for the spirit of the great Stephen to be poured upon us, so that whichever way we look we shall see the footprints of Stephen."

"This is what we shall do," answered one of them, Negru, of whom it was said that he had once been junior national Greek wrestling champion.

"Now," went on Darius, "we are called to do something else. We have three commandments for this night."

The fire smoldered in a barrel full of all kinds of recyclable materials, fossil fuels, and various other stuff. Their shadows flickered against the walls. They knew that they would have to conceal themselves, just as the Knights of Malta operated underground in their early days. An objective observer could not have helped seeing that the feature common to their faces was discontent. They were discontent with their reality and in times of discontent all kinds of ideas appear.

They looked at Darius and waited in silence. Some of them had known each other since childhood. Others were meeting for the first time that evening. But to all of them it seemed that everything they had learned in school, everything they had ever experienced, everything converged that evening, when they were called upon to prove themselves.

"The first commandment is that we shall visit a grocery store on First of May Boulevard and leave a message on behalf of Stephen."

There was no need to tell more. A few cheers erupted, even a round of applause.

They checked their motorbike chains, their baseball bats, their studded belts, their knuckle-dusters. One of them extinguished the fire, pouring water over the makeshift hearth.

They descended from the unfinished block, lighting their way with flashlights. They went silently, one behind the other, in single file.

When they reached the start of the boulevard, Darius gave a signal, and they gathered around him. He told them, "He's called Adnan. He's filthy rich. He came from Izmir two years ago."

The grocery store shone in the night. The shop sign, in Turkish, spoke of unintelligible things. In the window were painted green letters, in Romanian, which said, SAUSAGES, CHEESE, PASTRIES. Then, in red, NONSTOP. One of Darius's men went inside and carefully weighed the situation. He came back out and gave a signal: just two. All of a sudden, as if borne through the air by a miracle, a wooden post hurtled toward the window and, with an infernal sound, passed through the pane. A heap of tin cans poured into the street.

The watchman rushed outside. On the threshold he came eye to eye with Darius, who said to him, "Allah may be great, but why do you work for the unbelievers?"

And he struck him with a blunt object, which was shaped like a cross, but served only in such situations.

CHAPTER SIX

51
▾

The rest of the gang poured into the shop, and the last to enter was Darius, who shouted, "Where's Adnan? We know he's here tonight."

Then he said to the cashier, "Leave the till be, we're not here to steal."

"Look, there he is!"

"Is that the Turk over there?"

"Aha!" cried Darius. "Take him outside."

Small and swarthy, Adnan did not seem ready to put up a fight. It would have been hard for him, anyway, because his feet were not touching the ground, and his arms were held fast behind his back. One of the gang was holding him by the hair.

"So, Mr. Adnan. Do you speak Romanian?"

The immobilized man made a face that might have meant anything, but which in the context must have meant, "yes."

"Well, then. Is this your place? Or have others put money into it?"

"Mine," he said.

"What does the sign say? Have you seen what it says?"

"Sausages."

"I don't understand that word there," said Negru, bending over Adnan.

"In Romanian . . . on the window . . ." he was trying to say.

"Yes, but it's written in Romanian underneath. Look what it says up there. What language is that? I don't understand! Why don't I understand? That's not good. Here's what we'll do. Tonight, just ten of us came. Next week, there'll be a hundred, and we'll burn the whole place down. You've got enough time until then to sell the place, to gather together your chattels, and to leave Romania and never come back. And tell them, in the place where you came from, that you're not welcome here."

A moment of silence. Then, suddenly, Darius struck him on the forehead, hard, with the cross. They laid him on the ground and then left the shop without touching anything. One waved good-bye to the cashier.

"That was the first commandment," said Darius. "There will be other similar ones, but that's enough sport for today. Now we'll go on to the second operation."

They set off on foot for the Northern Station. It wasn't far. It took as long to get there as it would to smoke a leisurely cigarette. Darius gave the signal for them to follow him down one of the streets there, into a hidden place. It was a dark backstreet, with no street lamps, shaded by the abundant foliage of a linden tree. On the right there were some old, ramshackle houses. On the left, a piece of waste ground. From somewhere nearby a dog could be heard barking.

"It's here," said Darius.

They went into a courtyard, and Darius whispered to them, "Lights!"

There was a lopsided, mud-spattered stone cross on which could be descried an inscription in Cyrillic. They turned on two flashlights and with a match someone lit a few of those thick candles on which the Patriarchate has the monopoly.

"This is it." He pointed to the cross. "Let's go! To work, valiant warriors!"

The cross was placed in an awkward position. Darius threw his coat to one side and then passed a chain under the arms of the cross. He signaled some of them to pull and others to push the stone. They heaved it once and lifted it into an upright position. Then, they used their hands to raise a heap of earth at its base and keep it from toppling.

"What was here?" asked one of them.

"A church," explained Darius. "Built in 1620 by a munificent boyar. It was dedicated to Saint Nicholas. In the end it burned down, and in 1988 they were getting ready to build some blocks on the site."

A moment of silence. Then Darius said in a whisper, "Do you think we should move it from here?"

"No way," said the one they nicknamed the Knjaz, with a voice that hinted at deep piety. "The cross of a church is made to preserve the sanctity of the spot."

"But this is a rubbish heap. No one even knows to whom this place belongs. It's like a hole in Bucharest."

"This place belongs to this cross. We shouldn't take it from here. Let's lift it out of the mud, yes, but let's not take it away. The cross was sanctified on this spot."

Afterward, the ten shadows went to the bus station. As they waited for the night bus, they conversed. They too had heard rumors. They too knew what was being said. And it was said that a certain Teacher had gathered very many adepts and that he had moved into a villa in Lahovary Square.

"And who is this Vespasian Moisa?"

"He's impotent, deformed," said the Knjaz.

"An imposter."

"Some say he has powers."

"The hell he does!"

Each man lit his cigarette from the other's. Negru said, "We can't let it all go to his head. There are gullible people who would let themselves be led by the hand to church by the first one to preach to them."

Listening to them speak, Darius nodded and added, "Apart from anything else, it is not the right time. Our ideas require the city to be at peace, ready for us, virgin ground. We can't just let some liar convert the whole city to nonaction. We don't need another Gandhi. Our suffering is of a different order. We need to cleanse; we have to impose an idea, a moral model, with a strong foundation in faith. Romania's crisis is profound, and it is of a moral order. And so the third commandment for tonight is a visit to Lahovary Square."

"Very well," said Negru. "What are we going to do with a city whose senses are weary?"

"For tonight," said Darius, "there will just be some graffiti. If he wants more, we'll give him more. He needs to understand. Bucharest is ours."

"Let him clear off out of Bucharest," said Negru.

The next day, on all the walls in Lahovary Square could be read all kinds of insults about Vespasian Moisa. There were tar-black crosses everywhere, others in all the colors of the rainbow. The graffiti also contained threats, and fearsome lewdness. For whoever knew how to read this code, it meant without doubt a declaration of war.

■ □ ■ □ ■

CHAPTER SEVEN

FROM HIS VERY FIRST MEETING WITH VESPASIAN MOISA, THE PHYSI-
cian Arghir sensed that this occurrence would bring out the best in
him. He felt ennobled, a servant of a noble ideal, of an idea whose
brilliance would bring him the gratitude of posterity. This is why
he stopped telephoning his wife or maintaining any links with the
people back in Pitești. He no longer cared. His family was now the
people in the villa in Lahovary Square. He had to take care of them
and to be faithful and devoted to them. It seemed to him that he had
a lot of things to say, to recount, to write—dozens of books, to record
the countless experiences that the profound religious experience he
had undergone was bringing to light. He had been an atheist, and
now he had discovered Christ, and he saw his destiny differently. He
knew to which saints he had to pray. Some say, as he was listening
to the Teacher, an idea of genius occurred to him, one to enhance
the glory of this religious movement. If it had been a question of a
medical research laboratory, he would have known how to proceed.
If it had been a case of a hospital department, likewise he would have
known what was to be done. But now it was a matter of a religious
movement, and things were much more complicated. And he discovered that his role in the setup of the movement was to bring about its
swift recognition by all the public opinion–making bodies. He knew
what he had to do.

The next day, the physician Arghir wrote a letter to His Holiness

Father Teoctist, the Patriarch of the Romanian Orthodox Church. The document is registered in the Chancellery of the Patriarchate with the date May 14, 1993:

Your Holiness the Patriarch,

For centuries the mission of the Romanian Orthodox Church has not been a missionary one, which is to say our ancestral Church has never set off to preach to tribes of Indians, to bring new continents to faith in Christ. Perhaps the times or people have changed, because the time for a missionary order seems to have arrived. Whereas before a prophet was lacking, now there is one. Whereas before we did not have boundless faith, now we have it. Thirty-three years ago there came into the world, from two births at the same time, Vespasian Moisa. He had a Transylvanian birth and a Wallachian birth, just as in his veins there mingle two different kinds of blood. This man has the gift of foreseeing and is destined to make the city of Bucharest the second Jerusalem, for from birth he was born with the map of the city marked on his chest. I myself have been able to see, as a physician, undeniable proofs to support all I have said here.

This is why I beg you, Your Holiness, to summon Vespasian Moisa to an audience. He will bow and kiss the right hand of the Patriarch, and he will dedicate to the Church all those who tread in his footsteps. He is the only and the true prophet of our times. It is he that is called to lead the city of Bucharest to the heavens, as is told in the final book of the Holy Gospels. People believe this, and for many Vespasian Moisa has ceased to be a mere man. The Church ought to understand this and to recognize in him the one for whom it has waited two thousand years. For the hour has come.

Command, Blessed Patriarch, the Orthodox Church to found a right-believing order, and to the heavens shall rise pyres of thanks, and the smoke of the sacrifices shall make this city seem as it were fashioned from the spirit only. This city is summoned before the Lord, that it might be judged by its faith. Command, Blessed Patriarch, and the Benedictine, Jesuit, and Franciscan orders shall be swallowed up by history, shall be forgotten, because none of them has had a prophet who could transform the rod into a snake, give form to water, and walk upon the clouds. Vespasian Moisa is all these things, if not more.

With profound and right-believing Orthodox faith,

Yours, the pious etc.

Apolodor Arghir

This letter had not been easy to write, because it explored the translucent boundaries between demanding and pleading. But Arghir was satisfied with the results of his efforts. The reply from the Chancellery of His Holiness Patriarch Teoctist to the right-believing Arghir was not long in coming:

Bucharest, May 16, 1993

Beloved believer in Our Lord Jesus Christ,

It strengthens us spiritually to see such faith and such generosity on the part of a layman with such pure and unshakeable faith. We shall keep you in our prayers and we shall pray for the Lord's servants Vespasian and Apolodor, that their right-believing works may come to serve the poor and needy. May your care heal the wounds of those who are injured and may your deeds bring justice to those who have lost the Way. For Our Father that is in heaven will look down and rejoice to see the work of the Holy Spirit embodied in men of faith. We shall pray and we shall watch over the increase of your faith, together with the achievements and the alleviation of the suffering of those who have need of you.

May the Lord watch over you!

Teoctist
Patriarch of the Romanian Orthodox Church

cc: The Secretary of the Chancellery of His Holiness the Patriarch, Manoil of Snagov

On reading this reply, the physician decided to address other potential sources of recognition. Here is the letter the physician Apolodor Arghir wrote to the Director of the Soros Foundation for an Open Society, on May 18, 1993:

Dear Sir,

As part of your Foundation's programs to develop an open society in Romania, especial attention is paid to freedom of religious belief. The religious movement that follows Vespasian Moisa, called the Teacher, was born of the need for broad social structures in order to allow the populace to see its hopes fulfilled and illusions translated into fact. The frustrations of the decades of communism hinder the establishment of an open society in Romania today. Vespasian Moisa, in the unaltered space of the ancestral Orthodox faith, gives genuine spiritual fulfillment to all. The psychological context of this fulfillment is extremely propitious both for the Euro-Atlantic integration of Romania and the construction of an open society, in which free individuals will have the right to move along the vertical axis of creativity, as well as along the horizontal axis of the spiritual. These people need not so much God as much as His incarnate vision. They need not so much heaven as much as to see heaven. This is why, if you will permit me, I should like to advance through this exploratory document the idea of the opportunity of your organization providing a grant to the Orthodox religious movement that follows Vespasian Moisa. Financial support would allow us to open a conference room in which the movement's creative energies would be able to manifest themselves fully. A democratic framework for discussion would allow the energies of the participants to coagulate and enable them to express themselves freely as individuals useful to society.

Yours faithfully,
Apolodor Arghir

Specialist in the problems of an open society
Tidings of the Lord Movement
Lahovary Square, no. 9
Bucharest, Sector 2

This letter went unanswered. But nothing could discourage Vespasian Moisa's devoted adviser. He understood from the very first that his highest duty was to assist the Teacher, who had no knack at all when it came to such worldly affairs, and that he was foreordained to find suitable funding for the Movement and to ensure the most suitable interaction with all the fundamental institutions of state. He thought very long on all this. Every evening, in the mansard of the villa, he would sit down to write. A trusted courier, a man who prayed constantly with the name of the Teacher on his lips, would run off first thing in the morning to deliver the letter to the precise address indicated, so that these messages would be subject to no delay.

The third letter was addressed to the Head of Army Group I General Staff, and was delivered twenty-four hours after the preceding missive.

Esteemed General,

The two fundamental institutions of the Romanian people, the Church and the Army, have been called more than once during the course of history to lend their hands. Although our recent Constitution makes separation of the powers of State statutory, we understand very well that Church and Army are institutions that correspond to man's fundamental needs: the need for God and the need for a Homeland. Blessed are they that can dedicate their life to both pennants as if they were one. Blessed are they that tread in the footsteps of those who guide us down these paths.

I write to you in the capacity of a lieutenant-major in the reserve, having completed all the specialist military stages in a timely fashion.

The missionary order of the Tidings of the Lord came into being almost one year ago. One of our main activities is the series of lectures we have dedicated to Saint Andrew the Apostle. Our lecturers are experts in their scientific fields, prestigious professors and pedagogues. Our series of lectures has up until now explored subjects such as *God and Homeland, The Theory of Vibrations and the Prayer of the Heart in Orthodoxy,* and *Faith and the National Essence of the Romanian People.* I should like to take this opportunity to express our availability to hold a series of lectures on topics you deem useful at the military bases of your choice, perhaps with the overall title *Praise the Lord! Praise the Homeland!* The long-term effect on the troops can only be beneficial. Edified as to these matters concerning faith, prayer, and the afterlife, the soldiers will gain a deeper understanding of their mission to serve the country and will undertake the missions ordered by their superiors with a greater sense of abnegation. Our experts in psychology expect an extraordinarily positive effect on the troops.

CHAPTER SEVEN

I remain at your service with a view to analysis of the proposals presented above,
Apolodor Arghir
Scientific Secretary of the Order of the Tidings of the Lord

This had been the letter upon which the physician was pinning his greatest hopes. It seemed to him the most natural development of matters. Whenever he thought about it, this was how it seemed to him. From his army days he recalled the lectures he had attended. Once, on National Day, 1 December, it had been the turn of a staff major to speak about the Unification of Romania in 1918. He arrived with a three-page text he had prepared in advance and spoke tonelessly, unenthusiastically, before some three hundred soldiers, who, presumably, ought to have sat bolt upright. The text was dreadful, badly written, and chock full of clichés. And so Arghir knew very well the level of these sessions of so-called civic and patriotic education. But if Vespasian could convert people off the street, his persuasive effect would be greatly enhanced in barracks conditions. Vespasian's lectures would be like a machine into which you fed footsloggers at one end and which turned out authentic patriots at the other. The general would have to be sensitive to that. This is why, without consulting Vespasian, he decided that it would be best to get the Tidings of the Lord the greatest possible exposure. The lectures would be a mere bagatelle for them. If Vespasian was tired or couldn't do a tour of army bases, he himself would venture to carry out the task, in the absence of any other volunteer. Didn't they spend the whole day presenting inner prayer and the theory of the antiquity of the Romanian language to new arrivals anyway?

Great was his astonishment when he received not long thereafter the following missive, but, very strangely, not from the Army, as he would have expected, but from the Ministry of Culture. The official letter, with the letterhead of the Ministry, went like this:

Dear Doctor Arghir,
We hereby notify you that the Committees of the Ministry of Culture have unanimously voted to award your application for funding of the project entitled *Praise the Lord! Praise the Homeland!* a grant consisting of:

- One hundred thousand lei for current expenses

- A lecture room in the Faculty of Technology, at the campus in the village of Bragadiru, with thirty-six chairs and tables and a heater

- An ARO 10 1986-model jeep, in perfect condition

- As a place of worship for the Mission of the Teacher the Church of St. Anthony in Călăraşi has been allocated. Due to a temporary demographic crisis, the church is currently in a state of disrepair. In exchange for these premises, the Mission is required to repaint the church, put in windows, rebuild the chimney, and repair the woodwork, which is of particular historic value, as the church was constructed entirely from wood in 1902 and visited by Minister of Education Spiru Haret in the autumn of that year.

Please find the above services at your disposal,
The Minister of Culture,
(Signatures)

On receipt of this letter in the Order's chancellery, which now operated from the attic of the villa in Lahovary Square, Dr. Arghir hastily made the sign of the cross and gave a deep sigh. He thought of himself as a pragmatic man. He wanted to obtain something from all the state institutions, and he was convinced that he was now on the right track. And wasn't this a good start, to receive money from the Ministry of Culture? Perhaps it was not much materially, but from the political point of view, you never know, it might prove useful. And so Dr. Arghir was very happy with the results of his requests thus far. It was not until then that he shared with any other person information about his secret undertakings in aid of the Order. He discussed it with Professor Diaconescu. And, also as a shrewd political gambit, he said, "I think we ought to propose Spiru Haret for sainthood. It would be an important political move, and it would create a precedent that would oblige the authorities to grant us more attention . . ."

"What are we going to do, move all the way to Călăraşi?" asked Professor Diaconescu.

Arghir, overcome with a pragmatic spirit, answered, "Maybe later on. What we have to do now is conquer Bucharest. We can't afford to stop until we have this city at our feet."

"And what are we going to do about the letter? Aren't we going to take possession of what they've given us?"

The physician waved his hand.

"We'll take what we need—the money and the car—and keep the letter. Let others repaint the church. We've got serious business in Bucharest. What would we do out there in the wilds?"

CHAPTER EIGHT

"THANK YOU, DOCTOR, FOR YOUR TIME," SAID THE MAN.
He had taken a seat in the armchair in front of the desk and laid his document folder on his knees. It was the first audience that the physician Arghir, now secretary of the Order of the Tidings of the Lord, was giving that morning. The first on his guest list was Professor Pantelimon Rădulescu, who for twenty years had worked at the Academy's Institute. The professor was visibly a great lover of the faith. Dr. Apolodor Arghir received him as a distinguished guest, with excessive politeness and great attentiveness. The professor wrote a science column for the *Stop Press* daily newspaper, and for the physician, even if the daily in question had lately been losing readers, such a connection was extremely important. He would not even dream of letting the professor go away without having converted. As he wanted to charm his guest, he asked the Troubadour to stay with them during the interview. His mere presence had up until then proved on a number of occasions more effective than mere arguments.

"The pleasure is all ours," said the physician, cloyingly.

Pantelimon Rădulescu was a solidly built man, with a high forehead, thinning hair, a voluntary beard, and a rather fixed grimace. The physician measured him up with a single gaze. His new office as secretary of the Order was formerly the workroom of the businessman who had donated the villa. The physician had kept the massive mahogany desk and rare wood bookcase, which he had filled with old and more recent editions of ecclesiastical tomes, breviaries, and the *Lives of the Saints,* books reckoned to be needful for the entire religious order. He had made all the arrangements overnight, in order to keep things running at maximum capacity. He had as much assistance as he required: the courtyard was full of new converts. Some of them slept there in tents or in sleeping bags in the open. Saint Peter had been appointed head librarian, and he had introduced his own system of cataloging for the entire database. By the door of the office there was a computer with an extremely simple search engine, which anyone could use. In the room alongside, two former book editors, converts to the faith of Vespasian Moisa and the Lord in the heavens, worked day and night typing up *The Lives of the Romanian Saints* on Vasile Gheorghe's computers. In the room in which secretary general Arghir received the great man of science Pantelimon Rădulescu, the pattering sound of their keyboards was audible.

"The pleasure is mine," said the researcher, "because I have heard so many things about your ideas, and I am very curious to learn more. I'm interested in the direction of your thinking, from many points of view."

Pantelimon looked at the Troubadour. He was wearing a freshly ironed blue shirt, open at the neck. His smooth, bronzed chest was showing.

"Things have become more complicated," said the physician, "in the beginning it was merely a discussion of a religious nature, between ourselves, between the faithful, but in time we have come to understand much more. We believe that we have managed to range ever deeper into our ancestral belief, that we have elevated our understanding to the level of a doctrine with multiple extensions in various scientific fields."

"People are very persuaded by what they hear from you," said Pantelimon, with a fox-like look, nodding his head toward the window that overlooked the courtyard, whence came strains of song.

"It is the truth itself," remarked the physician sincerely.

"Yes, yes, of course," agreed the researcher, with the same cunning look.

"The truth has not reached people. And it would be hard for me to tell you how many have received it. There are days when I get the feeling that the whole of Bucharest has converted. We're besieged, and when the Teacher goes out onto the balcony, he is greeted with cheers.

Sometimes, the whole of Lahovary Square fills up with the faithful. It's something triumphal."

Pantelimon cleared his throat and settled himself more comfortably in the armchair. Perhaps he had not been expecting Apolodor Arghir to mention the conversion of so many people. He said, "I see that many aspects of your Order's doctrine speak of the theory of vibrations."

"Yes, and we have begun to understand more and more about it."

"Would you agree to talk a little about this?" asked Pantelimon.

"We would be delighted to! Would you like us to invite other members of the Order to join us?" offered the physician with a regal gesture of his hand.

"No, I would rather we tried to understand by ourselves how things stand, to see what it is all about first of all. Then, after we have understood how things stand, your friends are of course more than welcome. This story is somehow connected to certain things I'm interested in and which I've been studying my entire life. I began these studies twenty years ago."

He took from the table a glass of water. He took a sip, as if he needed a second to recompose himself, to breathe. He looked once more at the Troubadour's chest and went on.

"Back then I was working at the Academy's Institute, in the astrophysics and astronomy section. Every six months, we had to write an activity report. For a while, I was able to conceal the true nature of my research, but after a given point it became obvious from the nature of my investigations, so that those things raised a number of questions. I was investigated by the management of the Institute and subsequently called to order by the Securitate. Yes, dear sir, my research, although strictly theoretical, was in the sights of the Securitate. Things had become complicated. Then they offered me an amicable solution: for me to be transferred into industry. They said it politely enough, but I don't know how much of a choice I had. I wasn't holding the bread and the breadknife. They asked me why I didn't publish the results of my research. How could I have published them when what I had was in contradiction to what the vast majority of mankind believes, in contradiction with what everyone learns at school? We scientists have learned what there was to be learned from the story of Giordano Bruno. For a long time I worked in the Heavy Machinery Plant, then at the Automatica Factory, and after 1988 for the Railways, in the computer programming section. After the revolution, I was reinstated at the Academy's Institute as a researcher, and the Liviu Maior University did me the honor of appointing me to a professorship. I am telling you all this in order to put my research into context. Let us say a historical context. I paid heavily for the things I have researched and for what I believe. I have an entire history behind me, and what I am about to tell you this evening is a belief as dearly won as that of Galileo, who was so aware of the risks to which he exposed himself. There are some even today who would like to see authentic researchers burned at the stake."

He put the glass of water back onto the table.

The physician ran his fingers through his leonine mane and asked, with a spark of interest in his eyes, "Is it connected with the Theory of Vibrations?"

"Yes, and most directly. I shall explain to you where these vibrations come from and how the background noise that separates us from attaining the source-sound of the cosmic medium can be eliminated."

The physician frowned. He had read things about this, but never anything of this kind. For a moment he was worried that he was wasting his time with the professor. But he remembered the newspaper column and smiled.

"We read many things about the tenth planet of the solar system. Sometimes, unexpected calculations reveal distortions of the spacetime in the immediate vicinity of the solar system. It happened most recently with one of the Voyager probes, which was unexpectedly pulled in a different direction. A while ago, people talked a lot about that. But today those gravitational disturbances are regarded as anomalies, because we can't explain them, it seems like we have understood them, but we permit anomalies in our mathematical models. The rationalism of previous years is nothing more than a dictatorship at the informational level in circles at Pasadena or Baikonur. It's simple: they think that it is impossible for us to understand a poor little solar system with one star and nine planets. But wait a minute. How is it possible for us to send up a space probe which, at a certain distance from the Earth is thrown off its predicted trajectory? How is it possible for us to lose radio contact with satellites orbiting the Earth?

What are the vibrations that distort all these transmissions? How is it possible for a certain number of airplanes and ships to disappear in certain geographical zones of the Earth? What is going on in the Bermuda Triangle? Aren't all these things interconnected?"

The physician felt a golden bird alighting on his shoulder.

"It would be wonderful to be able to explain all these things by means of a unified theory."

"You have that theory," said Pantelimon. "You have arrived at it through faith, but you are not at all far from the scientific truth."

He rose to his feet, as if he were giving a lecture before a hand-picked audience. Clasping his hands behind his back, he went on.

"My theory is that the sun has a sister star, by the name of Nemesis, extinguished and dark, an emitter of vibrations, whose orbit is highly eccentric. The hypothesis of the existence of the star Nemesis was made by Johann Bermeyer, in a work published in the *Journal of Astrophysical Theory* in 1922. What he constructed there was a complete theory. He wrote up the equations for the motion of the eight planets (the number known at the time) in the solar system, according to the hypothesis that Nemesis exists. The article was published, but it wasn't much read at the time, and no one took it very seriously. In fact, Professor Bermeyer rather ruined his reputation, especially after he lectured on the same subject in 1925. He defended the existence of the star Nemesis until his death in 1929 from heart failure. It is hard to pinpoint the location of Nemesis. At very large intervals of time, Nemesis approaches the Earth, and then the conjunction of the two stars releases *global killers,* as must have happened with the extinctions of the Permian period or the meteorite that caused the extinction of the dinosaurs. We are talking about intervals of hundreds of millions of years. In any case, Nemesis is a star with the dimensions of the sun, which does not emit light but only sequences of vibrations. It is the source of the residual vibrations not only on Earth but also throughout the solar system. They have been documented and recorded for decades. There are all kinds of databases, but there is no unifying theory to incorporate them. They are predictable, ultimately, and must follow a certain pattern, but to all those scientists it's not at all obvious where they are coming from, although the source is much closer than Tau Ceti, for example. As a rule, we see everything that reflects light, but we can't see something that doesn't reflect but only vibrates in the darkness. And the strange part is that it sends out mini-vibrations through the entire solar system, and these are like bullets fired from a gun, ricocheting like billiard balls against the walls around, by who knows what arrangement of reflective angles, striking us and interfering with our radio signals, with all kinds of vibrations around the Earth . . ."

Apolodor Arghir listened, rooted to the spot. When Pantelimon Rădulescu fell silent, he asked, "And has anything of all this been demonstrated?"

"Yes, my results in this direction unfolded as part of a serious research program at the Academy's Institute. The most delicate thing was when I asked for a laboratory and equipment. I don't know how my results upset the communists, I mean, so there's another star, so what? What was the problem in that? I wasn't saying anything about their Marx or Ceaușescu. Ceaușescu probably couldn't have cared less how many stars there were. It was ridiculous. None of them understood anything. They packed me off to that factory without bothering to listen to what I had to say. And what I had was dozens and dozens of pages of very eloquent calculations. It's possible to work with the hypothesis that there is an emission source for this 'background noise' in the universe, and in this way a number of things become explicable. Even the Bermuda Triangle."

"Even that?"

"Even that."

"How?" said the physician, burning with curiosity.

"Unfortunately, I'm afraid that the aleatory discharges of energy are attracted by the Earth's energy poles, which are three in number. I know it sounds strange. I mean for the Earth to have three energy poles, but that's the way it is. One of these poles is in the Bermuda Triangle. Well, such discharges of energy can lead to the disappearance of matter in the form that we know it. It would be as if stone were suddenly transformed into vapor, as if all the humidity went out of wood, as if any object acquired a dual essence and the object were annihilated beneath our very eyes . . ."

"Is that what is going on down there?" said the physician, somehow disappointed. "A dual nature?"

"Yes, but for that I have no proof, just as I have no proof for what is going on with the planet Pluto."

"What's that about?"

"In fact, Pluto is the only planet which, when observed from afar, doesn't give any sign of Nemesis being nearby, although it's the closest to it. It seems that the planet is not affected by the presence of that heavenly body."

"How so?"

"I don't think we have enough data." The professor shrugged. "We would need a probe on the surface of the planet, to record the radio waves, sound waves, cosmic rays, everything that can be 'heard' on Pluto. We don't have anything of the sort. We just gaze at that chunk of rock, a little larger than the moon, and it seems to us that it is revolving undisturbed through space. But in reality, Pluto might mark exactly the halfway point of the gravitational field between the sun and Nemesis. The three must come into alignment at certain times, causing all kinds of strange positions, which mess up all our calculations here on Earth because we lack sufficient data."

Dr. Arghir covered his face with his hands and then, with an agitated gesture, he turned to his guest and said, "What I am about to tell you I have never before revealed to anyone. One day it will be known anyhow, and I don't see what would be bad in that. It is something that I have discovered by living for so long in close proximity to Vespasian Moisa. There is something unusual in his powers of concentration, in his way of reading people, of perceiving the profound psychological aspects of someone in just a fraction of a second . . . He has something wholly special, something never heard of before in Romania: he has the power to perceive all kinds of vibrations, all kinds of phenomena which those children torture themselves to capture with their countless apparatuses. On the heads of sharks there are tiny pores, known as *ampullae Lorenzini,* which allow the shark to perceive the weak electric currents given off by living creatures from a certain proximity. It is as if they feel the vibrations, even when they cannot see them. It is as if they see in the dark, as if they see movement. In the same way, on Vespasian Moisa's body there is a special organ that detects vibrations. It is something unique, similar to that shark sensory organ, and it takes the unusual form of a map of Bucharest. So, Vespasian Moisa was born with this extraordinary tool, with an additional sensory capacity compared with the rest of us. He probably hears everything we think, sometimes. He can probably hear us talking right now, here, although he is up in one of the rooms in the attic . . ."

"I didn't know anything about that organ the sharks have," said the professor. "And what can they perceive?"

"Vibrations, that is for certain, it has been proven. But it is highly likely they can perceive much more than that."

"You are saying that there might be people with such paranormal perception in the sphere of vibrations?"

"Yes, but there probably aren't many, only the very lucky ones, only the *chosen* ones."

"And they have a special organ for this?"

"It would seem so."

"Vespasian?"

"He does, without doubt!" confirmed the physician Arghir.

"Has he been studied? I mean, if I can put it like this, is it known what range of vibrations he can hear?"

"No, I have never seen him as an object of study . . ."

"With the deepest respect, doctor, allow me to tell you that what we have here is probably the great key to the understanding of many things. The stakes are so high that we should like to know what is happening. I say this with the utmost seriousness."

"I understand what you are saying, professor. We are talking about the same thing."

"A medical examination is necessary. A study of sensory capacities."

"And if, let us say, he happens to hear so many things, to be so highly endowed that he quite simply feels the vibrations of the stars, it is possible that he might not realize that he is different from us, from others. He is the Son of the Lord and his goodness is infinite. He is good and he believes that we should all save our souls and he wants to help us, and so on. He doesn't think about the differences between us, but rather about how he might help us."

With the same fox-like look, but this time cast at the floor, the professor said, "Yes, of course . . ."

On the bookshelf the tomcat was purring contentedly. It seemed as if he heard and saw nothing, although his ears were pricked up.

The Troubadour stroked him as he left the room.

COMING FROM AN OFF-KEY TIME

"What's happening in there?" asked Maximilian, whose turn it was to copy some passages from *The Lives of the Saints* on the computer.

"I've found out what Vespasian has on his chest," said Toni, standing in front of the closed door.

"The map of Bucharest, we all know that."

"He has a kind of ear with which he can hear vibrations. It's called Lorenzini's ampullae. All kinds of marine life have something similar. He can feel whether a man is good or evil, whether he's a criminal or a benefactor. He can see the past, present, and future."

"You don't say," gasped Maximilian.

"Oh, yes," said the Troubadour. "Listen to what I'm telling you. We're at the center of the world. We shouldn't sleep even for an instant. We should rejoice in every second of life, and thank the Lord that He has given us the Teacher."

All of a sudden, Maximilian clasped him in his arms and hugged him tightly for a moment. Then he began to weep.

■ □ ■ □ ■

In one of the attic rooms, the former owner of the house, former owner of the Robot Import Export Company, Vasile Gheorghe was doing his penance. The physician had imposed this obedience. Yesterday, he had given him a book of grammar to read. Today, he had gone on to more pressing and more important titles, within a rapid algorithm to attain lucidity. Julius came into the room and saw him dressed in a long black robe, with some kind of wooden beads around the throat, which he was fingering. He was rocking back and forth gently, as if parroting the multiplication table. The beads rested on his vest, which was poking, belly and all, through the robe.

"Excuse me," whispered Julius, "I was looking for a quiet place to read."

Vasile Gheorghe said nothing. He went on rocking back and forth. Eventually, he said, "I've never used this word."

"What word?"

"Look," he said, and showed him a book whose cover had wrappers made of newspaper.

And he said, "The word *intru*."

"Strange," said Julius, "but I've never used it either. What book is that?"

He closed the door behind him and went up to the chair on which the former manager general was sitting. He mouthed the words of the title on the frontispiece of the book.

"What a bizarre title! What does it mean? Who gave you this?"

With pure tears on his cheeks, Vasile Gheorghe said, "Arghir . . . He told me to read it and then to go describe it to him. I thought he wanted to help me understand, but I think that in fact he wants to punish me. I heard Vespasian saying that suffering brings understanding of doctrine more quickly than study. I'm afraid that this is the path that Vespasian has decided upon for me, and I think that Arghir merely brought the idea to fruition. If I want redemption, I have to suffer. I think that the Teacher told Arghir to make me suffer."

"Wait a moment, Mr. Arghir wanted to help you. I don't think Vespasian could ever have said anything like that!"

"I don't know, I don't know any more . . . The purposes of this world are a mystery, and the Romanian language is the key . . . The time has come for me to suffer."

The tears flowed down his cheeks, silently. He was prey to an inner unrest. Julius bent toward him and embraced him. He said, "Perhaps we should all learn new words. Romanian is such a rich language! Do you know how many words there are in the poems of Nichita? More than three hundred thousand separate words! It wouldn't be so bad if we had to learn the words that go in the poems . . ."

Then Vasile Gheorghe tapped his fingers on the book, shook his head, and said something that he would later regard as having been a very grave sin: "This doctrine is devilishly hard!"

■ □ ■ □ ■

CHAPTER NINE

ONLY ONE FLASHLIGHT WAS BURNING IN THE MIDDLE OF THE ROOM IN
the unfinished block on Victory Square.

"It's impossible," shouted Darius when he heard the news.

"It is said that the tombstone of Stephen the Great in Putna Monastery moved in that very moment," said Negru.

"Lord God in Heaven, it's impossible!"

The truth is that the idea of reincarnation is not exactly Orthodox.
The fact that they were talking about reincarnation unsettled them
all. At first, Darius would not believe any of it. He clasped his hands
to his head. He did not want to give credence to the rumor.

"Go on," said Darius.

The one who went by the nickname "the Knjaz," said, "It seems
that the man really does remember things that happened in the fifteenth century. The story began a few months ago, when he was hit
by a truck somewhere in Nicolina. They took him to the emergency
room and he lay in a coma for two weeks. A lot of people thought he
was done for. He had a serious head injury. But then he woke up, and
he was more coherent than before. Something had changed. He was a
different man, as if he had gone back to being what he ought to have
been, beyond the crust of everyday life."

"That's right," said Negru.

Darius looked at him for a long while. He could not see what there
was to approve.

"And what he remembered," the Knjaz went on, "were precise episodes from the past. He told a journalist from the *Jassy Chronicle* that at the battle of the High Bridge the Moldavian army had not sent forty thousand men into the fray, as is believed, but only twenty-eight thousand. He told the story of the battle in the minutest, most exact detail. The article was published two months ago. But yesterday he was on local television, and he confirmed that he is the reincarnation of Stephen the Great. He said that he remembers his entire previous life, precisely because he had reached that turning point between life and death where any barrier between lives is moved aside and the recovery of spiritual memory becomes possible. The physical memory is what the body remembers. The spiritual memory is what the soul has experienced during its long chain of reincarnations. This man can remember his last three lives. He was also reincarnated in the seventeenth century, but it wasn't an interesting life. On the other hand, what he says about the life prior to that one is astonishing. It looks like we're dealing with the reincarnated Saint Stephen the Great."

Darius cleared his throat. For some unknown reason, he did not seem very happy at this news. He said, "Are we sure it's like that? How can we know he's not just some loony who got run over by a truck and who's now seeing that historical film with Gheorghe Cozorici in the role of Stephen?"

"That's what I thought at first. But, after reading the interview and seeing the film recording made in Jassy, I for one was convinced. I think it's real. You know, there is something in it."

"I'd like to find out more before I rejoice as much as you, brother," said Darius.

"I got hold of his telephone number last night," said the Knjaz. "I spoke with him. I've invited him to Bucharest. I told him about us. He'll be arriving in two hours, on the Intercity. I think we should decide what to do."

"What else can we do? Let's get to the train station!" said Negru.

"That goes without saying," admitted Darius, in a voice less energetic than usual. "But how are we going to tell who he is and what he wants?"

A moment of silence. Then, with a playful smile, Darius said, "We'll receive him as if we were convinced that he is the Great Stephen. Then we'll bring him back here and talk to him. And we'll ask him about various historical events. Things we know about, things for which we have verifiable, clearly confirmed information. By the way, where's Neagu?"

"Neagu's at home," answered the Knjaz.

"Do you think Neagu knows enough about Stephen the Great?" asked Darius Georgescu rhetorically.

"Of course! Didn't he write an undergraduate thesis on him? Don't you remember how much he's stuffed our heads full of him? He's obsessed with Stephen the Great!"

"That's right. Negru, go to his house and fetch him. Bring him to the unfinished block in Icon Gardens at eight o'clock. We're going to the station to meet the train from Jassy."

"You do realize," said Negru, "what it means if it's true? You do realize? The Tidings of the Lord group claim they have the Son of the Lord, but that's not at all certain. But we could have Stephen the Great himself on our side! That lot from the Tidings of the Lord sit all day in a villa chattering and cooking up theories, and the streets are ours, they're all ours. Bucharest is ours. We've got them beat. We'll be the most powerful movement in Bucharest. We'll succeed. We've got them beat."

Darius laid his hand on his shoulders and looked into his eyes, as if trying to hint that it was a far more serious affair than might be believed at first sight.

"Maybe it's not a good idea for us to set off with preconceived ideas. Let's not set off with the expectation that Stephen the Great himself is really waiting for us on the platform at the Northern Station. Let's not expect to see what might not exist. If we're mistaken in this, then we're finished. Not even the devil will ever believe us again if we're stupid now."

"That's right. It's better like that," agreed the other.

"He's a man who got run over by a truck, I hope you do realize."

A deep sigh could be heard.

Then they started discussing the best way to get to the Northern Station. They decided to take the subway from Victory Square to the next station. On the way they didn't talk much. They were all deep in thought. If they discovered that it was all just a hoax or a case of insanity, would it not deflate all their enthusiasm for the Cause? This

CHAPTER NINE

75
▼

was what Darius was thinking. Of course, it wouldn't. A true warrior has to know how to face the enemy's diversionary tactics. The devil himself might send them a madman to confuse them. The cause of the true and authentic Stephen was not in doubt here. This was not what was at stake, but rather the truth. The lofty truth of the Romanian people—that was what was at stake.

In the subway, the wooden cross Negru used as a weapon fell out of his black raincoat onto the floor of the train. He swiftly picked it up. The other passengers pretended not to notice. The truth is that few had ever seen the like—a weapon in the form of a communion wafer stamp.

They finally reached the platform and waited for the arrival of the train from Jassy.

■ ◻ ■ ◻ ■

When the man alighted from the Jassy train, they recognized him on the spot. They were waiting for him on the platform and headed toward him. Although he was not tall, they spotted him from a distance. He was a small man, with broad, muscular shoulders. His long, blond hair reached to his shoulders. A bushy blond mustache illumined his face. His forehead was scored by a deep, vertical wrinkle. On his cheek he had a red scar, from the accident.

They remained motionless before him.

For an instant, none could speak. Then Darius knelt and made a sweeping gesture of obeisance before the mediaeval lord. He said, "Welcome, Sire!"

The others also kneeled.

"Hail, warriors," said the stranger, without appearing in the least surprised by the welcome he had received.

"Let us go," said Negru. "I think we'll all manage to fit in four taxis."

The Knjaz made a sign for the guest to follow him, and the latter, with a ceremonial air, gave a slight nod of the head. Negru lit a cigarette. He felt he needed one. They left the Northern Station and hailed the taxis.

■ ◻ ■ ◻ ■

Once they arrived in the unfinished block in Icon Gardens, they invited the guest to ascend first.

"What is this place?" he asked.

"It is our headquarters," replied Darius with undisguised pride.

They reached the fourth floor. There were ten cast-iron chairs arranged in a circle around a large, round chunk of concrete. In the corners of the room, which had been designed as a huge dining room, there were barrels ready to be lit. On the wall there was a torch at the ready. Negru went and kindled it with his cigarette lighter.

"We are on our way to closing the ranks," said Darius, who was following the guest from the corner of his eye.

"Do you go to church?" the latter suddenly asked.

"Yes, we sometimes go together."

"Every Sunday?"

"No, not quite, but we often go together."

"Do you stay until the end of the service?"

"No, we stay for about an hour . . ."

"It's very important to stay for the whole service and to take communion at the end. And to go to confession frequently. You are warriors and for you this would be well. It is very important how your souls travel through this world."

He then pointed at the Knjaz. "How often have you confessed this year?"

The tall young man with the swarthy face looked around him. Then he replied, "Never."

"What about last year?"

"Last year neither. I've never gone to confession."

"Aha," said the guest, running his hand through his hair.

He went up to Darius and touched his face. He pulled his eyelid down and looked carefully at the lower part of the pupil. He said, "It is likewise very important that you should shit regularly, to eliminate all the toxins from your organisms. You haven't had a shit today. Stand back. What's your name?"

"Darius, Your Highness."

Then Neagu smiled politely and asked, trying to change the subject, "We could hardly wait to meet you. Not in my wildest dreams did I ever think we would meet you. I would have liked to sit and talk with Your Highness like I did with my grandfather."

CHAPTER NINE

The guest smiled indulgently. Neagu, encouraged by the smile, went on. "Do you remember, Your Highness, the days when you commanded Filip Pop the Spatharius to cross into Szekler territory? What was it that happened after that? Tell us the story, if you please."

The blond man scratched his chin, as if he were recalling something that had taken place but the day before.

"Yes, I recollect it very well. All the armies that came to invade the land of Moldavia had always found as many swords as they needed in Szekler country. It was the year when I caught Petru Aron and shortened him by a head, for dealing in plots and writing letters to the boyars and Prince Cazimir to become ruler of Moldavia. Filip Pop was a trusty man, greatly skilled in combat: he knew how to guard his own hide and to flay that of the man he faced, and to thrust his men into the fray and bring them out again safe. And I gave him the command to take men from two villages of free peasants and to pillage the Szekler land to their hearts' content, damn those Hungarian nobles and their swinish font! Who was it that made up the bulk of the army that Mátyás brought to Baia? Who was it that made up the bulk of the army raised by Daroch János? Four thousand Szeklers. Who was it that wailed the loudest for Daroch János when our free peasants took his head? Why was it that each time Moldavia was invaded it was the Szeklers that were the most eager for battle? Tell me! Well, how could I not command Filip Pop to do to the Szeklers what the Tartars had done to us in the land of Hotin? We could play the Tartar too, if needed, the fucking curs! Was it not so that we could do that too?"

After a moment of silence, somewhat troubled by the tale, Neagu cleared his throat. "That's right, Your Highness," he said.

"Go on," murmured Darius, who for the first time had begun to be genuinely interested in history.

"Yes, it taught them a lesson," said Stephen, "for some years later, five thousand Szeklers came to join us in the battle at the High Bridge. It did them good. Fear too is a kind of love."

Neagu gave a discreet nod to Darius.

"Your Highness, if you don't mind, I would like to ask you something."

"Out with it."

Here, Neagu felt it fitting to rise respectfully to his feet.

"Tell us how it was in the war with Laiotă Basarab."

"Ah, that communion wafer of an old trollop!" said the reincarnation of Stephen the Great. "Many were the betrayals I saw in that life, starting with Crăsnaș the Dvornik, who thought not to go into battle as I had ordered him, and for that I had him flayed, but the greatest betrayal I was to see came from Laiotă Basarab. Not one drop of manly blood ran in his veins! The only thing he thought of from dawn to dusk was how to become *voievod* more quickly, how to crawl to the Hungarians, how to crawl to the Turks, how to crawl to the Polacks, just so that he could keep his back covered. I would not have lifted a single finger to help him if I had known what he was like and if I had got wind of the fact that after I had made him *voievod* in Bucharest he would set out with his army against me under the vile banner of Hadam Suleiman Pasha! But let me tell you how it was. No one had ever seen the like at that season of the year, but I set off with my army toward Wallachia in the month of November. It was at a time of year when the Turks would not have been able to cross the Rhodope Mountains very quickly to come to his aid. There was no way they could have come, and so the entire reckoning was between us alone, between Wallachians and Moldavians. And before putting him on the throne in Bucharest, I had made Laiotă swear on the Holy Scriptures that he would remain loyal to me, that he would never bow to Murat, that he would never break the laws of Christendom. And he winked at me. To which I told him, swear already, if not I'll break this cross over your head and anoint another prince to rule over this unwashed rabble. 'I swear, Your Highness, I swear!' And I left in the month of November and I reached Milcov, where the Voievod Radu was waiting for us with his army, the same Radu that had been Murat's bitch. And I crushed them in a single evening, so that even today no trace can be found of them, then I went on to Rîmnic, to Tîrgșor, and at last I arrived in the princely capital. There I found the walls defended by some of the Voievod Radu's nitwits. I got rid of them quickly, showering them with arrows and boiling pitch cast from the Genoese war engines. I stayed no longer than two weeks in that citadel when who should come running back than the Voievod Radu with the army from Rusçuk, in case the Lord of Moldavia should put down roots in the city of Bucharest. And he came with thirteen thousand Turkish irregular cavalry and six thousand Wallachians, from all over Oltenia, the whole lot of them enamored of the Voievod Radu and wanting

CHAPTER NINE

to see him anointed prince on the spot. I had to put them to fire and sword to rid the earth of them. And the last of the Wallachians laid their arms aside and said that they now recognized me as their master, 'long live Prince Stephen.' They held their arms aloft while my free peasants bound them. Yes, of course you recognize me as your master, after I scattered you and put your bitch to flight."

"How many were there?"

"I remember it as if it were yesterday," said Stephen with feeling, after a short effort to recollect. "There were two thousand three hundred men from the Dîmbovița River. I gave the order to prepare two thousand three hundred stakes, so that those tricksters from Bucharest would understand the political reality perched on top of them. It was on that day that I invented that saying about Romanians being mindful only after the fact."

"That saying comes from Your Highness," said the Knjaz, amazed.

"Of course it was from me. Who else? When I hauled the first one up onto the stake, the abbot of Tîrgșor, he started howling like a madman. You could see the stake had run through his stomach and burst it. The ones with a burst stomach howled like that, and out of fear and pity all the rest began to howl, bound tight as they were, 'forgive us, Your Highness, forgive us, Sun of Moldavia, you are our freedom, how good that you have rid us of the Voievod Radu and the Turk, now we don't want anything more to do with them, we want to be your subjects. We thought,' said they, 'that you were joking, but when you shoved the stake up the abbot's ass we caught on that it wasn't a game.' As if they hadn't understood that it was no game when I came to Milcov with my army."

Neagu was leaning one hand on a barrel. His mouth was dry. His face was scarlet. He asked, "And what did you do?"

"What else was to be done? 'Take them and impale them, my warriors,' I said. The one who goes over to the other side on the battlefield is not to be forgiven. Is he? When you catch him, you flay him there on the spot, because if you let him go tomorrow, he will come back and flay you. That's the way it has been since the beginning of the world. And so it was then, and so it is today. What, are you children?"

Hearing this answer, Darius Georgescu flung himself at his feet, and said, "Forgive me for having doubted you, Your Highness. But I wanted to be sure that you are HE. I wanted to sense you, to hear you, to see you, to touch you. I have dreamed of you a thousand times. I recognize your spirit. A thousand times I have wanted to be a soldier in your army of free men! I love you and know that it is you! I have no need of further proof!"

One by one, all ten men from the general staff of the devotees of Stephen kneeled. They bowed their heads.

"Rise, warriors!" said Stephen.

"Your Highness." Neagu began to weep.

"What's with him?" asked Stephen.

"He's an intellectual."

"Take him away," said Stephen, frowning, "and don't sleep next to him at night."

"That is what we shall do, Your Highness."

"And what's with this nonsense, with you meeting by night, among ruins, burning barrels of pitch, what's with all this nonsense? Are you the army of Stephen, or what the hell are you? Why aren't there any icons on the walls?"

No one ventured to answer.

"You behave like cowardly Bucharest folk. That's what you are."

"We've fought a few Turks. We're no cowards."

"That's nothing. You should fight them when they're many—that's what's required if you want to show your mettle. To fight them and to thank God for the joy he gives you when you throw yourselves into battle for the glory of Christendom. I give you my word that now, together, we shall conquer Bucharest in just three days."

"We love you, Your Highness," said the Knjaz.

"Words, words. It's easy to get words out of you," said Stephen. "Let's see: maybe one of you wants to perform a deed of valor?"

"I can, Your Highness," said one who had up until then been seated in the darkness.

"What is your name, warrior?"

"Isaia Faur, Your Highness."

"Are you ready to fight for an idea?"

"At your command, Your Highness."

"Then hearken! Take a pot of ink and conceal it about your person. Go into a crowded place, where the president of Romania is due to pass by. Pretend you wish to speak with him, to give him a petition, or something, then throw the ink in his face."

"I shall do it, Your Highness."

"And don't come back until you have fulfilled my command, otherwise your head will rest next to your feet. And if it takes you a year to get near the usurper of my throne, do not despair, but have patience and strive the harder. The Lord be with you!"

Isaia Faur bowed and vanished into the night.

Stephen sighed and turned to those who remained. He looked them over and saw nine boyish faces, young men who needed guidance through life, through these troubled times. With emotion, he said, "My warriors!"

■ □ ■ □ ■

CHAPTER TEN

SILENCE REIGNED AROUND THE TABLE IN THE MEETING ROOM. THERE were ten officers present, the top experts in intelligence on sects. It was the division's annual session for intelligence analysis, a very important moment for Colonel Focşăneanu. After presentation of the annual report, they proceeded to discussion. The coffee cups were empty, the ashtrays full. They had opened the window to let fresh, moist air into the room. At the head of the table, the head of the Romanian Intelligence Service's special operations was drumming his fingers on his coffee cup.

"What kind of sect are we in fact dealing with here?" asked General Mihalache.

"It's not clear," answered Colonel Focşăneanu. "It's not at all your common or garden sect, of the neo-evangelical variety. As I said in my report, it's all centered on one man, whose powers of attraction overwhelm all the rest. Our reports show a quite advanced organizational structure. It's called the Tidings of the Lord, and it currently has one thousand followers. It very rapidly got past the incipient stages of organization, and in just two to three months it won more converts than some neo-protestant sects that have been trying for decades. It's all concentrated around one man, the Teacher, a man with extraordinary powers of persuasion, a formidable speaker. Vespasian Moisa is never alone. He is always accompanied by a retinue of at least a hundred persons. Some of them go into the city to preach. They easily win new converts. It's something unprecedented."

The general scratched behind his ear and asked, "What the hell do they promise them? Eternal life?"

His question was only natural. He was the oldest person sitting at that green baize table. Only he was old enough to have attended that interesting atheism course that used to be taught at the school for party cadres in the olden days. It was taught very well. It even had interesting supplementary reading, like a book called *The Comical Bible,* by a Soviet author. It wasn't bad at all, he thought. It gave you a good idea of the world and of life. You could shield yourself from all the nonsense you heard at work, because, in general, in the job of gathering intelligence you could hardly avoid such nonsense.

"No, it's not the usual claptrap, with Lord have mercy and all that. It's something else entirely," answered Colonel Focşăneanu. "No one believes in that stuff anymore. Probably not even them."

"Do they give them drugs?" asked the general, raising his eyebrows.

"Our reports don't contain anything about that. We haven't caught them at it yet."

"Let's be serious. The whole of Bucharest is awash with substances. You're telling me that they don't snort or inject anything at all?"

"If they did," said Focşăneanu, "we'd be the first to find out."

All of a sudden, the general remembered something. "Well then, what's the point of an Orthodox sect that doesn't promise its parishioners eternal life? Does the Patriarch know about it?"

The colonel waved his hand in disgust on hearing the Patriarch mentioned and said, "He provides them with a special meaning. They make them believe they're in the proximity of someone who understands all the secrets of the universe, that he knows how to bring them to redemption. He gives them a theory, a doctrine that most of them feel at peace with, because it seems to them that they know what they're doing. I mean, once they have those explanations, it seems to them that they know what they're doing."

"Isn't this redemption the same thing as eternal life?" asked the general, surprised.

"Not for them, no. These people want to attain to the state of angelic matter by decoding the Romanian language," the colonel read from a report. "The majority of the sermons are about this. And by preaching this, Moisa and another two or three close to him have gained a certain authority."

"What authority?" The general banged his fist on the table. "It's not on. Has he ever said he is the Son of God? We could arrest him for that and bang him up in the nuthouse." Then, overcome by a fleeting doubt: "What is it that he says he is?"

"We don't have any report that says he has proclaimed himself the Son of God."

"Aha. So, you know what I'm thinking. He's not your classic nutcase. In the eighties I arrested fifty-six Napoleons and thirty Stalins."

"Yes, we could have nabbed him in the good old-fashioned way. Article Eighteen, Letter C, would have been a good idea, General, sir."

"So, what is it he says he is? When he talks to them, in what capacity does he address them? Why is it that this lot, who never listened to their teachers in school, listen to a down-and-out preaching on the street?"

"He says he's a teacher."

"What does that mean?"

"Maybe a kind of prophet."

"And what has the Church got to say about that? Do the priests know? Let's get the priests on his case."

"The Church hasn't said anything yet. For them, anything that gathers the faithful has their blessing."

"Is it enough to inform the Prosecutor's Office?"

"I don't know what article of the Penal Code we could class it under. They haven't actually done anything, nor are they threatening to do anything."

"We've handled cases of this kind before, not recently, it's true: usurping authority. Association with a view to committing something. For something like that, ten years ago they would have been arrested as quick as a flash."

"Allow me, General, to say that to me it's now clear that we need to be gathering data in this respect. The truth is that up until now they haven't committed any crime. They just talk. All of them, they talk a lot. Talking, talking, talking. They don't do what the others sects do. Not even any graffiti. No posters on the wall, no phone calls to con-

CHAPTER TEN

vert people, no missionaries on the corner of the street. They haven't done anything that could be classed as breaking the law."

There followed a moment of silence.

"Who is Vespasian Moisa, in fact?" said the general, in a low voice.

The colonel was confused for a second. "What do you mean?"

"What if he is really a prophet? I mean, one of those ones that can see the future. Or what if he's someone very clever, someone absolutely lucid, whose predictions might be of use to us? Do you think we could use him? Couldn't we use him to destabilize certain political forces? Couldn't we send him to Chişinău, to stir up disturbances?"

The colonel looked around the table. All the others were doodling.

"We haven't devoted any research to that," said Colonel Focşăneanu, confused. "We were thinking that it is a sect that endangers state security, and we've collected data to that effect. But if you like, we could move the inquiry in a different direction. Just give the order."

"But what do the real data say? What do you think? Your personal impression . . ."

"Allow me, General, to say that we haven't reached any definitive conclusion yet. I don't have a personal impression, although I've sent out our best spies."

The general turned and gazed out of the window. At the edge of the sidewalk, some children had set light to some paper and were now putting chestnuts on top of the fire.

"Is there anything you've forgotten to tell us?"

The colonel closed the dossier and squirmed in his seat. "It's true that one of our best-trained captains has resigned from the Romanian Intelligence Service while carrying out an infiltration mission." (A murmur in the room.) "Yes, I know, it is a disaster. A desertion to the side of the enemy in circumstances that have not yet been fully elucidated. But we'll soon find out what is going on."

The general leaned over the table. "And is it usual for me to find out from another department that one of your officers has gone over to the enemy for the sake of a hair-restoring lotion? Do you realize that the lads over in counterintelligence are laughing their heads off at us?"

"I was about to report to you on the matter, General, sir."

"Like hell you were."

"I wouldn't have dared not to."

"Shut up."

"At your orders."

There followed a moment of rather embarrassing silence.

"Let me tell you the news of the century," said the general. "Did you know that the people from the Ministry of Culture are giving them financial support? Did you know that the Tidings of the Lord has received a grant from the Ministry?"

At this point, the colonel stood up, as if he had difficulty understanding what was being said.

"How can they give money to the very people we've got under surveillance? What kind of tin-pot country is this? What the hell!" said Focșăneanu, his face distorted with fury.

"See for yourselves. Here's a copy of the document, signed and stamped by the Minister of Culture."

"That's just marvelous," said Colonel Focșăneanu, and sank back into his chair. "We're jousting with windmills. The goat's out of the pen, General, sir . . . It's out of our control . . ."

The general looked at the colonel in surprise. It seemed to him that there was something in his behavior that didn't quite fit the situation. He said, "Colonel, this is nothing more than an operational error, one that I consider very serious, but which can still be straightened out. Maybe it seems like a joke to you, but I say it's a very serious matter. We don't know when they applied for money from the Ministry of Culture. We didn't see the dossier to be able to intervene. You're the ones who should have found out, but you didn't. All I wanted to say was that in my opinion and given my experience, you're a damned inefficient outfit. You don't inform anyone else involved in a timely fashion. The information reached us thanks to a report from the intelligence service of the Justice Ministry, which has got the Agriculture Ministry under surveillance and found out about it by accident."

"That lot from the Culture Ministry throw money away any old how," said Focșăneanu. "They're unpredictable."

The general banged his fist on the table.

"Where have you ever seen anything like it before? Financing the target we've got under surveillance for undermining the national interest! It's madness. Think about it. You're giving money to precisely the people we consider a danger to the social order. What kind of country is this? Is there anything that still works in a country like this?"

"We need to reevaluate our strategy," said Focşăneanu. "You're right. I await your orders."

"I think that we should close the meeting here and that you should go away and draw up a new strategy. I want a complete, definitive, complex report, in which I'll be given a firm prediction as to the dissolution of this sect. That's what we need. Agreed, colonel? And please, no cheap heroics or fancy stuff. You know full well how many idiotic reports you make me read. Now is not the moment. These people might really turn out to be dangerous. They're growing in numbers and quickly too."

"Of course, General, sir. I've been working on precisely that."

"I want that report. When do you think it will be ready?"

"In a few days. We have all the elements," said Colonel Focşăneanu.

"Please, don't play with fire," said the general, pointing his finger at the ceiling. "Remember Pastor Tőkés in 1989?"

Around the table could be heard a number of disgruntled grunts.

"Then we can declare today's meeting closed. Colonel, I'd like you to stay behind for a little. We have something to discuss."

The other officers gathered up their files and left the room. The general gazed at them, gauging the bellies under their shirts, the bee-tled brows. After a while, he felt a need to gaze up at the ceiling. When only the two of them remained, the general asked, "Where do you get the bulk of your information from inside Moisa's sect, Colonel?"

The colonel smiled. The general was new as head of his department. There were certain things he did not know. In Colonel Focşăneanu's opinion, the opinion of a man who had seen many things in his life and survived a revolution on the streets, his direct superior was a general made to order, in recent times, on the wave of democratic politics. He didn't have much faith in him, but now that he was ask-ing, he had to tell him. One of the basic rules of intelligence gathering is not to divulge your sources. Maybe he should have kept his mouth shut. But if the general found out from somewhere else, it would end badly. And so he had no choice but to tell him: "We used a special cat, General, sir."

"You disguised a microphone as a cat?" said the general, pleasantly surprised.

"Oh, no, it's much more complicated than that. We have an officer disguised as a cat."

The general choked on his coffee. The spray flew quite some distance.

The colonel bowed politely then went on. "Allow me to inform you about the situation. The whole story began in 1991, in August to be exact. At the time I was working at the Foreign Intelligence Service, where I was detached for six months. I worked for the division for collecting information in the Soviet Union. The division operated from July 1990 until September 1991, when things changed and the USSR ceased to exist. At that time we had a number of officers on missions there who were fluent Russian speakers and found themselves cut off in various places. Those were turbulent times, and things were very tangled, especially when we had to gather information on the turf of the former KGB. Their counterespionage did not let anything get out of the country. They performed summary executions, because not one of those murders would ever be investigated. We had lost two young lieutenants in six months alone, each with a bullet to the back of the head. It was no joke. Well, Lieutenant Trăistaru was in Tashkent in August 1991, where he had recruited a colonel from the general staff of the city's garrison. We were interested in obtaining information about Soviet troop movements in Central Asia. At that time, their army was repositioning in the Central Asia zone. There were all kinds of cost-cutting changes. We were following all these."

"And what good was that information to us? I don't think you mean we were getting ready to invade Asia."

"To be honest, I don't know. We were ordered to get the information, and that is what we tried to do. Against the background of the breakup of the USSR, it wasn't a bad idea to see what was going on, to see what troops were being moved where. If they got the idea of tripling overnight the Fourteenth Army, it would have been good for us to know where those troops were coming from, what the logistics were, and the morale situation. In addition, we could come across information useful in negotiations between various parties. In any case, our orders were to get hold of the information, and Trăistaru was in Tashkent. At one point, he suffered an unusual mishap. He

CHAPTER TEN

was inside a civil building when he was attacked by a team of Uzbek counterespionage agents. What they were doing in Tashkent I don't know. In theory, it wasn't their area, but that's what we've been able to establish: they attacked him, tied him up, gave him a paralyzing injection, and took him to one of their laboratories. They'd caught him and they knew very well what his mission was. The source he hoped to recruit had probably been nothing more than bait. And now they intended to make him disappear. And in that laboratory it seems that one of the KGB's divisions was preparing a new weapon, something based on cosmic rays, absolute vibration or the devil knows what they called it. The fact is that they used Lieutenant Trăistaru as a guinea pig. They did an experiment on him. They irradiated him and turned him into a cat."

The general remained motionless.

"A cat?"

"Yes, a large ginger tomcat, with green eyes. Trăistaru had been blond with green eyes, it just goes to show . . ."

After a pause, the general asked, "And how did he escape from the laboratory?"

"They let him go. They weren't expecting his intellectual functions, voice, visual capacity, and other human characteristics to survive. They irradiated him, but they didn't completely turn him into a cat. Not the brain. Under that tomcat's fur it was still our Trăistaru, just as much of a patriot, with the same abnegation and spirit of self-sacrifice for his country."

"And what became of him?"

"He got back to Romania on a TAROM charter flight, stowed away in the cargo hold, and he reported back to me at the unit. He had gotten back from Tashkent unobserved, and I was the first person he spoke to."

The general regarded him at length.

"We had two options," the colonel continued. "The first was to keep him at my house and give him saucers of milk. The second was to send him back into the field, as an undercover officer, which is what he was trained for. I discussed all the options with Trăistaru. And he was interested in continuing to work for me, which is to say for me to send him on missions and for him to report back to me. The situation was unusual to the highest degree, and we adapted ourselves to it as we went along."

All of a sudden, there was a flicker of doubt in the general's eyes. "Colonel, are you sure?" he asked.

"It's a story for which all the documentation exists," said the colonel, smiling calmly.

"And where is Trăistaru now?"

"He's shadowing Vespasian Moisa. We know what and where he prays. We know what he eats. We know what he says in his sleep. We have the best possible information. Because Trăistaru is there on the stove in his room."

"Thank you, Colonel," said the general. "I understand the situation. We can now get to work. You've done an excellent job. I congratulate you on your intelligence gathering."

The colonel felt the volume of his thoracic cavity doubling. He stood to attention and looked straight ahead as the general left the room.

Somewhat troubled, the general returned to his office. He telephoned his secretary and told her, "I'd like to have a word with the ministry psychiatrist. Please put me through as quickly as you can . . . I'm afraid it's urgent."

■ □ ■ □ ■

Only two remained in the headquarters christened THE GOVERN-MENT. The others had left. The fires had gone out, and Darius was looking out the window at Victory Square. With the lights out, it was not even possible to tell that the block in which they had met was unfinished, abandoned by the authorities. It was unknown when and if it would ever be completed. The Knjaz took off his black overcoat, the one he called his "scandal uniform" and which was still bloodstained from two weeks earlier. Darius turned toward him and said, "Bucharest is so beautiful at night, viewed from up here . . ."

"I know what you are thinking," said the Knjaz. "It's our city. We'll convince them. They're ours. We've got them in the palm of our hand."

Darius shook his head doubtfully. "It's not quite like that, and you know very well that people are moving toward other groups, they're being persuaded by other ideas."

The Knjaz went to the balcony. Because the block was quite flimsy, he didn't have the courage to step onto the balcony. He looked out through the doorway, and said, "How are we going to convince them to support us more?"

"Through action," said Darius, with the same mechanical ferocity.

The Knajz placed his hand on his chest, as if he wanted to calm him.

"You're too angry, too tense. People sense it, and when they see people are angry, it doesn't encourage them to follow them."

Darius laughed. "Well, well, you're not so placid yourself. And there's something else. He's exactly like in the chronicle."

"Who?"

"Stephen. Do you remember what it says in the old book?"

"Of course," said the Knjaz. "You told us to learn it by heart. *The Voievod Stephen was a man not tall in height, quick to anger and to shed innocent blood. Many times at his feasts he slew men without judgment. Otherwise he was a man sound in nature, not idle, and he knew how to cover his doings, and where you least expected, there you would find him. In the arts of war a master, and where the need arose he thrust himself into the fray, so that his men would see him and not retreat, and for this reason rarely was he not victorious in battle.*"

"You see? That's the problem."

The Knjaz smiled.

"Why was that passage perfect as long as he was not with us but only became a problem when we found him?"

He didn't let him answer, but asked, "How old are you?"

"Twenty-two," said Darius. "You know very well. I'm a year older than you."

"You see?" said the Knjaz. "Who do you want to convince? In this country only the old duffers can convince. Only they get away with it on television. Only they have the opportunities. You can only be a senator or president if you're over thirty, and people will vote for you only if you're an ethnic Romanian born in the city. You've seen the statistics. Look, I was born in the country. How could the people of Bucharest follow the likes of us? Now and only now that he is with us do we have a chance."

At this point Darius punched the bare concrete wall with his fist. The other went on. "You speak to them about Christian charity, about Stephen the Great as a moral model. Have they got time for that today? They want a mute icon, an icon that doesn't preach anything. Any advice you might give them, it seems to them that you're imposing on them. And that's why we're here, and the old duffers are there." (And he pointed to the Government Palace on the other side of the square.) "But now, he is with us."

"That's about right. But, do you see, we don't have any more time to wait. If we grow old, all our energy will go to waste, everything we say, everything we might give to Romania. If the people followed us, we could give so much to Romania! We could lift it up to an unprecedented level!"

The Knjaz stroked his cheek. "You know what I have been wanting to ask you for a long time? If we're talking about the great Stephen as a moral model, why don't we live like him to the very end? Why don't we spend every night in the bed of a different woman?"

Darius took a step back. He stumbled over a chunk of concrete. He said, "That's what we ought to do. Except that we have to dedicate a great deal of time to the national revolution. We're taking the nation out of obscurity and bringing it to its maximum fulfillment. When we reach that point, the chicks will come by themselves."

"Look," said the Knjaz, "at Moisa's nuthouse there are more women than men. With us, there are only men. You'd think it was a military unit. Something is out of kilter. It looks like our message doesn't attract women."

"Yes, with us it's somehow more specific. The message we're conveying to the believers has a certain degree of difficulty. We're not all prepared to put on the shirt of death."

"And our personal life," said the Knjaz, taking a step back, "is in tatters. Think about it."

Darius heaved a sigh. Then, all of a sudden, as if he were chanting a litany, "You're right. Long live the great Stephen! We each need a woman. I'm off. Good night. Bye."

CHAPTER TEN

■ □ ■ □ ■

CHAPTER ELEVEN

THAT EVENING, THE PHYSICIAN ARGHIR TOLD VESPASIAN MOISA ONCE
again that all those theories were simultaneously true, that around the
Tidings of the Lord there occurred a phenomenon of collective en-
lightenment, whose outcome would be to capture the deepest secrets
of the universe, to explain once and for all certain scientific truths
within a close interpenetration with the revealed truth of the Scriptures. He told him all this trembling, feverishly, his eyes in tears, as
if he were communicating to him a vision, as if he had been transformed into a medium. All these components of the theory were con-
ceived and produced at the same time, in our time, and the time had
come for us to hearken to them and to understand that all arguments
are simultaneously true. "All of them!" he told him, his finger pointing to the ceiling. "They are the voice of our time, all these theories,
they have emerged from the ideatic universe of our time, and we are
fortunate that you have brought them to us, that you have made us
conceive of them!" A moment later, as if emerging from a tunnel of
darkness and grace, Vespasian Moisa showed himself on the balcony
of the villa in Lahovary Square, and he told the faithful who were
gathered there in the courtyard and outside, "The time has come for
you to speak. Your voices are the Truth. Do not be afraid, the Holy
Ghost will speak through you. The Church is nothing other than the
sum of all the beliefs and opinions of all Christians, however personal
these might be. Lord have mercy! Let the faithful speak. Are we not
here for our faithful? Let us listen to them. We owe them this. Enough

sermons. Now we shall do the opposite, our faithful, our master. We have no inquisition. We do not condemn anyone for anything that might contradict the Scriptures. We have faith. And we believe in the mind of man." After he had spoken from the balcony, he went out into the courtyard of the villa in Lahovary, and he gave the order for the bell-board to be hammered. And they all came. At that hour of the summer evening, some hundred followers happened to be in the vicinity. And he spoke to them in the courtyard: "This is the Great Revelation. The Moment has come for me to tell you that all your ideas are simultaneously true, for when we tell you to love your neighbor as yourselves, it means above all to accept your neighbor's truth, as if it were simultaneous with your own truth, even if it is in contradiction with your truth. Love your neighbor even when what he wants is exactly the opposite of what you want with all your soul." His words floated above the multitude *like a linden flower within an abstract thought.* "The time has come for you to speak." This is what he said. "Ascend, each of you in turn, onto the balcony and speak. All of you, come and tell all the truths for which you are ready to lay down your lives. This is the word of the Romanian people." As if in the grip of a fever, he pointed somewhere far away, in the sky. Then he pointed at them, and at the sky once more. Next to him, Professor Diaconescu was gesticulating in the same way, and from the balcony, Dr. Arghir was gesticulating even more wildly. The first to ascend was Marian Tudose, that young man from Jassy, who had twice failed to be admitted to university, but who presented a perfect, superb, simple demonstration of Fermat's Great Theorem. He commenced with a reductio ad absurdum and, after a series of syllogisms, he delivered checkmate to that riddle which has stumped mankind for two hundred years. It was a demonstration they all understood, because it used many sixth-grade notions. Then the physician Apolodor Arghir demonstrated that the oldest language in the world is Romanian, that nothing is older than Romanian, that Latin is a derivative of Romanian and that Romanian contains in codified form the cure for baldness. Then Miklós Lakatos, a Transylvanian Magyar, ascended to the balcony, and they all listened to his tragic story in his approximate Romanian. He had not been able to study in his native language, and in the army they had forced him to learn the dreadful idiom of the majority, a language that only the gypsies spoke in his native village of Sfînta Maria. This traumatized him as much as the growing pains peculiar to adolescence. He begged the audience's forgiveness, but insisted on saying that Romanian had violated him and that only an accident of history meant that he was speaking it now. In Bucharest, he had been able to devote himself to his oldest passion: engines. He became a mechanic, after learning the internal anatomy of the creations of General Motors and Renault from a manual written in a language unfamiliar to him and whose secrets were revealed to him by a black man, a Cuban immigrant to Romania. After ten years of repairing Dacia cars, he was able to buy his own garage, a hangar far from the world, which in a short time became a Mecca for forgotten makes that no one else knew how to fix. He told how he had been alongside Vespasian Moisa constantly, and then he told of his secret laboratory and his most daring project. "We mustn't believe anything we learn in school," he said, in an almost unintelligible accent. "We have to experiment with everything for ourselves." His first experiment had been with an explosive liquid of huge power, which he never tested at its full capacity and which, he believed, drew upon ideas current in sixteenth-century Transylvania. A whole series of other experiments brought him very close to re-creating the forgotten Weissdorf clock mechanism, a *perpetuum mobile* which could measure time without being wound for hundreds of years, and whose unique and essential secret was a spring that recharged itself with potential energy with an efficiency of almost one hundred percent. And nonetheless all these were mere playthings.

"Angelic matter exists, and these things can be demonstrated. If you like, I can show you," he told the multitude, who were listening open-mouthed.

All this came to pass in the evening, and the shadows danced upon their faces. They were all pierced by an awkward emotion, by a chimera, by multiple hopes, it seemed to them that they were at the center of the Universe and that everything that was to be said that evening Would Be Essential. Miklós came down from the balcony, to make a demonstration. He was a little nervous. He said that he had performed the experiment dozens of times, before many people, and that on each occasion a genie had poured like smoke from the lamp, a genie of ethereal and illusory consistency, barely perceptible to our senses. Then he related how he had seen it, how it existed, how it breathed, and how he knew from the very first instant that it was an angel. It was dancing like the flame of a candle, like a phantom, translucent and tall, clouding the places over which it passed like a breath of wind. "I saw it and I understood that, from all that illusion, everything is true," he said. "I watched how the angel was embodied before my very eyes, how its shadow entered into me and let itself be inhaled and exhaled, how it purified me and touched me within, and I fell to the ground and I understood that now I knew everything, everything is true. And the angel spoke to me and said, 'Miklós!' Then," Miklós went on, "I wrote a letter to the Lord God: 'This is why I am writing to You, because You have revealed to me this chronicle and with it I present myself before You, for You have called upon me as a witness, all at once a believer, heretic, and inquisitor: angels exist.' I confess that I tried to manufacture gold, but from the experiment something else came out, this angel emerging from the glass. I had no way of escaping. And if it is heresy, I confess belief in it, for with my own eyes I saw it. And the Catholic priest, the one who baptized me as an infant, told me to go to the Romanians, perhaps they would believe me, and he told me that I was rummaging in devils' shit, that's what he told me. And here I am, before you. It's not the case that I was astray and that my soul needed salvation. For each of us is plunged in an illusion: no one is living his real life, but only a life of smoke. No one gets what he wants from life, but something lateral, no more, no less, only something lateral, and reality is the result obtained by shifting all our alterations in destiny to a global scale." Miklós was the first speaker of that evening to be applauded, as though at the theater, so that the square resounded with whoops and hoorahs. The people were happy. They were laughing like children upon whom new toys have been showered, even if the demonstration with the smoke did not quite come off. That was of no importance, of course. The important thing was the ideas. Miklós kept rubbing the lamp until late into the night, to show the angel to the crowd, but nothing came out.

Then Visarion spoke. He brought into the discussion the vexed problem of Atlantis and its identification somewhere among the Canary Isles and the Iberian coast. What he was proposing was a plan to bring Atlantis back to the surface, by successively raising landmasses. One of the ideas was to displace some volcanic rocks by means of massive hydrogen balloons, whose lift would be sufficient to budge them.

It was not clear who would attach the steel cables to the underwater rocks and how exactly the landmasses would be brought out to sea. These were technical details he was still working on. But it was clear that if Atlantis was geologically stable before the great earthquake, then this stability could be regained, just as the Dutch had reclaimed so much land from the sea, with their dikes. Practically, Atlantis could be brought back to the surface using balloons.

After Visarion, Pamfilie came to the microphone and recounted how he had studied Farsi for ten years. He was a specialist in oriental languages. He read *Omar Khayyam* in the original and knew by heart a host of verses, which he declaimed in a pleasant nasal-guttural tongue that no one had ever heard before. He told them that Farsi is twenty-nine thousand years old, that it was invented by God Himself and that it contains in its basic formulas a code that unravels the nucleus of the planet. This idea was not well received by the audience, who began to boo and yell. From somewhere in the second row, someone produced a large Romanian tricolor, with a hole in place of the former communist emblem, and raised it above the heads in the crowd. An angry bearded man shouted in a baritone voice, "It's Romanian that's twenty-nine thousand years old! Romanian!" His words were repeated by dozens of voices, the whole crowd speaking simultaneously. To calm them, Professor Diaconescu began to say the Lord's Prayer, but few could hear him.

It was then, as the evening of free opinions was drawing to a close, against the backdrop of the crowd's unexpected reaction, that Vespasian Moisa collapsed, convulsed by shivering, in a trance, his teeth chattering and his eyes rolling, their whites reflecting death and the sky. The tumult died away as if by miracle, and all eyes fastened on the balcony, where the Teacher seemed to have been possessed by a demon. Through the imitation Doric columns it could be seen that he was quaking and writhing out of control. The Teacher was sprawled on the floor of the balcony, among the legs of those who were crowded there. A large ginger tomcat, appearing from nowhere, approached him and nosed his lips, sniffing to see whether he was still breathing. As if afraid, the tomcat licked him once, then vanished into the gloom of the evening, while Apolodor Arghir forced his way through the crush, bent down, and stuffed a handkerchief between Vespasian's teeth, so that he would not bite his tongue.

Margot drew Toni to one side, and pointing to the rest, said, "It's a complete madhouse here. I'm not sticking around any longer. There's nothing else for us to see. Let's get out of here."

The Troubadour bent toward her ear and recited a line from a secret song, but she said, "That's stupid. Leave it out. Let's go."

Toni ran his fingers through his hair and said, "I believe in the Teacher. I'm staying."

Coming up to them, Barbie pressed her brow to Toni's shoulder. Margot said nothing. She kissed her on the cheek and vanished into the night.

■ □ ■ □ ■

CHAPTER TWELVE

VESPASIAN MOISA WAS SITTING ON THE FLOOR IN THE FORMER DINING room of the villa in Lahovary Square, with a compress on his brow. He had not fully come to. He was still exhausted after the shock of the previous evening. It seemed that he was praying, but two paces away the television was turned on, and it would have been impossible for him not to hear it. Doctor Arghir was watching him from a corner, with a certain amount of disquiet. He had been wanting to speak to him for more than an hour, but it seemed to him that the Teacher was unable to concentrate and that to converse would have been impossible. The television was broadcasting the news. The anchor, a man with thickly gelled hair, was reading an item entitled, "Large-scale witch hunt." After a short pause for effect, he went on: *The witch hunt in the Congo has to date claimed 843 victims. Armed forces from neighboring Uganda have had to intervene to stop the slaughter, arresting seventy persons. The violence has been targeted at villagers accused of employing witchcraft to kill people, torturing them to sign over their property. Those accused of witchcraft and their accomplices were chopped into pieces.*

Vespasian Moisa opened his eyes. He saw the suffering and heard the weeping for real. He was close even when he was far away. He was everywhere, and he understood everything. He had moments when he breathed through that highly sensitive tissue on his chest, which some said was just like the map of Bucharest. Through that tissue he sensed pain from afar. His closed eyes would then open within.

It had been his fault the previous evening, the physician reproached himself. He should not have allowed Vespasian to be exposed to the ideas of those people. They shocked him and traumatized him, with all their idées fixes. Not all of them were on the wavelength they ought to be on. Not all of them. He reproached himself for it now.

The voice of the television anchor had become even more solemn. He was now reading another item. *The Vatican has issued strict guidelines to reduce unauthorized exorcisms and healing by heretical methods. The guidelines came in the form of seventeen pages of instructions from the Congregation for the Doctrine of the Faith, the department formerly known as the Supreme Sacred Congregation, which used to control the Inquisition. In the ten disciplinary guidelines, the Congregation says that it is legitimate for the faithful to pray to the Lord to cure illness or alleviate suffering, but groups gathered for this purpose must receive authorization from the bishop of their diocese, and there should be no cults built around individuals. Although no one was specifically named, many of the guidelines seem to be aimed at Archbishop Emmanuel Milingo, a controversial healer and exorcist from Zambia, who is currently in Rome.*

Vespasian took the remote control and turned the volume up. The news seemed insane to him. He wanted to hear it better. For a moment he thought that if he could hear it better, if he could understand it better, the absurd nature of the news would be diminished.

We now return to news from Romania. This afternoon in Matache Square there was a pitched battle between gangs of youths of differing religious orientations. The most aggressive of the gangs is the so-called Stephenists. At around two o'clock this afternoon they attacked on a patch of waste ground where, it seems, last night a sect of Satanists had buried a live cat and held a ritual to conjure up Beelzebub. The battle resulted in a number of wounded, who were taken to the Emergency Hospital.

After this account, images from the emergency room were broadcast. For a second, it was possible to see the Knjaz lying on a stretcher, being pushed by two nurses, one of whom was holding a drip. A physician, Popescu by name, appeared on the screen, a microphone thrust before him. In a calm, detached voice, he said, *The injured are not in any immediate danger. None of them has life-threatening injuries. Up to now, we've had fractured skulls, sprains, countless contusions, but no internal lesions or open wounds, the kind of injuries we always get after a Rapid v. Dynamo match, for example. These cult members are tame by comparison.*

CHAPTER TWELVE

Then the camera showed a hospital ward with wounded Christians and Satanists lying in beds all mixed up together. You could tell which were which by the chains around their necks, by the tattoos, by the faces. They looked like two separate decks of cards shuffled together.

"Oh! This doesn't bode well," said Maximilian, who had been watching the news over Vespasian's shoulder.

Doctor Arghir looked at his watch and left the room, giving Maximilian a discreet sign to keep an eye on the Teacher.

The image on the screen then cut to one of the beds, in which was lying a mean-looking, broad-shouldered man with a large gold cross around his neck. In the next bed was a scrawny youth with spiky hair and an arm in plaster. A tattooed pair of horns was visible on the youth's shoulders, a swastika on his forehead.

Maximilian laughed at what he saw.

"The Lord be with them!" said Vespasian, his eyes closed.

The tomcat stopped purring. He peered at the television screen, his large green eyes wide open.

On the screen flashed the words, *Live from Matache Square*. And for an instant the image remained fixed on a bouquet of flowers in the studio. Then the frontispiece of an old, ramshackle house at the edge of Bucharest appeared, in front of which was standing a reporter dressed in a denim jacket.

This morning, Matache Square was the backdrop for a bloody clash between two gangs. From our investigations, we have discovered that one of the gangs is Satanist in nature, the other neo-Christian. The gendarmes are trying to restore order in the neighborhood, but the street fighting still continues. The clashes are more violent than those this morning, with knives and clubs now being used. Events are still unfolding. We shall keep you up to date with the latest developments.

At this point, something exploded off camera, probably a firecracker. There was a scream, and the camera panned to show a man in a black overcoat lying on the ground, clutching his knee. What kind of firecracker could that have been? The camera now moved in to give a close-up of his face, distorted with pain. All of a sudden, in the background a man mounted on a white horse appeared. The rider was of middling stature, middle-aged, with long blond hair, and wearing a red cloak. Behind him came a whole host of youths, running and whirling chains and clubs. The rider shouted something to them, but nothing could be heard. Next to the reporter someone was cursing and asking where the hell this band of men had come from.

At the end of the street there was another band, all dressed in black, but seemingly in a different way. They were shouting, too, whirling chains and clubs. Their tattoos were visible. From a side street, a line of police emerged, holding shields and wearing helmets. At their head was an officer with a loudspeaker. At first it was not possible to make out what he was shouting, but when the megaphone turned in the direction of the camera, the words became clear:

—*Stand quietly in your places!*

The order had an exacerbating effect on the rival gangs. The rider on the white horse turned and signaled to his followers. Behind them, the street filled with police, who advanced in orderly fashion along the street. After the running and smoke of but a few seconds before, the image on the screen now seemed unearthly.

—*Into the fray, warriors!* was heard from off camera.

—*Aaargh!* was heard next to the cameraman.

—*Watch out for the tear gas,* said a choking voice not far from the reporter's microphone.

Then the camera jolted and went black.

Cut back to the studio. The anchor, his face stiff, had an announcement to make:

—*We have just received a telegram from the commandant of the division of gendarmes. The populace of Bucharest is assured that riot-control forces have intervened to restore order in the capital. Thanks to the professionalism and dedication of our officers and troops, the guilty parties will in the next few hours be arrested and an inquiry will commence into the circumstances of the street fighting between rival gangs. Our goal is for the capital to get back to being the peaceful city we all know within the shortest possible time. The police have escorted transports of bread and mineral water to shops in the areas affected by the fighting.*

The image in the studio now cut to a heavily made-up young lady, who read the following information:

—*So far, there have been recorded twenty-six people wounded, who have been taken to the emergency room. There have been no cases of serious injury and, fortunately, no deaths.*

—*We now have a message from the Third Millennium Party, communicated to our newsroom five minutes ago. Our Party expresses its alarm at the repeated infringements of human rights committed by the police today during the demonstration for the civil rights of the populace of Bucharest. The police used tear gas, which is banned by European legislation, and arrested persons who were then prevented from gaining access to adequate medical care.*

All of a sudden, another young lady appeared in the frame, dressed as elegantly as the other, in a cherry-red *deux-pièces,* with a miniskirt, but less stridently made-up. Standing behind the other, she said, *I didn't authorize this item, and I don't know how it came to be broadcast.*

—European legislation guarantees the right . . . the other tried to go on, but the woman behind her tried to snatch the sheet of paper away from her.

As she was tugging at the paper, the words LIVE FROM THE STUDIO began to run across the bottom of the screen. The two women were locked in equal combat, one sitting, one standing. Seeing that she had no other way of emerging victorious, the woman who was standing grabbed the other's hair and began yanking it determinedly. The woman who was sitting let go of the paper, stood up, and grabbed her assailant's hair. In her turn, she began tugging the other's hair every which way. The camera cut to the bouquet of flowers at the edge of the frame.

"What was all that?" asked Maximilian.

"A beginning," said Vespasian Moisa, from the armchair.

Maximilian looked at him, and it seemed to him that Vespasian had never been ill. Indeed, it seemed to him that the Teacher was radiating energy, that he was well and that nothing could stop him . . .

■　□　■　□　■

Senator Laurențiu Morariu had been waiting for ten minutes in the library, together with his host, who was very honored by this visit. Mr. Vasile Gheorghe, now dressed in a black evening suit, with his air of being a Bucharest business big wheel, liked to show how thanks to his generosity an entire religious movement was housed in his villa in Lahovary Square, and the senator was welcome anytime. The senator was wearing a dark blue suit, of consummate elegance, and a necktie of violet hues. A gold tiepin, in the form of a mermaid, stood out against his pale blue shirt.

"Does Mr. Moisa have another meeting scheduled?" asked the senator, with one eye on the clock.

"Oh, no, at least not as far as I know. He is due to meet you now." The door swung wide open, and Professor Diaconescu entered, followed by Dr. Arghir. They both rushed toward the senator to shake his hand. The senator hurried over and embraced them.

"I'm overjoyed to see you," said the senator. "Where is Mr. Moisa?"

"At this hour, Vespasian is in his office. He will arrive presently."

At that very moment the door opened once more, and the senator saw a burly man enter. He was wearing a gigantic cross on a gold chain around his neck. Behind him, the senator recognized Vespasian Moisa, whom he had previously seen only in newspaper photographs. He was wearing a silk dressing gown and had a somewhat weary air. The senator rushed up to him and embraced him. He issued a few oriental courtesies and then said, "It is a great honor for me, Mr. Moisa."

The others smiled. The senator embraced Vespasian once again, before allowing him to take a seat in an armchair. The senator also took a seat, but the others remained standing. The burly man, who seemed to be some kind of bodyguard, positioned himself behind Vespasian.

"You can't imagine how happy I was, Mr. Moisa, when I found out that the latest opinion polls rank you as the most respected public figure, appreciated by more than ninety percent of the population of Bucharest. Since January 1990, no one has achieved such a credibility rating. It's something unprecedented for a populace with such a fluctuating memory. And, what's more, it's something inconceivable for someone who has never appeared on any talk show, who doesn't have his own television program, or even a newspaper column. It's something my party's sociologists just can't explain. You're familiar to the whole of Bucharest and you enjoy fantastic credibility."

Here, Vespasian made a slight bow, still seated in the armchair, and looked the senator straight in the eye. "Not me, but the Lord. It is the credibility that the Lord God enjoys, for I have come in His Word. If He had not wished it, I would not be here at all. If the Lord had not sent me, then I would not be surrounded by so many wonderful people now. It was the Lord Who sent me, and it will be He Who summons me to return, back into the mist whence I came, when there will no longer be any need for me."

On hearing these words, the burly man with the gold cross emitted a noise like a samovar and fainted, sprawling full length on the parquet of the villa. Vasile Gheorghe leaped up and sprinkled him with a little water. As if apologizing, he said, "The lad is very religious. We hired him for Vespasian, because he is a believer and you can put your trust in him. He probably fainted when he heard death being mentioned."

"It's plain that people love you," said the senator. "And we love you too. It's in our party—a party with a strong Christian outlook—that you're probably best loved. Categorically one hundred percent."

"I know very little of politics. I've never been very interested," said Vespasian.

"But you're interested in people, aren't you? You're concerned about people having a better life, so that each will be able to dedicate himself to the faith, aren't you?"

Vespasian nodded.

"Only a well-fed man, who has hot water and heating in the winter, who earns a wage comparable to the average in the European Union, is able to pray, to dedicate himself to unending prayer, so as to be able to reunite with the atmosphere of the Initial Vibration, which restores to us our position as wonderful citizens of the cosmos."

"Ah, how beautifully you put it," said Professor Diaconescu ecstatically.

Dr. Arghir looked at the senator with a certain amount of envy. I mean, damn it, how quickly he picked up on the theory.

"It's from the heart," explained the senator, bowing, placing his right hand on his chest. "I have been thinking about all this for a long time, before coming to see you. I know what our people need, and I would like to help you, to put you in a position to help the people of our wonderful city."

"I shall do it with love," whispered Vespasian.

"The parliamentary elections are coming up. The years pass so quickly . . . For me it is an honor to act as spokesman for our party, with the request to invite you to stand as our candidate for election to the Senate in Bucharest. It's an eligible seat, please believe me. We would not have dared propose any other."

Professor Diaconescu looked at Vespasian, ready to shout, "YES!" in his stead. Vasile Gheorghe had lifted his hand to his heart, visibly overjoyed. Arghir remained a block of stone, his eyes narrowed, surprised by the proposition. Vespasian smiled and said, "The Kingdom I bring is not of this world."

"But it can help this world."

"I already do so, perhaps more than others," said Vespasian in a firm voice.

"You will be able to help build churches and feed the poor! Think only of these extraordinary aspects! And your charisma will mean you'll be backed in parliament by numerous members of our party, who will support you in all your projects. Our party is a tool, a tool destined to help people as you wish."

"My only tool is faith, and my voice is prayer," said Vespasian.

Here, the senator waved his finger as if to say, "Yes, yes, of course," and went on: "Well, politics is good for something, too. So many good things can be achieved through politics . . ."

"What interests me is people's souls, not their average wage," said Vespasian.

"But how can you reach the soul except through the average wage?" said the senator, patting his stomach. "Ask your friends here."

Vespasian looked around him. Although he was not looking at the physician in particular, the latter said, "It's not a bad idea at all, dear. We ought to think about it a little."

"And then, what is encouraging," the senator went on, pointing his finger at Vespasian, "is that you are young. Young and in possession of extraordinary credibility and an immaculate reputation—in a country like ours, which has an elderly president, which is to say, one with an abysmal past, you realize what that means? You realize how people's trust in you could be exploited?"

Vespasian shook his head and looked at the senator as if he were a great distance away. He said, "Trust is not the same as faith. Throughout history, our beloved clerics and our beloved laymen have mixed things up."

"The exceptions only serve to strengthen the rule, my dear sir," went on the senator, unruffled. "We find ourselves at a moment in time when the political paradigm is shifting in Romania. Things are changing; people's outlooks are changing. Like kittens, when they first open their eyes. We're at that point in our political life when we're only just beginning to see."

"Quite right," said Vasile Gheorghe, helping the bodyguard to rise to his feet from the floor, at last.

"The political paradigm has been changing from one day to the next ever since the time of Saint Andrew the Apostle. You can't rely on that," observed Vespasian categorically.

"I understand," said the senator, as if negotiating. "I'm prepared to listen to your conditions, with a view to your acceptance of our political offer."

"No, no, perhaps I haven't made myself understood," said Vespasian. "I don't think I'm suited to your offer. My answer is no, no, no once and for all, a categorical no."

The senator ran his fingers through his hair, without shedding his smile, and said, "Allow me, then, to present to you a project that might interest you. It is an initiative by our party, one of the most substantial projects for the coming electoral cycle."

As he spoke, the senator took from his briefcase a thick file, bound in red covers.

"I am talking about the Cathedral of St. Andrew, patron saint of Romania, which we intend to construct in the middle of the round-about by the University. It will be even taller than the Intercontinental Hotel on the other side of the square, and it will completely solve the traffic problem, because we will systematize the boulevards and build an underground passage under the cathedral, thus without blocking off the intersection. From the architectural point of view, it will be a combination of the Byzantine and Gothic styles, with neo-Gothic features, a bit like the Cuza Palace at Ruginoasa or the Palace of Culture in Jassy. Moreover, it will bear a certain resemblance to the Hagia Sophia Cathedral in Constantinople, as well as to the cathedral in Cologne, if you take a look at the spire, here. From a distance, it will be visible that the second skyscraper in central Bucharest is an Orthodox spire. It will dominate the city."

"Superb," said Dr. Arghir.

"How much will it all cost?" asked Professor Diaconescu, pointing at the plans.

Vespasian rose to his feet and said, "None of this is for me."

"But, dear Mr. Moisa," said the senator, "I ask you kindly, tell me at least what you think of my political proposal. We could do so many things together. Look at this cathedral. I know, you are probably thinking that so many religious construction projects have been bandied about over the last few years, some of them are being built, others are still at the discussion stage . . ."

"This is a lie."

"Pardon?"

"A lie from one end to the other," said Vespasian.

"It's a splendid cathedral, on a historic site, sanctified by the blood of our young martyrs during the revolution."

"If Andrew heard what use you're putting his name to, he'd double up with laughter."

"Which Andrew?" asked the senator.

"Saint Andrew," said Vespasian. "Didn't you say that it was going to be called the Cathedral of St. Andrew?"

"Ah, yes!" admitted the senator, tapping his brow, as if punishing himself for his oversight. "Or perhaps his blessed effigy is happy, up there in the heavens."

"He wouldn't be happy at all," Vespasian contradicted.

"How so?" asked the senator.

"I've met him and ass-kissing isn't much to his liking."

There was a moment of silence. They were all looking at Vespasian. He had said it with the utmost gravity. The doctor asked, "You know Andrew?"

"Yes, very well, too," emphasized Vespasian.

"Where from?" asked the doctor, breathlessly.

"Perhaps in a dream," added Vespasian, as if he did not want to divulge more.

"But let's not get overwhelmed by the technical details," said the senator, in a different tone. "I think that we can look forward to, for our Orthodox believers and our Romanian Orthodox money, a certain reinvigorating trend in one of the country's most important political parties. Sincerely speaking, you have convinced me. I am yours. I, personally, would wish to see the Tidings of the Lord movement growing and transforming the Romanian Orthodox Church into a militant institution, one more involved in the nation's problems, or, as we Romanians say, one with bigger balls. The militant component, this is what we're lacking, and we can regain it only by each becoming more involved. I wish to become a member of the Tidings of the Lord, and I ask you kindly to place me on your records forthwith. But why do you all not want to become members of our party?"

Vespasian turned around and said, "We don't have any records."

Dr. Arghir cleared his throat and said, "I have taken the liberty of making some notes, of a strictly personal nature, of course."

Vespasian looked at him with unexpected harshness and said, "Please destroy them."

"I thought that . . ." said the doctor, with his hand in the air.

For the first time, they say that Vespasian was losing his composure then. He went up to Arghir and shouted, "Destroy them, otherwise I'll throw you out into the street. We're not here to play politics or cut deals, of any kind or with anyone. This is not what we are here to do!"

"Dear Vespasian," said the doctor, "have you seen those people outside? Someone has to provide them with something to eat. There are almost two hundred people in the yard of the villa. They've also filled the cellar. They've put up tents on the man's lawn. They've laid sleeping bags on the steps. And there are another twenty or so sleeping on the pavement outside. All these people are here for you. They pray when you tell them to, they listen to what you say, they go to church when you tell them to. We have a responsibility toward them. They're like my own children. I have to know who my children are."

"But don't keep records. No! And if you raise the issue one more time, I'll go out onto the balcony and tell them what you've done. It's not the case here for us to become an institution with records and attendance sheets."

"Legally speaking, it would be a good thing for us to become an association or foundation," said Vasile Gheorghe. "What do I know? It couldn't do any harm."

"No! I'm not having anything like that. Enough of this nonsense."

Turning to the senator and shaking his hand, he said, "What is happening here is not for you, nor is what you do for me. I respect you and wish you success, but we have different paths."

And as if Vespasian were in a hurry to get somewhere, he went out of the room, leaving the senator with his hand still outstretched.

"Well, what do you know," said Professor Diaconescu.

"Senator, sir," said Vasile Gheorghe, "let's keep in touch. We'll see."

The senator smiled and gave him a discreet wink. "Of course, Mr. Director," he said, inclining his head, with a brief smile. "They're not ideas that can be accepted lightly. I understand that."

"You know, that's not a bad idea about the foundation," Dr. Arghir told Vasile Gheorghe.

"No it isn't, no it isn't," he answered, getting ready to conduct the senator out of the villa.

The senator heard them and smiled.

Vespasian went back to the room reserved for him, with the ginger tomcat purring and rubbing up against his legs. There, Maximilian was watching the television news, an interminable broadcast.

"You can't imagine how hot things are getting," said Maximilian, pointing at the television set. "Those two broads were fighting like madwomen. One of them was left with her bra showing."

Vespasian sat down in the armchair and listened.

—In the last few hours, among the crosses in University Square a strange statue has appeared, representing a sun with inwardly pointing rays. It looks like a sphere pierced by numerous holes. We have invited to our studio Professor Pantelimon Rădulescu, from the Romanian Academy Institute, to explain the significance of this statue. Later, in our other studio, we will have a surprise guest, who will take part in a discussion on the subject. Over to you, Professor.

—Thank you. Indeed, in the very center of Bucharest an esoteric statue has turned up, an ancient symbol of the dark star Nemesis. It is the first time public opinion in Romania has been confronted with such an image, has seen such an image, and I thank you for the opportunity to explain its significance.

—What is it all about, Professor?

—I think it is a case of the dark star Nemesis, which marks the emergence in Romania—a country which has lately become profoundly spiritualized, as spiritualized as Tibet—of a new sect. This sect worships Nemesis and brings to the fore the vibrations emitted by the star Nemesis toward Earth. Without doubt, we will not be mistaken if we describe the

CHAPTER TWELVE

orientation of this sect as satanic. This is not what I wish to discuss, but rather the wholly special situation with the star Nemesis.

—Where is this star located, Professor?

—Nemesis is situated twice as far from the sun as the distance between the sun and the planet Pluto.

—Is its existence documented?

—Not by direct observation, no. But by means of calculations, its existence has been wholly proven since the 1920s.

—Isn't it just a theory?

—No, it's a certainty.

—So, Professor, you give credence to this theory.

—Entirely.

—Thank you, Professor. We are now going over to studio six, where our colleague Mihai Pelican has a special guest.

"Each of us has an idée fixe," Maximilian told Vespasian. "We are living in a time when many people have one and the same idée fixe. The air in which we swim scorches us."

Vespasian wrapped himself more tightly in the dressing gown that had been a gift from Vasile Gheorghe. He seemed cold. The fever had probably returned.

—Good evening, viewers. This evening we have in the studio as our special guest Professor Radu Pirgu, the head of the mathematics, physics, and astrophysics section of the Romanian Academy. Good evening, Professor, we're delighted to have you here as our guest in the studio. Did you follow Professor Rădulescu's declaration?

—Thank you for the invitation, Mr. Pelican. For me it is a privilege to make a number of important clarifications. I hope that by the end of the discussion Romanian public opinion will have been completely enlightened. That scoundrel Rădulescu was kicked out of research twenty years ago, and for very good reason. His pseudo-theories are nothing more than out-of-control psychoses. The man is sick. He doesn't know what he's talking about. There is no theory about Nemesis. There are no proofs from the 1920s. He is a liar.

—But what about the statue in University Square?

—How the hell are we supposed to know? It's a problem for City Hall. If it isn't authorized, then they should remove it. But what I wanted to say is that the solar system is made up of the sun and nine planets, i.e., Mer-

cury, Venus, Earth, Mars, Jupiter, Saturn, Uranus, Neptune, and Pluto. There is no Nemesis. It's a big lie, invented by idiots for other idiots.

—Thank you, Professor. Your explanations were very useful. Now, back to the main studio.

—Thank you, Mihai. Professor Rădulescu, what is your reaction to the declarations of Professor Pirgu?

—First of all, madam, allow me to say that I'm glad the old duffer's still in the land of the living, just as vile as ever, but still hale and capable of listing the planets. Unfortunately, since the discovery of Pluto in 1930, other things have taken place in science. Obviously, I stand by what I previously said. I have nothing to add.

—Thank you for that clarification, Professor. Now over to Mihai in studio six.

But rather than the voice of the young reporter, the cracked voice of the academician could be heard, breaking into the broadcast:

—If I'd known you were inviting me here to confront me with that old baboon, I wouldn't have come. There isn't any theory about Nemesis or any theory about the sun having a twin. He's lying and trying to make propaganda through nonuniversity channels for an idea that failed at the academic level. He's a toad, whom, when I catch him, I'm going to thrash.

With that, he shook his stick in the air. The presenter leaned away and said, Thank you, Professor.

The screen now split in two, with images live from each studio. From his armchair, clutching the microphone, Professor Rădulescu began to bellow, You can't accept other people's ideas, and you know very well that you've never been able to accept them! You've never been able to carry on an honest intellectual discussion! All you can do is to lay down the law, based on the authority you imagine yourself to have. The whole lot of you—you've played with the orthography of the Romanian language, with Academy prizes, with institute budgets, with the Academy library, with everything! You ought to be put on trial for lying to the nation!

—You're a fine one to talk, you ox, quoting nonexistent works! You obtained your shitty little doctorate with Ştefănescu in '64, after Ştefănescu got himself made a Ph.D. supervisor as a reward for grassing people to the Securitate!

—You idiot, there's nothing you can teach me. You've never in your *whole life been capable of giving a decent lecture. All you've ever done has been to show up to your lectures drunk and splatter the blackboard with snot!*

—*You cretin, how did you come up with the calculations that the ecliptic of Pluto proves the existence of a binary star? Don't you see that it would be thrown off orbit if that were the case? What's it meant to be, a hypothesis by means of the absurd, or what?*

—*When did you do that calculation so as to know? Haven't you ever heard that it's possible to construct a model with binary stars, that there's an admissible stellar mass for Nemesis, which allows for the same orbit and the same structure for the rest of the solar system?*

—*And how much would this mass be?*

—*I can prove to you that it can be between 1.22 and 1.46 of the mass of the sun. Do the sums and you'll see that it works out. In fact, you did similar calculations yourself in your 1974 paper, but now you pretend you've forgotten.*

There was a moment of silence. The academician rubbed his forehead, as if straining to remember something. He leaned his cane against the table and, somewhat deflated, said, *It's true. I did work on a binary star model back then. I studied it, but not its applicability to the solar system.*

—*You predicted all this, and, if you'd taken the calculations to the very end, you'd have seen that the theory you argued for is not contrary to what I've been saying here.*

—*What was that reference to some work from the 1920s?*

—*Blaschke defends it too, you know.*

—*In what form? Maybe not specifically. I don't believe that.*

—*Yes, old chap, we could meet some time, to talk about the technical details. I'll convince you in five minutes, because I can prove to you the admissible limits of the ecliptic of all the orbits in a bipolar model, and you'll see there's no contradiction.*

—*Are you sure you didn't divide by zero?*

Professor Rădulescu began to laugh.

—*Come off it! That would have been a good one.*

Maximilian looked at Vespasian, without speaking.

—*You have been watching a live debate on the significance of the star Nemesis in the contemporary imagination, brought to you by our* station in order to provide a better overall picture of the recent events in Bucharest.

"What can you do to help a mad world?" said Vespasian. "What can you do to help? If you teach people something, they don't get it. If you tell them something, they don't hear it. If you pray for them, your prayer flows away like sand."

—*We now go over to sociologist Johann Knaster of the Institute for Study of Romanian Society, in studio eight.*

—*Good evening, Dr. Knaster, and thank you for being here with us tonight in our studio.*

—*Thank you.*

—*What is your opinion on the discussion we have just been following?*

—*It's clear that within the scientific community there are certain things that are as yet unclear and certain ideas that give rise to lively discussion. But what seems to me extremely significant at the moment is not the current model of the solar system, but the situations produced by the contemporary imagination. It is not the scientific truth that counts, but the impression that certain scientific facts create upon the broader population. It doesn't matter whether the star Nemesis exists, or whether this star transmits vibrations to earth. What matters is that there is a group of people, sociologically speaking, that believes in it. This is why the technicalities we hear in a discussion about astronomy are irrelevant. It is not this discussion we are interested in. What we are interested in is something else, namely the fact that a group of people has set up a satanic symbol in University Square, a place of symbolic importance for Romanians since the 1989 Revolution. This is what is in discussion here. We seek to understand the nature of this imagery. What is it that motivated them to attack a space sacred to the national community, inserting a symbol of this kind there? That is the question.*

—*Why did they do this, in your view?*

—*To be honest, I don't know very much about this phenomenon. But I think that it might be an idea that has filtered out of scientific circles, an idea that has been poorly understood and poorly interpreted by all kinds of social misfits, people marginalized by society who have now come to claim for themselves a portion of the public space.*

—*How do you see this social phenomenon evolving in the future?*

—*I don't think this will be very easy to predict.*

CHAPTER TWELVE

—Is there anything else you would like to tell viewers, in conclusion?
—Yes. Without exaggerating, I would say that history is repeating itself. The excesses of the past might have helped us to understand and not to repeat something that formerly thrust us toward tragedy. Genuinely to take responsibility for the past means to understand every historical fact and every idea that might return to trouble us now. These ideas can come from anywhere, from the field of science, from the utopias or heroic deeds of other ages. They can come from anywhere at all, because today's society allows the large-scale dissemination of an epidemic of ready-made ideas. And some social groups, made up of individuals suffering a profound crisis of identity, revive these ideas, rather than learning something from past tragedies, and incorporate them, sometimes at a fundamentalist level, into their group identity or into the identity of each individual within the group.

—What you are saying, beyond the academic terminology, a language probably impenetrable to our viewers, is that it is hard to predict what might come next.

The sociologist remained silent, seeming to have frozen in front of the cameras. The camera panned back to the presenter, who said, *Thank you, Professor, for having taken part in our news program.*

At this hour of the evening, Colonel Focşăneanu was in his office in Romanian Intelligence Service headquarters, together with Major Baldovin and a secretary. They were all standing and watching the television, a color portable. The colonel was on his fourth black coffee of the day. His eyes were bloodshot. He pointed to a folded piece of paper and said to the major, "This is the report I received an hour ago. Statistics made available by the police. Now we have graffiti, too."

He read from the report, "Graffiti depicting a sun with inwardly pointing rays has been appearing on the walls of all unguarded buildings in Bucharest: on the walls of the Ion Luca Caragiale National College, on the fence behind Romanian National Television, on the fence of the former presidential residence of Nicolae Ceauşescu on Primăvara Boulevard. The Romanian Intelligence Service has identified two hundred and twenty-two cases of fresh graffiti within an interval of twenty-four hours, scattered throughout the whole of Bucharest."

"Yes," said the major, "it looks like the work of a Satanist sect, one that is well organized and capable of vandalizing buildings, not to mention doing battle with those nutcases from the Northern Station."

"Damned life," said Colonel Focşăneanu, looking at the map indicating the places where graffiti had been found. "A sect of Satanists—do you know what this means? A sect about which we don't have a single report from the inside . . ."

And then, in a tone of genuine concern, "Do you know what that lot do to cats?"

Colonel Focşăneanu turned toward the television and saw a scene that few of us will ever forget.

A troop of masked police had surrounded a short, stocky, blond man. They were holding him and trying to handcuff him. All of a sudden, the man yelled to the camera at the top of his voice, *Get your paws off me! I am Stephen the Great!*

Across the screen once more rolled the message that this was a live broadcast from Matache Square. The broadcast cut to another reporter at another point in the city, somewhere in the middle of a brightly illumined boulevard. A line of police had blocked off the traffic. The reporter was saying, *A religious war broke out as night fell in the emergency room, where it seems that the Satanists and ultra-Orthodox conservatives had been made to share the same ward. The fighting broke out spontaneously and was impossible to predict. Ten minutes ago, a doctor on duty was thrown from a second-floor window. He landed on the awning of an ice-cream stall and bounced off it onto the top of our television van. Our colleague, Carmen, was on the spot to give him first aid, and here he is now to say a few words.*

The camera showed a man wearing a white coat, lying on his belly on the hood of a van, with his legs somehow twisted up in the air. The reporter moved the microphone to the man's mouth. *Good evening, doctor. Can you tell us who threw you out the window? Who were the aggressors?*

—I don't know. There were too many of them. I didn't have time to see much.

—What were they doing in the ward? What did you see when you entered?

—Fighting.

—Which of them?

—All of them.

CHAPTER TWELVE

—*What do you think is the solution?*

—*I don't know. I'm a specialist in head injuries. I don't know anything about insanity like that. They're spoiling for a fight. You don't even have a chance to tend to their injuries.*

—*That's all for the moment from the emergency room. A minute ago, special forces went into the hospital, to bring the situation under control. Now back to the studio.*

The television screen hissed for a moment, and then the camera showed once more the flower arrangement with the petunias. In the background could be heard chords from Ciprian Porumbescu's *Ballad.* Then, a blonde, middle-aged reporter warbled, *There now follows a poetic interlude.*

CHAPTER THIRTEEN

THE NEXT MORNING, AT THE CRACK OF DAWN, COLONEL FOCŞĂNEANU had on his desk the executive summary of a file on the so-called Northern Station Satanists. The entire staff of the division had worked through the night on the materials. The colonel's head was aching. On the desk there was also a press bulletin. On the first page there was a commentary by an Italian editorialist, who wrote about the events in Bucharest thus: "The time has come for Romanians to laugh at themselves, as we laugh at them." There's nothing to laugh about! What nerve! What a lack of political understanding! He leafed through the dossier on the Satanists and read the entire list of warnings about the movement, their secret messages and signals, which he had not taken seriously. Which is to say, he had been expecting the heart of the action to be elsewhere when it came to the sects. He had thought he knew the dossier by heart. Now, on seeing it for the tenth time, things seemed to be coming together: a gang of Satanists, appearing out of nowhere, was fighting a turf war with neo-Orthodox fundamentalists (as they were called by one of the dailies). Some of these events, presented in that voluminous file, were authentic news items, taken from the mass media and then, coming under investigation, meticulously documented by specialist officers. This was how Colonel Focşăneanu discovered that there were different kinds of Satanism, a western and an eastern version, just as there is a western, Catholic, and an Eastern Orthodox Church. Here, for example, was a passage from a newspaper article dated September 21, 1992: *Exactly one week ago, Officer*

Flavius Popescu, assigned to guard the State Archives building in Baia Mare, shot dead four of his comrades before turning his gun on himself. Investigators are following two leads: the killer's possible membership of a Satanist sect and drug use. Initial information shows that Flavius Popescu was a fan of Marilyn Manson—a singer known for his Satanist messages—but official investigations have so far not uncovered evidence that the soldier was affiliated to any movement of this kind. A fellow soldier has declared that Popescu often used to meet with men of his own age who wore Satanist rings, chains, and other insignia. As he read, the colonel clapped his hand to his forehead. There you have it, there are Satanists even in the ranks of the forces of law and order now. We've got them all: madmen, Satanists, fundamentalists, idiots—the whole gamut. In a number of reports, there were various accounts of the same kind, about how various groups met and conducted all kinds of services and ceremonies. It was only to be expected that one fine day they would erupt and make headline news. It's easy to call up such a soldier and post him to some military unit or other, where he'll have access to firearms and cause a tragedy. Here, the colonel felt personally guilty, and if not guilty then at least responsible. What about that Vespasian Moisa: was he dangerous or not? This was the major unknown factor. Might he mobilize that huge mass of people under his sway to attack, for example, the presidency? Why not? Vigilance should never slacken. The colonel had to anticipate all the moves. However, it was not a matter of Vespasian here, but of the Satanists, who had managed to unleash a street battle. And against whom! With the lumpen proletariat, with the salt of the earth, the most downtrodden of mortals, the worshippers of Stephen the Great! You don't mess with them, not even if you've got backing from Beelzebub himself! The colonel closed the file. It was phantasmagorical, interminable. Let us suppose, he told himself, that tomorrow we arrest them all. Would that solve the problem? Of course not. Because it is ideas that give rise to these groups, sects, manifestations, or whatever the hell they are, whatever the hell you call them. In short, are we not dealing once more with the same human behavior that was known in the Middle Ages as madness, in various guises and forms of organization? Precisely. Why do they organize, thought the colonel, why do they come together to manifest their fixed ideas in a group? Is it because the individual is powerless when alone against society? In Budapest they have problems with skinheads. Here in Bucharest, all kinds of sects, street gangs, and fanatics of every shape and color have come to the surface. Do these movements incorporate the entire gamut of madness latent in man? Does a sect such as that of Saint Stephen the Great incorporate the crisis of identity of a category of disappointed and disaffected youths? Yes, it's one thing when you see them on the television beating each other with chains, another when you listen to a psychiatrist discussing their fragile souls. It's not the same thing. Look, for example, at what an individual out to wreak havoc is capable of. From the report dated June 11, 1992: *A Satanist murder was committed in Germany. The two killers, Manuela, twenty-two, and Jens, twenty-five, held a satanic ritual and brutally murdered a car salesman, aged thirty-three. His body, cut into pieces and with sixty-six machete and hammer wounds, was found in the couple's flat in Witten. "The victim was unrecognizable," said one policeman. The body was found lying next to a black coffin, with plastic skulls, inverted crosses, and Nazi rune stones. The police also found a list of fifteen persons that the pair intended to kill as part of satanic rituals. Manuela and Jens were apprehended and arrested near Jena, in eastern Germany. The car salesman was a workmate of Jens and had been invited to the flat under the false pretext of a party, without suspecting the terrifying fate that awaited him. One of the police investigators said, "The walls were covered with black cloth. The slogan* When Satan comes to life *was written on the window."* Well, that was a real news item. It really happened. It was an authentic newspaper article, processed by our specialist officers at the time. It happened and it will happen again, because the ideas are out there. The superstitions, the prejudice, the necessary context. And now we can imagine one lot of madmen, who unearth the forgotten crosses of Bucharest, coming across the other lot of madmen, who were in the process of burying a live cat. This kind of crisis can't be kept under control. What can you do with them? How can you predict their madness? And the president shows up tomorrow and says, what information have you got, Colonel Focşăneanu? He could pull out this file, with its long list of ritual murders, mass shootings followed by suicides, sacrificial ceremonies, ceremonies without sacrifices, in Baia Mare and Witten and Chişinău and Craiova and Belgrade, and even in Rome, where they scrawled all kinds of inscriptions over the walls of the Vatican Library. That's what he would tell the president, the devil take him too. They all want something or other. But nothing could be done, that much was clear. Nothing could be predicted. The entire task of intelligence gathering didn't mean anything anymore, not today, and in any case not in this kind of situation. I mean, what can you do when individual instances of madness begin to group together? All of a sudden, Colonel Focşăneanu began to sweat, realizing that, given the global population explosion, the phenomenon was ineluctable.

"We're toiling for nothing . . ." he murmured, thrusting the file to one side.

■ □ ■ □ ■

It was a superb morning in Bucharest. It had rained a little at dawn, and the grass in the parks was wet. A summer sky, lofty and blue, like in the times before pollution, crowned the city like a Byzantine cupola. Drop by drop, the traffic in University Square was, as usual, clogging the intersection, and, as usual, more than twenty illegally parked cars had been towed away first thing in the morning. They had been removed from all over the city, and now it was being announced on the radio news. The Dîmboviţa River, without water, looked like a festering rubbish pit. From afar came a flock of seagulls. It circled the riverbed before going to cool off in the stagnant lake in Cişmigiu Park. The summer heat wilted the city, leaving its vital rhythms, but retarding it, a gigantic, exhausted body, overwhelmed by numbness.

■ □ ■ □ ■

Around this time, the situation of Vespasian Moisa's Christian sect, known also as the Tidings of the Lord, was about to complicate the international situation in a highly unexpected manner. In the faraway Emirate of Salibaar, a former British colony and now a member of OPEC, new reserves of oil had been discovered since 1990. The statistics showed that Salibaar was beginning to compare with Kuwait. Luckily, Salibaar enjoyed a much better geographical location and was one of the few countries where the desideratum of a thousand-year peace had real chances of fulfillment. The House of Salibaar had come to power in 1711, at around the time when Prince Dimitrie Cantemir of Moldavia took refuge in Russia and the Turks were very busy in Europe. The first emir came to the throne not by bloodshed, not by alliance or lineage, but thanks to a power vacuum, for that rock, one similar to Saint Michel (situated not only between earth and heaven, not only between land and sea, but also between Normandy and Brittany), had for centuries been a place where nothing happened. Oil was discovered there after the Turks and the British had left the region, and so there were no struggles for supremacy as far as the House of Salibaar was concerned. The only problem was of an administrative nature: that part of the world had never been very populous. When the emir came up with the idea of building a motorway from Salibaar City to the outlying town of Sabah, he had serious problems finding the manpower. In that period, for the first time in Salibaar's history, Indian laborers were brought in. They had numerous advantages: they were Mohammedans, they did not demand medical insurance, and they could be paid half the wage of Iranians and a fraction of the wage of Britons, if anyone had had the crazy idea of hiring Britons to complete the Sisyphean task of building a motorway in the middle of the desert. In the sixteenth century, the first Portuguese explorers had named that place the Coast of Death: at first sight, everything seemed dead, and nothing could ever have budged it from its inertia.

In such an environment, labor shortages were nothing new. After 1967, when a host of tensions between various European countries and the Arab world complicated the political equation between Europe and the Orient, Romanian experts entered the game, as a workforce in the service of developing Salibaar. They built the first section of the motorway, as well as the ring road around the capital and a suspension bridge over the Al Akhir Gulf, a kind of Golden Gate with architectural details that recalled the descriptions of *A Thousand and One Nights* and the legacy of Anghel Saligny. It was also Romanians that began to work there in the oil industry, at a time when Romanian laborers paid eighty percent of their earnings to the Romanian state in taxes. After 1990, the situation changed, and Salibaar became one of the favorite destinations for Romanian oil workers. At first, there were only eighty of them, mostly maintenance workers for oil drilling equipment. Then there came more oil workers, experts in water treatment, cooks and waiters, and builders, all the people needed to construct a country from scratch. One of the bizarre laws of Salibaar was that any worker who had worked for five years under contract to the government could ask for emirate citizenship. And so it was that a Romanian minority came into being in Salibaar, and it was only because the emirate did not hold free elections that there were no representatives of Romanian desert workers in the parliament there (not that they had such a thing).

The rock of Salibaar had been inhabited since ancient times by a Bedouin tribe, which, over the course of time, had produced fanatical devotees of the cult of Islam. Among their demands, which the emirs had been obliged to pass into law, was that no Christian church or Israelite synagogue was ever to be allowed in the emirate. And so the greatest surprise in the entire history of the emirate was the rumor that Emir Jaber al-Salibaar was a secret sympathizer of an obscure Christian sect, about which he had learned from his adviser, a construction engineer, initially hired during the golden age of the motorway construction project and later becoming a kind of unofficial minister of emirate public works, the highest post ever to be held by a Christian in Salibaar. He had told the emir of the fascinating theory of vibrations, how everything is made up of vibrations, which explain so many things, from the emergence of life on earth to the current geopolitical situation. He even succeeded in explaining to the emir why there is so much oil beneath the rock of Salibaar. The rumor agitated spirits in various local religious circles. What would become of Salibaar if the emir were secretly to convert to Christianity? Only the televised images broadcast every Friday of Jaber IV prostrating himself in the mosque went some way to calming public concerns . . . An emir of Christian sympathies would be inconceivable, illogical; it would be a nebulous excrescence on centuries of glorious history, of sustained piracy against Christian ships in the Indian Ocean. Things are not so simple when an idea as unusual as the Theory of Vibrations transplants itself in a different culture . . . The emir, however, was a discreet man, whose wisdom was the equal of that of an eagle in flight. With the greatest discretion, he sent a special emissary to Bucharest, a man with the genuine ability to be invisible, the holder of seven passports and seven parallel lives, and this silent emissary took with him seven million dollars which he donated to Vespasian Moisa's team. Colonel Focşăneanu was the first to find out about this, thanks to his specialist sources within the sect. The situation produced panic in intelligence circles. The Romanian Intelligence Service recommended that the Supreme Council for Defense should freeze all the accounts of sect members. The president rejected this proposal: in any case, the money was not being kept in any bank account and, besides in a confidential report, it had left no trace. The only perceptible change had been the appearance of two Mercedes-Benz limousines in Lahovary Square, both registered in the name of Dr. Arghir. The reports noted that Vespasian Moisa did not know anything about this unexpected donation, that all the wheeling and dealing had been carried out by Moisa's inner circle, and that only they knew where the money was hidden.

"They were donated to us by one of the faithful," explained Dr. Arghir to Vespasian, pointing at the limousines.

"I hope it wasn't one of those syrupy politicians you keep bringing here."

"Oh, no, not at all. Isn't it obvious? It's a different style entirely . . ."

"Send them back," the Teacher was recorded in the report as having said.

"Let's keep them at least for a little while . . ." Apolodor Arghir had said.

On the evening when the money arrived, for the first time the three hundred people gathered around Vasile Gheorghe's villa had been treated to champagne, whiskey, caviar, and fine pâté. In Lahovary Square, there was an open-air reception, besides which those of the next-door Scientists' Palace paled in comparison. From the street, the cameras of three television channels discreetly broadcast images of the feast, while three or four patrols of police wandered back and forth in front of the villa, in stupefaction and without any specific orders, inhaling the rich aromas through the palings.

CHAPTER THIRTEEN

■ □ ■ □ ■

CHAPTER FOURTEEN

AT FIRST, IT WAS JUST A RUMOR, WHICH SMACKED MORE OF A TALL tale, but in time it became a legend, as generally happened with all stories in the village of Dîrmănești. The people from thereabouts were in the habit of tangling things until the point where they became legend, but this time it was something bigger than what they were accustomed to. At the time when this story came to light, they say that the more simple-minded among them lost their minds. Ana was Victor Radu's daughter. She was four years old when her father was taken away to a prison camp, before the war, for some political affair he had gotten mixed up in. Like a peasant simpleton, he had gotten mixed up in it, in such a way that he could be found guilty before he had even managed to do anything. He came back, but in the years that followed he was in and out of prison. Her mother was left with all the worries of the household on her head. But the strangest thing of all was yet to begin. When Ana was seventeen, she got pregnant. Her father was out of prison at the time, and he beat her so that she would tell him who the father was. The girl insisted that she was a virgin. Victor Radu was having none of it, although he was a religious man and he prayed many times each day. In prison, he had made a rosary from grains of rice strung on a thread. He could not get anything out of his daughter. Maybe she was right, for the manling Ana Radu gave birth to had wings, golden hair, and blue eyes, and looked very different from the rest of us. They hid him in a grown-up's smock, because they did not want anyone to know that the girl had given birth to an angel. It was in the autumn of 1959. The secret police got wind of it, and two truckloads of soldiers came and surrounded the house. It is said that they ordered Victor Radu to come out with his hands up, and that was what he did. And they shouted for everyone to come out of the house, not omitting the one who had unleashed among the peasants of Dîrmănești such a dangerous outbreak of mysticism.

The heavens opened and a divine light poured from the upper air, throwing to the ground all those who were there with guns in their hands. And they all heard the voice of the Archangel Michael commanding the soldiers to leave the child in peace, to go thence and to tell the rest of the world that there was nothing to be seen there, for only this news would allow the child to grow. "Get ye hence and tell them!" thundered the voice, "swear ye that there is nothing here, otherwise I will find you wherever you are and turn you to dust."

And the story goes that the wee lad grew up in Dîrmănești and went by the name of Mihail Radu. And the shirt he wore hid not a hump but a pair of large white wings, like an eagle's.

On reading all this, Colonel Focșăneanu threw the report at the ceiling. The pages scattered through the air. The colonel began to laugh like a madman.

"Not another sect! This report just came in today! Another sect! Another! We had a new sect only yesterday, about some other madness. Where am I going to get the men?"

"Orders to open a new investigation, Colonel, sir?" asked Major Baldovin.

"We don't have the men for yet another investigation. I already have nine officers assigned to the Stephenists, fourteen plus the tomcat on surveillance of the dangerous sect of Vespasian Moisa, seven at Maglavit investigating the supposed reincarnation of Petrache Lupu, and six elite officers on the trail of the Satanists. Where am I going to get a team to shadow the son of the Archangel Michael himself? It's just not possible. We don't have the resources to keep this new religious outbreak under surveillance, let alone under control. No one ever foresaw that in Romania so many idiotic ideas would appear all at the same time. It's unimaginable. We don't have enough men to report on them, let alone to take action. Something, somewhere, will always slip out of our control."

CHAPTER FOURTEEN

"But these kinds of activities are precisely the objective of our department," said the major, in a disappointed voice.

"Yes, that's right," said the colonel. "We've ended up working harder than the department that deals with irredentism. We've got more Romanian sects than irredentist movements. You'd think it was a Spielberg film about aliens. I for one am sick of it. You barely manage to finish a dossier and a new problem crops up. We've got more lunatic Romanians than restive Hungarians. How am I supposed to allocate men for each new outbreak of lunacy?"

"At your orders, Colonel, sir."

"It all comes from the Patriarch. The Patriarch is to blame. I've never seen such a dish of porridge for a man. He's soft and weak and panders to them all. He answers their letters, he gives them audiences, he allows priests to bless them, he blesses them himself, if they come to him on a Sunday. It's unprecedented."

"Have we got the Patriarch under surveillance?"

"No, no. We don't need to deploy men to tell us about him. Most of the time he tells it himself. The problem is with all these movements. Tomorrow you wake up with a hundred thousand people outside the government building, one holier than the next, each one demanding something different, each with a banner and a beard down to his knees, each holding a candle and singeing the next one's beard. I can see the prime minister now, shouting for Colonel Focşăneanu to get into his office. And what will I tell him? That an entire department wasn't able to keep tabs on a single sect? That we were numerically overwhelmed by how many new religious ideas have been cropping up in the last few years? Lord, what am I to do?"

On saying this, the colonel made a broad, priestly sign of the cross over his belly. He looked as if he was going to burst into tears. Large, blue bags hung beneath his eyes. Major Baldovin gazed at him with cold eyes. The colonel had changed in the last few days.

"Do you know what yesterday's report is all about?"

"I'm not up to date on it, Colonel, sir."

"Well, it's happening in the very heart of the city, beneath your very eyes, beneath everyone's eyes, and I receive a report from the Intelligence Department of the Justice Ministry. We're a laughingstock."

The major was standing to attention, as if frozen to the spot, while the colonel seemed to be melting onto the carpet. His hair was disheveled, his necktie loosened, his eyes bloodshot.

"Look, this is how things stand. Yesterday morning, in front of City Hall, a sect called the Diogenists showed up. There are fifteen of them, for the time being, but they're proselytizing like you wouldn't believe. They preach by the power of example. Picture fifteen barrels in front of City Hall. People come on business to the mayor's office and they see fifteen filth-caked Diogenists, each living in a separate barrel. The report says that they do their business in the barrel and then move it a short distance away, as if what they left behind them isn't theirs. The report describes how three days ago one of them crossed the road with his barrel around his body hiding his nakedness. In the middle of the busy traffic on the boulevard, suddenly a barrel appears, with a bearded man inside, trying to cross the road. The report also gives details of how one of the men in the barrels started jerking off just as a respectable lady was passing him on her way toward City Hall. Well, this is one religious group we don't know anything about."

"We have nothing to reproach ourselves for," said the major. "We've done everything humanly possible. We can't cure twenty-three million mental cases."

"Absolutely! As I was saying, the history of mankind has known all kinds of exaggerations. All these excesses are nothing new. They were well known to physicians down the ages. What is highly specific to this place and historical moment is the fact that all the excesses are taking place simultaneously, and our great misfortune is that our task is to keep track of them and to anticipate when these mobs are going to take to the streets. Not even the devil himself could keep track of them."

As if he wanted to resolve the affair right there and then, the major asked, "What are your orders to deal with the Diogenists?"

"Firstly, because they're very close to here, I think it would be our duty, as true intelligence professionals, to go and take a look at them. We'll inspect the situation, then we'll call the police to come and arrest them."

"Shall we open a file on them? How shall we proceed?"

"Let the police deal with them. A legal solution needs to be found, damn it. People shitting on the sidewalk is a matter for the police. Our specialty is in much more subtle matters."

As he spoke, the colonel stood up and walked over to the coat stand. He had taken his hat and was making to leave the room when the door opened and General Mihalache appeared.

"To what do I owe the honor, General, sir? I wasn't expecting you."

"No rush, my friend," said the general, with unwonted warmth.

The colonel now saw that behind the general was standing a solemn man, with glasses and a black suit, like a gravedigger, and two burly types, one of them wearing a white coat.

"Allow me to introduce Dr. Horza, an old friend of mine. I recommend you put your entire trust in him. He's an excellent professional, and he can help you. These are his assistants."

The colonel looked the newcomers up and down, trying to understand what was going on. Then, all of a sudden, he let out a desperate cry, rushed to the window, opened it, and said, "Help! The last bastion of democracy and freedom is in peril!"

"Please, Colonel," said the general. "You can't imagine that anyone will save you. Do you know how many people have cried for help from this building over the years? And has anyone ever leaped to their aid?"

"Help!"

"Please, gentlemen, it's your turn," said the man in black.

"Don't come near me! I'll kill you!" said Colonel Focșăneanu.

One of the burly men leaped from a distance and felled the colonel like a skittle. The other, the one wearing the white coat, jumped on top of him and began wrapping him in a strait jacket.

"So, what were you saying? Talks to cats, does he?" said the gravedigger.

"Yes, it's a long story. You'll hear things you've never heard before."

"I'd be surprised if I heard something that surprised me," the other said, shaking his head.

The general turned to Major Baldovin, who had remained standing to attention all the while, and said, "Major, please accept interim command of this division."

"Help!" cried Focşăneanu, on hearing this.

"I serve the motherland!" replied the major, his chest puffed out.

The two burly men lifted the colonel from the floor and left carrying him between them.

CHAPTER FOURTEEN

■ □ ■ □ ■

CHAPTER FIFTEEN

"IMPOSSIBLE," SAID PROFESSOR DIACONESCU. "HE HAS COME HERE himself?"

"Yes," said Maximilian. "I could hardly believe it myself."

They were standing on the steps of the villa in Lahovary Square, lost among the other hundreds of people. In a corner, two men were praying aloud. Not far from them, the Troubadour was kissing Barbie, who was wearing a pink dress.

"Should we invite him inside?" asked the professor.

"Do you think we ought to?"

"Why not?"

"Well, he's been tried and convicted for his role in the repression during the revolution."

"Yes, but now he's a free man. And he has the soul of a Christian. Why shouldn't we receive him? We receive everybody."

Saying this, the professor assumed a triumphant air and crossed the courtyard. He headed to the Dacia 1300 motorcar parked on the sidewalk, behind one of the limousines. He bent toward the backseat window and said, "Welcome. Please come inside."

"I would like to speak to Mr. Moisa, if possible," said the man in the motorcar, without making any move to alight and follow the professor.

"We'll do everything possible, of course. I don't know what schedule he has for today, but we'll do everything we can."

"Is it true that lots of people want to see him?"

"Oh, yes. That's what most of the people here have come for."

And he pointed behind him at the compact mass, almost a hundred people, who formed a thick queue winding around the courtyard of the villa.

"Perhaps it would be better if I came another time," said the man in the motorcar.

"Please, come inside now. I am Professor Diaconescu, and I am one of the founding members of the Tidings of the Lord movement. I assure you that we'll have time to talk at leisure, at least the two of us."

"Thank you, Mr. Diaconescu," said the man.

He got out of the car and extended his hand, introducing himself. "Eliad Bărbulescu," he said.

Of course, the professor knew him from television. He had seen him many times, the last being at his trial, which had been broadcast live, but before that he had often seen his photograph in the newspaper, watched him on television, heard his voice on the radio. Eliad Bărbulescu had been prime minister for exactly four months under Nicolae Ceauşescu, but now it was not very clear what he was. In any case, he had made an end of his reckonings with the law, after having been imprisoned, it would seem, for two years. The professor did not have very many details.

They made their way through the crowd with difficulty. Eliad Bărbulescu was wearing a broad-brimmed brown hat and opaque sunglasses. He had aged so much compared with how the professor had known him that no one recognized him. Anyhow, no one in the courtyard of the villa cared about anyone except Vespasian Moisa.

The professor opened the door of the villa and invited the distinguished guest inside, to the basement.

"Please come this way."

Eliad Bărbulescu hesitated for a moment but followed the professor down the steep steps. The professor turned on the light. They passed a group of young people who were tuning their guitars and entered an annex that was now transformed into a kind of monastic cell. It was a small, whitewashed room, in which there was a bed, a table, and a chair. On the wall there was an icon of the Mother of God at the foot of the Cross, which was illumined by rays of light seeping through a small window near the ceiling. Through the window, which gave onto the backyard, a hum of voices could be heard.

CHAPTER FIFTEEN

"Please, take a seat."

"Thank you," said the guest. "I don't want to take up too much of your time, and so I'll get straight to the point."

He sat down on the chair, and the professor perched himself on the edge of the bed.

"I would like to make a confession," said Eliad Bărbulescu. "I would like to see a priest."

The professor laughed awkwardly.

"We don't have any priests here."

"None at all?" said the guest, in surprise.

"None at all, because we are a lay movement. It is a lay order. It's something new to Orthodoxy."

The former prime minister nodded.

"Yes, I understand," he said. "But I would like to ask you a few things."

"Please . . ."

"I was an atheist my entire life. You see, given the life I led, I didn't give such matters much thought. When you're busy with other things your entire life, you don't raise the question of faith."

"I understand," said the professor. "I was the same. For a long time it didn't interest me."

"Yes, and you end up thinking that this is how things are meant to be. That there isn't any afterlife, that the only things that exist are the things you can see, that we live in a material world without any mysteries."

"I can remember feeling exactly the same thing."

"Well, when I was in prison, I began to pray. One evening, as I was praying, it seemed to me that from somewhere in the corner of the room a greenish light began to shine, as a kind of signal. I was convinced that it was not an illusion, that it was something real. I felt that someone was listening to me from the world beyond. I felt that, if I spoke, I was not alone, that something in me was not mortal and transient. That something would remain."

The professor remained silent, unflinching, listening. The guest went on: "Beyond the world we live in, beyond what we have to choose in this life, there are much deeper things, there are higher stakes and more essential choices. We gamble our soul in every moment. Now I know this. And this is why I wanted to ask you what is the story with the theory of vibrations and with prayer?"

"For centuries, the monks of the Eastern Church have perfected a technique of prayer that seems to produce genuine miracles—if it is performed correctly and if the mind concentrates on what it has to do. We believe that through prayer the soul of man can come to capture a part of the resonance of the primordial energies that come from God. We also believe that these prayers gain in value if they are uttered in Romanian, because we reckon Romanian preserves the encryption of a precious code."

"Interesting theory," said Bărbulescu.

"My own," admitted the professor modestly.

"Yours?" said the former prime minister admiringly.

"Yes, mine."

"And what exactly have you discovered?"

"I have discovered a part of the medical code of the Romanian language. The primordial code is combined with a medical code, a code that contains, in the name of each illness, the name of the cure. It is as if the name of the poison also contained the antidote."

"Phenomenal!"

"Yes, please believe me. It is something apparently unbelievable."

"And what does Mr. Moisa say about all these things?"

"What does he say? He preaches them! He came and he reevaluated them, he put them in a different form, he presented them to the world in a different way, and now they are the flesh and soul of a theory that is proving to produce the most extraordinary religious phenomenon in Romania. It is the very substance of the eternal Romania! Did you see those children with the guitars? They sing about it. What other theory has ever made people sing about it?"

"But there is something special about Mr. Moisa, isn't there?"

"Yes, there is," said the professor. "He is a special man. I am convinced that he is a chosen man."

"Some say of him that he is the Son of God."

"They say many things," said the professor. "All will be revealed to us at the appropriate time."

Eliad Bărbulescu rose to his feet and said, "I would like to be a part of all this. I would like to be a small particle of it. Please, help me to live alongside you, to be with you, to pray with you. I feel in my heart that Vespasian Moisa is the Son of God, and I desire, by serving here, to redeem the sins I committed in the past."

The professor laid his hands on his shoulders. "If only you knew how much I understand you!"

"Thank you!"

"Yes, I understand and admire your honesty."

Then the former prime minister burst into tears. He not only wept but also whimpered softly.

"You see, at the moment we have a little problem with space. Sometimes I get the feeling that not even the House of the People itself would be big enough. It's full up here. We don't have any room to house people, and we need to do something about it. But what I propose is something else. I'll telephone you when we have more space available. Maybe we can find other premises somewhere. I know we have all kinds of plans, that there is talk of the Tidings of the Lord moving outside Bucharest. Perhaps we will have better conditions soon."

"This is my number," said Bărbulescu, handing him a visiting card.

"I promise."

"Thank you."

The two men shook hands, as if in a gesture of supreme understanding.

"There is one more thing I would like to ask you," said the former prime minister.

"Please do."

"What I would like to understand, at the level of ideas, of course, only at the level of ideas, is the story about the Romanian people being the chosen people. How is it that the Romanian people are the chosen people?"

Professor Diaconescu frowned. "I don't think I have ever said that."

"That's what I heard," insisted Eliad Bărbulescu, in a confident tone of voice.

"No, it must be some kind of mistake. What I said was that the Romanian language is extremely ancient, that it is seven thousand years old, and that it conceals a code."

"Could it really be seven thousand years old?"

"No, it *is* seven thousand years old," said the professor. He had gone through the arguments many times and he no longer had any doubt as to the veracity of the theory.

"How can we be sure of it?" asked the former prime minister. "A long time ago, I used to be up to date with all the new theories, but I don't recall having received any information about what is, let me say, such an epochal discovery."

"Let us suppose, absurdly, that the Romanian language were new. How then could it be decoded? Why would an understanding of it produce cures? This is the main argument. Moreover, this argument is connected to our understanding of the theory of vibrations. In the world there exist vibrations left over from the time of the creation, and we can reach these vibrations via a suitable code. And this code, which unshackles and clarifies everything, proves to be the Romanian language. For, if you will allow me, we have not said the Romanian people are a chosen people, but that the Romanian language is a chosen language, a miraculous language, which contains all kinds of key poetic lines. These poetic lines have healing powers, and whenever they occur in everyday speech, who knows where, who knows when, they come to convince, to possess a huge power of persuasion over, those who listen to them. We can't see them, they are invisible, but they are present and have an incredible magical content."

"Give me an example," said Eliad Bărbulescu.

"We have established with precision that the formula *The years have passed like clouds over the plain / And never will they come again* has an anesthetic effect on eighty percent of patients. It acts at the level of the cortex and anesthetizes, in some situations, acute pains, and causes paralysis for a few seconds. Contrariwise, a formula that has an excitatory effect on ninety percent of subjects is the following: *Let not God by His holy hand / Make us demand blood, not land! / When we shall no longer endure, / When hunger to revolt does lure, / Were you Christs, still will you be damned / Even in the grave!*

On hearing these lines, Eliad Bărbulescu rose to his feet, transfigured by emotion.

"You see?" said the professor. "It is very important to know that these magical formulas, once firmly implanted in the subject's small brain, at the primary school level, give convincing responses on various occasions, even at an advanced age. The mechanism is connected with the theory of vibrations, because it reproduces at the human level a form of preservation of uncreated energies, which relate to the situation of celestial bodies in the ether. This distinguishes man from beast, for the beast is not sensitive to such formulas. Man, however, perceives these energies when he is touched by the magical formulas submerged within the chosen language. Blessed are those who discover them."

The eyes of the former prime minister filled with tears. He said, "Thank you very much. I feel as if I have been freed from a great misunderstanding. I am beginning to see. I am beginning to understand these complex situations. Everything seems to be coming together. It seems to me that not one single moment of my life has been lived in vain, that nothing has been wasted. It seems to me that failure does not exist, that I have done well in serving the Romanian people in various honorable positions."

"Of course, of course," said the professor, patting him on the shoulder.

"I feel at peace, reconciled."

"Think what a healing effect this superb theory might have on the hundreds of alienated young people who come here, singing folk songs full of magical formulas, seeking the truth brought to us by Vespasian Moisa. Think how this comfort is brought to them by a prophet whom we believe to be the Son of God. And we are merely awaiting the day when this will be revealed to us through a revelation."

"It will be revealed?" asked Bărbulescu. "How so?"

"Not even we know how it will come to pass."

"But what will happen?"

"Let us have faith in the Lord our God," said the professor piously, "the Lord who led the nation of Israel into the land of Canaan and who strengthened Stephen the Great at Baia and the High Bridge, who gave succor to Brîncoveanu in the face of the foul heathen, in his final moment. So too let us have faith and let us be strengthened."

"God grant," said Eliad Bărbulescu timidly.

"And do not forget that these formulas are barely the beginning of a string of discoveries. We do not know how many there are and how many are to come. But we do know for sure that this is the reason why Romanians have so many problems communicating with the outside, why there are so many misunderstandings between us and the rest of Europe."

"Because of the code?"

"Yes, of course. Because the magical formulas of the Romanian language are untranslatable, and nothing can cross over into another idiom—neither the relaxation nor the excitation formulas. We are more isolated than the speakers of Korean. We are doomed to loneliness and unhappiness, because we are the bearers of a code with manifestations so particular that no other nation can perceive them."

Here, the prime minister felt the need to embrace the professor. He rested his head on his shoulder, and a few moments later the professor felt him sobbing. He caressed his hair and said, "Weep, weep, brother, until you calm down."

Eliad Bărbulescu sobbed for quite a few minutes. It was as if he were convulsed with chills. Finally, with a baritone snivel, he blew his nose and declared, "You are a great man, if you have been able to forge such a theory."

"Well, yes," said the professor, modestly.

"And you live here, under the stairs . . ."

"It's not a problem. That was how Blaga translated Goethe . . ."

"Yes, but, even so . . ."

"Please, no more."

"You are a great man!"

Then, Eliad Bărbulescu straightened his necktie and put on his sunglasses.

"I think it is time for me to leave."

Dusk had fallen. The buses that turned around in Lahovary Square, near the villa where it seemed there was a perpetual demonstration, had thinned out. The chords of a guitar could be heard somewhere, as if someone was preparing to play. The people in the bus station kept to one side, not mixing with the mass of demonstrators. The latter, sitting on the sidewalk, seemed overcome by perpetual torpor, as if they were a colony of salamanders in the sun.

That evening, one of the sub-officers on duty patrolling Lahovary Square was warrant officer Ionescu. The officer did not believe in nonsense. For him, they were all lunatics who interfered with traffic circulation, and two platoons could have solved the situation swiftly and without right to appeal. He could not understand all this politeness toward madmen. Maybe there were demands by the European Union at the bottom of it, and it is better not to meddle in such things, if

CHAPTER FIFTEEN

you don't want headaches. And so the warrant officer watched them with patience and calm.

"Pst, pst," he heard from a rosebush in the garden of the Scientists' Palace restaurant.

The officer turned but could see no one.

"Pst, pst," he heard once more.

This time, the officer placed his hand on his pistol. He had heard clearly, but he could not see anyone.

"Mr. Officer, please help me. I'm Lieutenant Trăistaru of the Romanian Intelligence Service. I'm working here undercover, and my liaison officer hasn't turned up to the last two rendezvous."

The officer could not see anything, and the voice seemed to be coming from thin air, as if someone invisible wanted to speak to him. Cautiously, he released the safety catch of his Carpați pistol, still in its holster.

"Where are you?" said the officer.

"Here, close by. But listen. I am one of your comrades, an undercover officer. Leave the pistol alone."

"If you're an officer, then you know very well that I'm merely taking a precautionary measure."

"I'm afraid you will lose your composure when you see me," said the voice.

"Cut out the nonsense," said the officer. "We're not children."

"All right," said the voice. "I'm coming out."

The rose bush swayed, and from beneath it appeared the whiskers of a large ginger tomcat, whose eyes gleamed brightly in the semi-darkness of dusk.

"Where are you? I can't see you," said the officer, staring at the tomcat. He could not see anything else moving in front of him.

"It's me," said the tomcat, and the officer saw its whiskers moving to the rhythm of the words and its throat bobbing up and down to the vibration of human vocal cords.

Then the officer drew his pistol and from no more than six feet fired. One shot, then another. The tomcat leaped to the right, then to the left, zigzagged across the cobbles and jumped over the fence of the Dorobanți Hotel in a single bound. The officer ran after it, but it was now nowhere to be seen.

The gunshots could be heard from a distance. They echoed against the wall of the twenty-story hotel, which vibrated briefly and bounced the sound as far as Victory Avenue, where the old buildings caused it to glide along the vibration highway that causes sounds audible in the Antipa Museum to echo along the banks of the Dîmbovița. The sound of the two shots was for an instant obturated by a group of furious Stephenists, caught outnumbered, then it was drowned out by a pneumatic drill, boring its way toward a recalcitrant pipe in the bowels of the earth; but the sound of the shots rose once more and thence, borne on a cosmic vibration, struck the windows of the second floor of the Romanian Intelligence Service headquarters.

"What was that?" asked General Mihalache, sitting at the head of a green baize table.

"Some idiot warrant officer, probably," said General Pavelescu, sitting to his right.

It was a new meeting of the division for surveillance of religious sects and movements. The two generals had arrived five minutes earlier and had been greeted with an official report by Major Baldovin, who had taken up the interim command and who was now hoping to be appointed division commandant. For him it would be the most important moment in his life. He could barely wait, and this was why he was a little agitated and excited.

"Gentlemen, allow me to present Lieutenant Colonel Filip Pop, who has worked at the Foreign Intelligence Service for many years. He speaks seven foreign languages fluently and is a black belt in judo. I have the honor to present him to you as your new division commandant."

On hearing this, Major Baldovin slumped in his chair, but the other officers, some ten in number, stared wide-eyed. They measured up his fixed expression, with the air of an *unredeemed skeptic of a world in agony* that the lieutenant colonel gave himself, and they all pictured him on a judo mat. It was visible that Filip Pop was, under his freshly starched shirt, all muscle.

"Lieutenant Colonel, you have the floor. Please present your plan of action."

"Thank you, General," began Filip Pop, bringing to the air of the room the vibration of a pleasant, tenor timbre. "I never would have expected to be working in the last bastion of reason in the struggle against the generalized dementia that has overwhelmed Romanian society. I am honored by the trust you have placed in me, and I would like to thank the Supreme Defense Council and the president personally for this appointment. Having said that, I would like to underline from the very outset that I will not tolerate any insubordination. What has happened in this division is unbelievable, unacceptable, hilarious. An officer has defected to the enemy camp, having been converted during the course of an undercover mission. This is worrying and indicates very poor ideological training. An officer should carry out his mission without misgivings, without personal opinions, without allowing himself to be snared by the dangerous ideas of sects. For, ultimately, what are we? What do we represent in Romanian society? I see our mission as being one of great subtlety, as an agency to regulate the disturbed functions of the social organism, as an elementary antibody in the exercise of this function. Why do you think the Romanian Intelligence Service scores highly in public opinion polls? Because people want us, because people expect us, because the social organism needs to be penetrated and to see its information gathered by those who know how to do so best. People seek us; people need us. This function cannot be fulfilled by the press. The press has absolutely no role in this social organism. The intelligence services are called upon to gather what the anxious citizen barely expects to give them. We fulfill a social role as important as that played by the food store, because we bring the citizen something without which he could not live, something as important as bread. We are the shoulder on which the Romanian citizen cries during the time of economic and political transition, and we are called upon to keep watch so that the holy ancestral faith, which has held together the body of the nation over the course of history, shall be protected from heresies, from deviations from the line of Orthodox faith. Who else is there to do this? The Church? The Church is for nonaction. It prays. No, it is not the Church that is called upon to preserve order, but rather us, by gathering information, analyzing it and joining all the pieces together, dealing the appropriate blow by outflanking the enemy, purifying whatever is to be purified. Just as the president stressed in *Revolution and Reform,* everything that exists is information and acted-upon information. Well, gentlemen, this is what I believe we are called upon to do. These are the two-thousand-year-old values that we are called upon to defend."

Lieutenant Colonel Pop, with a very grave mien, concluded, "For my part, I ask you to imagine that I am the reincarnation of a boyar of Stephen the Great and that I have been called to arms. This will be the abnegation with which I shall execute the orders of my superiors and with which I expect you, gentlemen, to obey your orders."

As silence descended over the room, the evening wind carried from afar the sound of a guitar, as if no other sound would have ventured to travel over Bucharest at that hour of the evening.

CHAPTER SIXTEEN

"I DON'T BELIEVE YOU, I DON'T BELIEVE IT'S YOU," SAID THE KNJAZ, clutching his jaw.

He was standing two paces from their guest and measuring him with an angry gaze.

Of the general staff of the Stephenists only five remained. The head of the Knjaz was encased in an enormous sarcophagus of plaster, and he was having difficulty articulating. Neagu had his right arm in plaster. Stephen had been arrested the previous day. Negru seemed intact, but he was limping and his face was full of plasters, which covered some ugly cuts. The Tiger had a corset around his waist, like those worn by ladies in olden days. The halest of them all was Darius. As commanded by the *voievod,* they had installed electricity in the flat in the unfinished block and placed numerous icons on the walls, real icons, recently stolen from a church.

Before them, seated on an upturned barrel, was Professor Diaconescu.

"It is me," said the professor. "I have come to speak to you about a number of shared interests."

"Don't listen to him," said Neagu to Darius. "It might be a trap."

"It is not in my interest, gentlemen, to play a double game," said the professor, more affectedly than was the case.

"All right," said Darius, who up until then had kept to one side. "Let's see what you have to say for yourself."

The professor turned toward him and bowed respectfully.

"Gentlemen, I have come to the conclusion that the rivalry between our projects might be deadly to us all. We have far too many enemies. We have far too many internal problems, and adversity between us would be destructive now."

He waited for a moment, to see whether his words had produced any effect. None of the adepts of the great Stephen said anything. The professor went on. "If we look more closely, there are a number of shared aspects to the ideas that have brought us here this evening. Gentlemen, we have all abandoned our families and jobs to dedicate ourselves to ideas. Do you realize how noble this self-abnegation is? How extraordinary this self-denial in the service of an idea is?"

They listened to him closely, and it seemed to the professor that his old gift of reaching the hearts of men had returned to him.

"You have proved that you are ready to lay down your lives for the idea in which you believe. You have fought the police and the devil himself in order to restore order to Bucharest. Well, I say to you that together we can conquer this city. And you will not have to change your way of being or your beliefs, because this is the prerogative of great religious revolutions: all camps are in the right. From the very start I have argued that we are all in the right. Many are the unorthodox movements in Bucharest today. None can count them. But it is we who have the most solid ideas. I am the author of the ideas at the base of the Tidings of the Lord, and you are the minds behind the healthiest national revolution. We need one another."

Having said that, he joined his hands together.

"Agreed," said Darius. "We're listening. We're ready to talk."

"I know that they have arrested Stephen."

"Yes, an egregious villainy on the part of the police."

"Let us free him," said the professor.

"How are we supposed to do that?" said Negru, bursting into incredulous laughter. "We were thinking of getting a lawyer. He risks from two to five years inside."

"I have another idea, which will lead us to a solution of a political nature." The professor smiled.

The five looked at one another.

"This is no longer politics," said the Knjaz to Darius, speaking with difficulty from his plaster cast. "It's us or them."

"Let's not approach it in that way, gentlemen. History offers us multiple solutions to get around such difficulties. You are just a handful of men, after the latest battles and arrests. But you have something very precious and important: you have an idea, a national idea, the idea of reviving Romanian morality by setting out from an unmatched prince, from a holy *voievod,* from the healing example of the most extraordinary figure of Byzantium after Byzantium. Yes, gentlemen, this idea is extremely precious. I appreciate it at its true value, and the merit of having revived it falls entirely upon you. But your idea and its strength have come to depend upon the release of Stephen."

"That's right," said Neagu.

"How about we bring the entire Tidings of the Lord movement, thousands and thousands of people, to demonstrate for the release of Stephen in front of the Interior Ministry?" suggested the professor.

After a moment's thought, Darius said, in a businesslike voice, "Vespasian Moisa would never agree to that."

"Yes, perhaps," said the professor. "He has always preached non-action and prayer. But now is the time for action, not contemplation."

"Can you convince him to do this?"

"No," admitted the professor. "I don't think I could."

"So," said Darius, "all this is nonsense from one end to the other."

"Not quite," went on the professor. "If someone were to take Vespasian from among them, the Tidings of the Lord would be like a decapitated snake. Only then would the thousands of people pour to the Interior Ministry and demand the release of Stephen."

"If Vespasian went missing, why would they demand the release of Stephen," wondered Neagu.

"It's clear," said Darius. "Because we would take Vespasian hostage, and we would wait for them to demonstrate before we gave him back."

"Not a bad idea!" said the Knjaz, tugging at his plaster cast.

With a cry, Darius leaped to his feet and said, "It's a terrible idea! Don't you realize it would put us off course, and what's more it would bring us into enmity with the Tidings of the Lord, something that could lead to an irreparable situation? Because when we freed Vespasian, he would tell them."

"So what if he did?" said Negru. "What, are we afraid of them? In the past we'd have wanted to fight them, but there wasn't anyone to fight, because they're all sniveling cowards."

"Well, gentlemen," said the professor soothingly. "You will have a few days at your disposal to make friends with Vespasian. You know, he's a very convincing man."

"We'd end up fighting on too many fronts," said Darius. "We have to fight a battle in the Bucur Obor District with the gang of the Son of the Archangel Michael, and then we still haven't mopped up all the Satanists around the station; there are still about twenty of them. We have to eliminate those shit-stains from in front of the City Hall. There are still twenty or so shop signs in Turkish around Bucharest. Hostage-taking is the last thing we need. We don't have enough men to fight all of them. Let alone the prophet of some of them. It all amounts to too many things to do. Even on our best days, we were barely more than one hundred determined men. But now more than half of them are in hospital or laid up in bed. Aren't these too many things for just a handful of men?"

Looking in his eyes, Negru said, "Listen to me, Darius. We need to talk. Just the two of us."

"Now?"

"Right now."

Negru headed into a different room. He descended the stairs of the unfinished block and moved aside the boards that stood in the doorway of an empty flat. He advanced into the darkness, turned to Darius, who had followed him, and said in a whisper, "Listen here. Our greatest enemy is Vespasian Moisa. It's a rare opportunity to get rid of him in an exemplary way."

"How? Why?"

"By a trial. We bring him here. We try him and prove that he is not the Son of God, and we sentence him to death by impaling on a stake. And then all his followers will come to follow us."

"Why will they follow us? Why will they follow the ones who executed him?"

"They won't know. We'll take care of both Vespasian and Professor Diaconescu. We'll execute them separately. They'll be two separate trials."

"For what?"

"One for being a false prophet, the second for treason."

Here, Darius burst out laughing.

"Do you want to try the professor for having betrayed Vespasian Moisa for our benefit?"

"That's not bad," said Negru. "It's a great idea."

"And what will Stephen say?"

"He'll applaud it. On his release from prison he'll find himself with thousands and thousands of followers. And if not, then at least we'll get rid of the Lahovary Square problem. Why do you think he might be discontented? What does one stake more or less count, given how many people he's impaled?"

"Yes, but in the end people will still find out that we executed Vespasian."

"Then perhaps it would be better not to execute him, so as not to stir up resentment. Perhaps it would be better to pretend to execute him."

"Exactly," said Darius. "Think about how we might kidnap him and thereby eliminate him from the hearts and minds of all his followers, but in such a way that we won't be guilty of anything, even when it comes to light."

Negru grasped his shoulders.

"I know! We try him and record it on video. We'll prove he's lying. Then, we'll sentence him to death. But we'll release him in shame and dishonor, after seeing to it that the whole of Bucharest finds out he's a liar."

Darius pulled his hair back in a ponytail. He fished in his pocket for a hairclip. When at last he found one, he said, "Not bad. And what will we do with Diaconescu?"

"His own people will take care of him," said Negru. "Damned lunatics."

Darius laughed sarcastically. "If they're lunatics, why then do we want them to support us?"

"They won't support us. They'll disperse. Perhaps it's better that way."

After this discussion, they returned to the upper floor and smiled at Professor Diaconescu.

■   □   ■   □   ■

The gate to the villa in Lahovary Square opened, and Professor Diaconescu entered, followed by three burly men. The professor bade people a good evening, right and left, among the sleeping bags, tents, and field kitchens, and made his way to the door. There, he met Julius, who was carrying under his arm a card index of Nichita's kisses. The professor patted him on his shoulder and continued on his way, signaling the three to follow him.

"This way," he said.

Once they were inside, the professor showed them the stairs to the upper floor. In the semidarkness on the stairs there was not another soul. In Vespasian's room, the only other person was, as usual, Maximilian, who lately had become a kind of all-purpose secretary. One of the bruisers whacked him over the head and then dragged him under the bed. In less than two minutes, the three descended the stairs, lugging a Persian carpet, which must have been extraordinarily heavy, given that three brawny men were having such a hard time carrying it. Behind them came a large ginger tomcat, agitated to the point of madness. One of the men carrying the carpet bade a good evening to some nice-looking girls drinking chamomile tea on the steps.

When they were no more than five minutes away, from the upper floor of the villa was heard a scream, a woman's voice. It was Barbie, who had discovered that Maximilian had been knocked out and that the prophet Vespasian Moisa, whom they believed to be the Son of God and a miracle-worker, had been kidnapped.

"It's the work of the secret police," said Professor Diaconescu from the balcony. "The Securitate!"

"How could we not have sensed anything?" said a voice from the darkness in the courtyard. "We should have had our own bodyguards."

"That's right! Our own bodyguards!" said the others.

They had all gathered under the balcony of the villa, trampling underfoot what until a few minutes ago had looked like a seaside camp. Faces woken from sleep, bewildered faces, people who could not grasp what was going on.

"Let us learn from our mistake," said Professor Diaconescu, "and let us use our common sense. Let us go to police headquarters and demand the release of all religious prisoners. Let us demand the release of Vespasian and all those who have been arrested in the last few days. Let us demand from the European Parliament the release of all political prisoners in Romania!"

"What business do we have with the others?" said Dr. Arghir, who had until then been standing in the darkness.

"It is a matter of principle," argued the professor, his voice vibrating with rhetorical fervor. "Vespasian taught us to pray and to be pacifists. Now the moment for action has come. Let us go there and let us demonstrate for the release of those prisoners!"

"That's right! Let's go!" a number of voices were heard from below.

"Diaconescu is right!"

"Wait a moment," said Maximilian, who had emerged onto the balcony leaning on Barbie and clutching his head. "Something is not right. I was in the room when Vespasian was kidnapped."

There followed a moment of stupefaction. No one said anything.

"There were three of them. Professor Diaconescu opened the door of the room where Vespasian was getting ready for bed."

A wave of boos and whistles rose from the mass of people in the darkness below, as they trampled underfoot the sleeping bags and demolished a number of tents.

"No, no! It's a misunderstanding," cried the professor.

"Is it?" asked Dr. Arghir.

"Wait and see," said the professor. "Things are not quite like that."

"Tell us! Is it?"

"Is it?"

"Listen to me!" cried the professor. "We have to go and demonstrate in front of police headquarters, we have to demand what I've told you, so that all will be well with Vespasian. As for Vespasian, be not afraid. He is in the hands of friends. He will convert them, too!"

"How could you do such a thing? How could you bring them here?" said Maximilian. "What kind of friends are these? They hit me and kidnapped him."

"So it's true!" someone shouted.

"Treason!"

"Treason!"

"Nonsense," said the doctor. "I can't believe you did such a thing."

"What if they were from the police?" said Julius. "They were really mean-looking."

"No, they're not from the police," reassured the professor.

"They're from the police!" shouted one of them and ran up the stairs toward the balcony.

"That's right!" said the others, crowding after him.

Someone from the courtyard had penetrated to the balcony, and without any further introduction he grabbed the professor by the hair and dragged him toward him. The doctor tried to drag him the other way, by the shoulders. A mêlée broke out on the balcony, with confused yelling and groaning. A broken pipe belched steam up into the June sky. A window shattered. The plaster beneath the balcony cracked and began to fall. A brick loosened and fell into the courtyard below with a crash. The balcony shuddered, and the balustrade gave way on one side. The whole group, some two dozen people, tumbled pell-mell over the broken balustrade on top of those in the courtyard below. Police whistles could now be heard, for a number of patrols had gathered on the other side of the fence. In the distance the siren of an ambulance blared. In the courtyard, the heap of bodies was struggling to get up. All of a sudden, tiles from the roof of the villa began tumbling down on them. It was as if the heavens were bombarding them with blunt objects at random. Below could be heard shouts of horror. Vasile Gheorghe was crying, "Don't trample the flowers!"

"Stand back! Get away from there!" said an officer who had clambered up onto the fence.

But the crowd did not budge from the courtyard of the villa. They all seemed bound to that place, seemed determined to die crushed to death rather than abandon the place where they had spent the last few weeks.

All of a sudden, there was an explosion in the basement of the villa, and huge flames belched from the ground-level windows. Window jambs and shards of glass flew through the yard. It was probably a gas pipe or some act of sabotage. The balcony rocked once more and then collapsed into the courtyard below with a deafening boom, raising dust into the sky and smothering the screams in debris.

"We're under attack!" the voice of Dr. Arghir was heard. "Everyone take refuge in the embassy of the Emirate of Salibaar!"

Those still standing fled from the courtyard and poured into Lahovary Square, halting the traffic, jostling with policemen and onlookers. They scattered in all directions. Some were running as fast as their legs could carry them.

An officer pulled an old man from under the rubble of the balcony. Dr. Arghir assisted him, although he was shaking violently and could barely stand up.

"He's dead," said the officer.

The doctor recognized Professor Diaconescu.

"Friend! Brother!" said Dr. Arghir, and burst into tears.

Then, trembling as if in a fever, he said, "Now how can we know where they have taken him and what deal you made with them?"

On her knees beside him, Barbie shouted something. An officer came and yelled something about the scene of the crime. A frightened ginger tomcat jumped on him and scratched him. The officer drew his pistol and fired a warning shot.

■ ▢ ■ ▢ ■

"You should be ashamed of yourself," said Negru. "This whole taxi is smeared with cooking oil."

"Yes," said the driver, visibly put out by the Persian carpet they had crammed into his trunk. "It is. A few days ago I gave a ride to some people who were carrying bottles of oil by the sack. One of them must have broken. I haven't had time to clean it up."

"Shamelessness," said Darius. "My trousers are all wet with oil. The whole seat is wet."

"Yes, I know," said the driver. "I'm sorry, but that's the situation."

"Stop here," said Negru.

"It's right in front of the government building. We can't stop here in the middle of Victory Square."

"Stop here," yelled the Tiger, who was sitting up front, placing a knife to the driver's throat.

He slammed on the brakes. It was obvious his passengers were very irritated. For the whole way, from Dorobanți Avenue to Victory Square, just a stone's throw away, he had sensed an incredible nervous tension. If he had not seen they were so tense, he would have asked them what they had inside the carpet in the trunk. The three leaped from the cab, dragging the carpet onto the cobblestones, which fell with a heavy thud.

"I hope there wasn't too much in that injection," said Darius.

They hauled it up onto their shoulders and then vanished into the darkness of the entrance to a block. Amidst the rusting iron of the unfinished building they made their way to the stairs. Negru said, "Let's put him down. We have to climb four flights of stairs with him."

"Why is he so heavy?" wondered Darius.

"Do you think he is?"

"I remembered Saint Filofteia," said Darius, in a tremulous voice. "It is said that although she was a girl of twelve, she grew so heavy that not even the strongest men could carry her."

Negru began to laugh. "Cut out the nonsense. We've got a job to do. Let's finish it. This isn't Saint Filofteia."

They heaved him up and almost sighed in relief once they had placed him on their shoulders. They set off up the stairs. When they reached the third floor, they heard a voice. "Is it you?"

It was the Knjaz. They recognized his voice.

"Yes, it's us. Light a match or something."

The Knjaz brought a flaming torch closer.

"He's heavy."

"Take hold of him here."

"I can't," said the Knjaz, tapping his plaster cast with his finger. "I can't bend down with my head."

"Step out of the way, then. Give us some room."

They entered an abandoned flat, in which the Stephenists had arranged some tables and chairs, as in a courtroom.

"Has he come?" asked Darius.

"Yes, he's here."

"In person? The vicar of the patriarchate?" asked Negru. "Excellent."

"Yes. He didn't think twice. He came straightaway," said the Knjaz.

In a matter of seconds they had rolled Vespasian Moisa onto the cement floor. Neagu gave him another injection, in his upper arm. In a short while, Vespasian Moisa came around. He said nothing.

"Good evening," said Darius, smiling. "I am Darius Georgescu. You will be tried this evening."

CHAPTER SIXTEEN

153
▼

"Me? Tried? By whom?"

Vespasian saw rings of light, lowering darkness, shadows, and faces. He did not recognize anyone.

"Get up now," said Darius, giving him his hand.

From somewhere a cat could be heard mewling. Darius looked in that direction.

"There is no one but us here," said Neagu.

"How many of our people are here," asked Darius.

"More than two dozen. That's as many as we could muster."

"Send an armed patrol to the entrance of the block downstairs. Let another patrol inspect the other flats on the landing and another block access from the roof. We want to be sure. In any case, no one will find us here."

"Do what you have to do more quickly," whispered Vespasian coldly.

"Don't worry," said Darius. "This time, it's very serious. I know what I have to do."

He took him by the arm and led him into the courtroom. Vespasian was dazed. When he opened his eyes, he saw a room lit by torches, with many icons on the walls. One of the icons was of the Mother of God and the Child. Another showed the Ascension of Christ, on a bluish cloud. Vespasian's eyes moved from one icon to another, as if he were seeking strength in them. Gazing at them was for him what drinking a cup of coffee is for others.

"Good evening," a voice was heard from the judge's table.

"Good evening," said Vespasian.

"We have not had the honor to meet. I am Manoil of Snagov, and I was invited by these pious Orthodox to take part in this evening's debate."

Vespasian allowed himself to be led up to a table. On the other side of the room, opposite his table, there was another, longer table, where the three who had brought him there now took their seats. He recognized Negru, Darius, and Neagu, all three of them in a state of increasing excitement. At the back of the room stood the public. Vespasian measured them with his eyes. They were all dressed in long black overcoats over black shirts and wore large crosses, some made of gold, some of silver. One of them was filming with a video camera mounted on a tripod. They looked like a disciplined army. A commando of hard men. It struck Vespasian that their faces all resembled one another. They all looked like men who knew no doubts. And then, for the first time in a very long while, Vespasian became afraid.

"Can we begin the debate, gentlemen?" asked Manoil.

"Before anything else," said Vespasian in a confident voice, although one that hinted at fear, "I have a question. What kind of trial is this? What kind of court is this?"

"Oh, Mr. Moisa, we were just about to explain it to you," replied Manoil, rolling up his sleeve above one of the holy books. "It is not a trial. It would be incorrect to say that. It is a discussion about heresy, according to the ancestral code of the Holy Church."

"What law applies here?" asked Vespasian, shrugging.

"It is not a question of law, of guilt and punishment. Not at all. What we are called upon to establish here, on the basis of the Holy Scriptures and Holy Tradition, as it has been passed down by the Romanian Orthodox Church, is the value of truth. We want to establish who you are. Or rather what you are. What you have been doing to the faithful of the Romanian Orthodox Church."

Vespasian looked around the room. None of those in the black coats had anything to add.

"So, this is a discussion about the truths of the Church."

"Not quite," said Manoil. "We will try you, and our references are those of the Orthodox faith. What we are trying is a situation, a social situation, which the Tidings of the Lord has produced in Romanian society."

"Why was it necessary to bring me here, then?" asked Vespasian.

"What," said Manoil in amazement, "did you not come of your own free will?"

After a pause, Darius cleared his throat and said, "Are you afraid to talk about all these things in the presence of His Holiness the Vicar of the Patriarchate? Are you afraid of losing?"

"There's no question of that. But how am I to know that it hasn't all been fixed?"

Here, Manoil thumped the table with his palm. In his baritone voice, he said, "You know very well who I am. I have not fixed anything."

"Yes, but I don't know what's going on here. I don't know who is working with whom."

"And we don't know what's going on in Romania, in this sick society where everything is upside down!" answered Darius. "We want to understand who you are to disturb Bucharest."

The cleric rose to his feet and said, "Let us pray. Let us join hands and say the Lord's Prayer. Let us proceed to a just discussion, in which we shall clarify in our souls all the questions we have."

They all rose to their feet. They moved to the middle of the room. Vespasian happened to join hands with the cleric, on his right, and Neagu, on his left.

And they prayed together.

At the end of the prayer, Manoil of Snagov said, "And so help us, Lord, may the truth light upon us in this room."

Each went back to his place. They took their seats. It was not until then that Vespasian noticed that on the table in front of him lay a Bible. He felt the need to take it in his hands. He opened it at random, but he did not recognize the script in which the book was printed. These were neither Greek, Slavonic, nor Latin characters. What the hell had they placed in front of him?

"Please begin," the bishop bade them.

"Where is the file?" asked Darius in a loud voice.

"Are you going to read it, or shall I?" asked Neagu.

"You," said Darius.

"Very well," said Neagu. "I shall speak extempore." Then, to Darius, "What file? We don't have any file."

Then, to the courtroom, in an affected voice, he declaimed, "Your Holiness, honorable guests, let us examine together the situation that has occurred in Romania since the emergence in Bucharest of the religious movement led by Vespasian Moisa, known also as the Tidings of the Lord. As is well known, the religious life of Romania is very rich. We are a nation of intense spirituality, which is now undergoing a second Christianization, or rather conversion, because people nowadays are converting to all kinds of things. Numerous groups, large and small, have put forward various theories, some more interesting than others. What makes the presence of Vespasian Moisa in the public space all the more interesting is the fact that he in his turn puts forward a theory that is ascribed to by numerous converts and that he regards himself as holding a privileged position on, let us say, the ladder of truth. Am I right?"

The room filled with approving murmurs. Someone whistled. It was as if he spoke in the name of all of them. Manoil of Snagov said nothing. He was following the scene with the gaze of a coroner confronted with a corpse.

"What we believe, and by this I think that I am in agreement with my friends and brothers gathered here today, is that Vespasian Moisa does not in fact have a theory but a hodgepodge of notions which, who knows how, manage to coagulate in the minds of some and, paradoxically, fasten themselves to the Christian root. In the second place, we further believe that the flock of the faithful that follows Vespasian Moisa has been diverted from the straight path of the ancestral church. It is unbelievable how some many hundreds of people have followed him and continue to come to him. Finally, we do not believe that Vespasian Moisa is any kind of prophet or worker of miracles and other follies, as has been claimed about him. These are the three questions we wish to debate."

"Very good, bravo, keep it up," could be heard from around the room. There was a continuous hum of voices, and the public was in its element.

"And there's something else," said the Knjaz, who had risen to his feet, leaning on one of his comrades. "The Tidings of the Lord has produced and distributed a baldness cure lotion, which we consider to be witchcraft. If we go by the holy books, this is the sin of sorcery, and this man has committed it!"

"That's right!" shouted someone. "Sorcery!"

The Knajz pulled from his pocket the incriminating evidence: a bottle of the offending lotion. He asked Vespasian, "Is this it?"

"I've seen such bottles before," said Vespasian. "They're the ones they sell plantain syrup in at the pharmacy."

As if all of a sudden irritated, the Knjaz confronted him. "Here's what I think of your baldness cure lotion."

And as quick as a flash he poured the contents of the bottle down his throat in one gulp. As he leaned back, his plaster cast popped.

"You shouldn't have done that," said Darius in a barely audible voice. "You'll get a hairy intestine now."

"So, it seems that these are the accusations against you," said Manoil to Vespasian. "What do you have to say about them?"

Vespasian rose to his feet and cleared his throat. "I am now certain that I do not find myself among friends. It is all the same to me whether I speak to those close to me or to those who have already convicted me."

"No! Not so!" protested the bishop. "We do not begin our journey with preconceived ideas. It is a free debate. We are believers who are seeking an answer in Christ. Remember the Synod of Nicaea. Orthodoxy has passed through much harder trials."

"Yes, very hard trials!" mocking voices in the public were heard to say.

"So," resumed Vespasian, "the theory about which you have been speaking here is nothing more than a natural adaptation, in contemporary terms, of the inner prayer, of the pearl of Eastern spirituality. It is true that at one point I have mixed into my ideas facts and images borrowed from science. This does not mean that what I have said is something severed from the tradition of the Church. These things are at most questions which we all might ask ourselves. However, I am convinced that all those present believe in the power of prayer, because it is to prayer that I have most of all urged people. I have brought them to the Church. That is what I am. That is my work."

"Yes," said Neagu, "but you have also invited all kinds of people to preach their theories to others."

"People need to express themselves. I helped them. I invited them to speak before others. It is true, I did this."

He waited for the reaction of those present. They were listening to him tensely.

"Please continue," said the bishop.

"The second accusation was that I led astray these people who follow me, that I led them away from the Church. Well, you will see that most of those who are waiting for me now in Lahovary Square had not been to church for a long time and that when we gathered together and prayed together they were concerned with the salvation of their souls and with loving their neighbor. We have not taken any parishioner away from the Church, but rather we have filled a space left empty by the Church in this world."

"Heresy!" cried the Knjaz.

"Please, gentlemen," said the bishop, tapping his spectacles on the table. "Silence, please. You will speak only when it is your turn to speak!"

"Lastly, the third question is the hardest. You ask me who I am. You ask me this, and you say you do not believe I am who I am said to be. I don't know what each of you has heard, but I can tell you merely this: I am a true Christian, and I pray every evening for our Father to show me the path. I wait for a sign from Him, an idea, a step. Because I am ready. If my future points toward death, then so be it. I am ready, and I have no doubt that the fate that awaits me will be useful to the faith."

Not a sound could be heard in the room.

"Yes," said Neagu, "but they believe you are the Son of God."

"We all are. I am a marked man. To be precise, I am marked with something that binds me to this place, to Bucharest. I do not know what it means, and every evening I pray to find out. More than that I do not know."

"He's lying," said Darius.

"Please, gentlemen," said the bishop. Then, to Vespasian, "Go on."

"That is all I have to say."

"Well, hmm, let us see. So, is that all?" The bishop wanted to assure himself.

He smiled at them as if they were all children. He cleared his throat and said, "You see that there is no misunderstanding between us? It is very good this way. Nothing serious has happened, and I propose that we should rejoice together, in prayer, for the discovery of this spiritual communion, in which the ancestral Church, through my presence here, is also part."

Here, Darius scratched the back of his neck and said, "It doesn't seem to me that we have reached any agreement."

"Yes we have, my dears, yes we have. We are in complete agreement," said the bishop. "Anyone can say anything at all and can link his ideas to the faith, because this faith is in us all. And it is good when men pray together. It is a sign of a rich spiritual life to ask Our Lord God every evening what your role is in the world. We are all Romanians. It seems to me good that we are here together this evening, and I hope that our meeting shall be the first in a long line of concords between the Church and the new generation of laymen. We are proud of this new generation of laymen, who are so profound, so aflame for the ancestral ideals of the Orthodox faith."

CHAPTER SIXTEEN

159
▼

"The devil take him, what is he rambling on about," said the Knjaz, in a rather loud voice.

"No, gentlemen," contradicted the bishop. "I am speaking to you from the heart. May the Lord help us to find concord, forever and ever, Amen!"

He rose to his feet and thrice made the sign of the cross. Then he said, "Do you think you could call me a taxi?"

"Accompany His Holiness," said Darius to one of the men.

He placed his hand on Vespasian's shoulder and pushed him back into his chair.

Manoil of Snagov vanished, not before blessing all those in the room. The hurried steps of the bishop could be heard receding into the distance. Darius paced around the room for a little while and then, out of the blue, punched Vespasian in the stomach.

"That was church nonsense. Now, let's dispose of matters between ourselves. We'll have a second trial. Knjaz and Tiger, you'll be the judges. Negru and myself will be the prosecution. You'll be speaking in your own defense. Now we'll see what's what, now we've got rid of that prattling priest."

In the room could be heard whoops of joy. At last, things were being played out more to the liking of the audience. One of them sang, "Oh, yeah, baby!"

"So," said Neagu, "who the hell do you think you are, and what do want with all those people in the middle of Bucharest?"

"Yes," said Darius. "Do you realize you've stolen all our rock bands from the Magheru area? All the ones who used to sing *Stephen, Stephen, the great prince, / Peerless in all the world* are now crooning *Lord have mercy* in various alleyways. Do you realize how much damage you've done us?"

"You'll realize soon enough how much damage you've done yourself," said the Knjaz, rubbing his plaster cast.

Vespasian closed his eyes, and his lips began to murmur something.

"Bravo, that's the way," said Darius, "when you're not man enough, you hide wherever you can. He closes his eyes like an ostrich."

"Do you know what we're going to tell that lot in Lahovary about you?" asked Neagu. "We're going to tell them that we gangbanged you the whole night long."

"Maybe that's what we really ought to do to him," opined Darius.

"You first," said a voice from the back row.

"Well, yes," said Darius, "let it be known who's a man around here."

They burst into laughter. Then Darius said, "A prophet. Is this a prophet? He's just dishwater."

CHAPTER SEVENTEEN

"HOW EXTRAORDINARY," SAID LIEUTENANT COLONEL POP, AFTER listening to the report of the Romanian Intelligence Service psychiatrist. It was the first time he had received him in matters relating to an official case.

"Commandant, sir, the case seemed so bizarre," said the doctor, "that I wanted to signal it."

Dr. Radovan had worked for almost thirty years with military personnel subject to conditions of stress. He said, "In the last week, we have had three agents with nervous breakdowns, including Colonel Focşăneanu. It's a tough job, especially when you're dealing with all kinds of lunatics and strange things. The mind goes astray immediately, if you're not trained to hear such things. Our officers are not always trained to come into contact with the demented ideas of our times, and that's why they're very fragile, very impressionable."

"Yes, and that's precisely why things need to be kept under tight control. I don't even want to think about what might happen if such information leaks out to the television stations and these so-called doctrines are presented to the wider population. We have twenty-three million potential psychiatric hospital inmates out there. As it is, they've been cast unprepared into a world set aside for them by history—what are you supposed to do with them now, subject them to perverted ideas? Phooey."

The doctor perched his glasses on his nose and, consulting his notebook, said, "So, about Lieutenant Petrescu. He was brought in to me this morning in an advanced phase of disturbance, with convulsions, and I had to intervene twice so that he wouldn't swallow his tongue. What is interesting is that his theory somehow makes sense. It seems that behind his delirium there are real facts, whose coherence might interest you."

"I'm listening," said Filip Pop.

"Lieutenant Petrescu followed a surveillance target of Russian nationality into the ELCOM refinery. He described him as being tall, blond, and a good Romanian speaker. Inside the plant, Lieutenant Petrescu was spotted by other Russian citizens, with very good military, technical, and sharpshooting training. They opened fire on Lieutenant Petrescu, and he shot back at them in self-defense. There was an exchange of fire, as documented by our investigation team, and you will probably receive the first part of their report very soon. What are interesting are Lieutenant Petrescu's ideas about what he thinks he discovered. After that night, he reached a theory. This theory seems to explain a number of matters in recent history, and Lieutenant Petrescu is convinced of their veracity."

"That's what they all think," said Lieutenant Colonel Pop, waving his hand in disgust.

"Well," the doctor went on, "Lieutenant Petrescu recounts that last night he discovered, listening to the Russian agents, the existence of a bomb timed to detonate in three generations, in the sequence EXPLOSION—ACCUMULATION—REPLICATION. It is an ideological bomb, which, according to how Petrescu described it to me, works like this: first, a genius or a group of people, an association or a party, creates a certain expectation in society, then, in parallel with the creation of this expectation, accumulates money or power, in such a way as for their legacy to explode in three generations. The first such explosion was programmed by Lenin. We are now in the phase of the final accumulation of energy here in Romania. An explosion will follow, but we don't know what kind. The agent discovered all this listening to a conversation in the place where he exchanged fire with the Russians. The Russians then fled. The bomb mechanism has been planted in Romania. Something like that. This is what Petrescu said."

Filip Pop said, "It's hallucinatory. I don't understand anything."

"You're right," said the doctor, closing his notebook.

CHAPTER SEVENTEEN

"It's one more case of madness to add to my list of all the others I've heard and which characterize Romania today."

"You never know. I am merely reporting it to you."

"Could I talk to this Petrescu?" inquired Pop.

"Of course, commandant, but I warn you, because your time is precious, that this man might be incurable."

"What idea is it that Petrescu says the Russians have planted here in Romania? What is it that's going to explode in three generations' time?"

The doctor consulted his notebook once more and said, "He says that the Russians are the ones who implanted religious fanaticism in Romania. Well, as if we didn't have anything of the sort! If we look at the two-thousand-year history of the Romanian people, when have we suffered from fanaticism? When have we gone over the top? This must be the Russian idea. This is what Petrescu thinks he overheard in the refinery. He thinks that the Russians are not refining petroleum, but making all kinds of chemical compounds to amplify Orthodox religious fundamentalism."

Then, with a certain amount of skepticism, closing his notebook, the psychiatrist concluded, "There are cases and then there are cases. No one needs the help of anyone else to start spouting nonsense. I have a colleague in Pitești who is writing a book about it."

Filip Pop studied him, and for a moment it seemed to him that this doctor was not in his right mind.

■ □ ■ □ ■

CHAPTER EIGHTEEN

ON THAT JUNE EVENING THE SKY ABOVE BUCHAREST WAS BOUNDLESS
and diaphanous, and in it could be glimpsed the depths of the cosmos,
the entire solar system—all the visible planets and all the perceptible
asteroids. There was not a single cloud in the heavens. The Milky
Way rose above the horizon, as broad as seven rainbows, against the
infinite black depths of cosmic space.

Of the villa in Lahovary Square not much was left. The explosion
in the basement had demolished almost the whole of the walls. There
was no habitable room left. The floor had caved in and the basement,
where it was not choked with rubble, had flooded with water.

"I know where he is," Barbie whispered to the Troubadour.

"What?" he asked, as if waking from sleep.

"I think I know where they took Vespasian."

They were sitting in the courtyard of the villa in Lahovary Square.
Around them were mounds of rubble, shards of glass, roof tiles, pipes,
and bricks. Not far away, Vasile Gheorghe was sitting on the steps,
holding his wife, who was bawling her lungs out. The Troubadour
bent down and whispered to his lover so that no one else might hear,
"How do you know something like that?"

"I just know."

"Hey," he whispered. "Didn't you promise you would tell me everything? What are you hiding?"

He cupped her face in his palms and said, "Hey, my love. Tell me."

She drew back and answered, "First promise me . . ."

"Promise you what? This isn't a game. This isn't the time for that."

"I'm not playing. Things are as tangled as can be. Promise me that if I tell you everything, you won't hate me . . . That's all I want . . . To know that you won't hate me . . ."

He took her in his arms and kissed her. It was that secret kiss that he employed to make women melt in his arms. Then he said in a voice softer than he had ever used with anyone ever before, "I promise."

"All right," she said, just as softly. "You ought to know that I know Negru. I know him very well."

"Who's Negru?"

"One of those lads who believe Stephen the Great has been reincarnated. Apart from that lunacy, he's a very nice guy."

The Troubadour ran his fingers through his hair.

"Where do you know him from?"

"Please, don't ask."

"So, that's it?"

She made no reply. After a moment, as if she were asking or pleading, she said, "Please don't hate me."

"All right," he said. "When did you last see him?"

"A few days ago, before all this chaos began and before Bucharest was crisscrossed with soldiers and police. Before he went off to battle, as he said. I didn't know what to believe."

Toni clutched his head in his hands. He realized all at once that he had been cheated on, that his lover was not his lover and that you can't put your trust in any woman. His heart filled with bitterness, and he said in his mind that he hated all women. He stood up and went away from her. He sat down on some broken masonry a little way off.

"But what has this got to do with Vespasian's kidnapping?" asked the Troubadour.

"I thought I saw his outline a few hours ago. He was wearing a kind of large cloak, like a monk's, but in bad taste. I'd recognize him in a thousand, for the way he walks. I know him . . . And that's why I went out of our tent after him, because it seemed to me that something fishy was going on. That's how I reached Vespasian's room when they had already vanished. It was me who sounded the alarm. I think that if I hadn't gone to check, it would have been hours before anyone found out that Vespasian was gone."

The Troubadour hugged his knees with his arms.

"So, you think it was them."

"Yes, I think it was them."

"And were they thinking about this a few days ago?"

"No, not at all. Negru never said anything to me about it. On the other hand, he suggested to me countless times that I should leave you all and follow him. He told me that he would conquer Bucharest. He told me that one day he would be Minister of Culture. That's what he told me."

The Troubadour burst out laughing.

"But seriously," said Barbie, "why not? He's such a delicate boy, if you get to know him up close . . ."

Here, the Troubadour's smile froze on his lips. In a bitter voice, he said, "How long have you known him?"

"Since high school."

"Since high school?"

"We went to the same high school."

"Have you seen each other in the past year?"

"Yes."

"Many times?"

"Many times. Please, don't ask me more."

The Troubadour rose to his feet once more and began to pace around the courtyard. The tone of his voice had said everything there was to say. He had no further questions. He kicked a roof tile, which went flying over the heads of some people waiting at the bus stop on the other side of the fence. He turned back to her and said, "You can't trust anyone anymore. Not anyone."

With wide eyes, she said, "You can trust me, because of what I'm going to tell you now."

"What are you going to tell me? That all this time you've been talking about love and there was no love? You told me it was love in a way that others don't understand. You told me that when all three of us are together it's me you love and me you feel. Who can believe in you anymore? You cheated on me with a Stephenist!"

"I know where they've taken Vespasian," she said.

The Troubadour ran his fingers through his hair.

"Where?"

"I think it's somewhere either in Icon Gardens, the Northern Station, or Victory Square. And if they decide to execute him, which is highly likely, I think they'll do it on the Hill of the Patriarchate, for it to be as symbolic as possible."

The Troubadour looked around him, because now help was what he needed. But he saw no one who could have helped him. In Lahovary Square there was nothing but a destroyed villa, on whose ruins the owners were weeping, and the host of people that had for a time been the strength of the faith of the Tidings of the Lord had scattered. Of that multitude nothing had remained.

On the sidewalk an old sergeant could be heard telling a young soldier, pointing at the rubble with his cane, "Look at the havoc their madness has wreaked! See what drugs lead to!"

Then, scratching under his cap, "In the old days, they wouldn't have dared. I remember the summer of '68, when here in Cosmonauts' Square we had problems with the hippies. Well, back then, we shaved their hair off and tore up their jeans. Nowadays, they destroy houses and nothing happens. It's all because of the drugs."

From the courtyard, the Troubadour whispered to Barbie, "What idiots!"

"They're unreal," she said. "Imagine they don't exist and that Vespasian is still here."

Toni answered, "Yes, but he isn't here anymore."

■ □ ■ □ ■

CHAPTER NINETEEN

THE CAR WITH THE OFFICIAL PENNANT OF THE HOLY SEE CLIMBED THE
Hill of the Patriarchate, preceded by four police motorcycles. Bishop
Manoil had come out to greet the distinguished guest. After the door
of the car had been opened for him, the guest, who was none other
than the High Representative of the Holy See's Congregation for the
Doctrine of the Faith, the celebrated Bishop Giuseppe Marianini, the
Pope's right-hand man, alighted. In perfect Romanian, he said, "So
glad to see you again, my dear friend. May the Lord be with you!"

It was said that he spoke seventeen languages and that he had traveled all over the world. He knew everything about everything. Now,
before being received by the Patriarch for a brief audience, he was
going to speak with Manoil of Snagov.

The Romanian bishop conducted the guest into the protocol room,
which was a modest cell for prayer. A Cantacuzino Bible lay open on
the table, and on a shelf carved with interwoven cross motifs there
were other priceless holy books, including a Slavonic Gospel from the
time of Matei Basarab and Varlaam. The two armchairs had red velvet
coverings, with gold tassels, likewise the oak table. A carpet depicting
Voroneț Monastery lent the whole room an air of freshness.

After exchanging courtesies, the guest said, "The Church should
take notice when new currents of thought appear in the world. In
particular, we should pay attention when those ideas are so close to
the interests of the Church. The Holy See follows with the greatest
interest all those ideas from around the world that are close to our

own doctrine. This is why, on the basis of the numerous reports the Congregation has received recently, I would like to ask you to be kind enough to act as a mediator between myself, as a representative of the Holy See, and Romanian citizen Vespasian Moisa."

Learning only now the reason for the visit of the distinguished guest and knowing one or two things about what events had been coming to pass under the sun, Bishop Manoil spoke melodiously, as follows: "I must confess that nowadays many things in Romania are in disarray. Among them, things connected to the faith and to those who serve the faith, whether priests or laymen. Matters are complicated. What I find the most disturbing is the huge quantity of madness that holds sway at every social level, at every stratum of this constantly changing world. Yes, there is a strange madness that manifests itself everywhere, and which is all the more strange given that it brings together groups of people with fixed ideas in common, with mental illnesses in common. Sometimes, by the very nature of the situation, of their trade, such people are brought together within an institution, working together for the common good. When has history seen such a storm, such a dangerous tide of mental maladies? I understand, of course, the beautiful madness of the poets, who, overwhelmed by worldly love, come to fashion beautiful poems, which we read with the same pleasure as they wrote them. We understand such beautiful madness. But we do not understand the madness of those who do evil, of the Satanists, of warring football supporters. This is something we do not understand. Of course, these are visible forms of madness. But there are also more subtle forms of madness, invisible madnesses, which bring people together, and the more their minds were twisted before getting there, the more they are twisted after they arrive. It is as if someone were to wring out a cat to make it dry, to use an image from a folk saying."

Here, the high prelate of the Holy See nodded and smiled knowingly. He said, "I understand you very well, and I admire greatly your consummate diplomacy. I understand that you are warning me, discreetly and with Christian concern, not to allow the Holy See to carry out any investigation into one of those madnesses that twist the minds of men. Oh, yes, I understand you, and I thank you for your exquisite concern. But, having reached this point in the discussion, I do not see why I should not inform you of the proofs that the Office already possesses. You see, we have acquired extraordinary experience in detecting fakery and heresy from the very first sight. We daily receive at least one false report of a previously unheard miracle performed by a candidate for canonization. All kinds of local witch doctors converted at the last moment to the holy apostolic Roman creed play all kinds of tricks meant to look like miracles after their deaths. We deal with such things, and we have our own weapons against them. We know which are the tricks and which are the true miracles that the Lord sends us as a sign that his servants are well received in the heavens, along with their deeds."

Inclining his head, Manoil of Snagov said, "The Romanian nation possesses certain very strange particularities of temperament. Above all, it is incomprehensible how such strong national feelings can manifest themselves in a nation so given to emigration. It is the same with miracles here in Romania. They follow no regular pattern."

"Oh," said the guest, laughing politely, "but it is no different among the Italians . . ."

"What I find disturbing with Romanians, and this is something that would warrant more careful investigation, is precisely the fact that collective madness has every chance of manifesting itself in a people with strong tendencies to gather in a herd. And what is more, it is strange that neither psychiatrists nor sociologists nor political scientists nor anyone else can give any clear answer: what is wrong with these people? No one has analyzed carefully the causes of this profound crisis of ideas. For a crisis of ideas it is. It is sufficient for some idea to be floating around for a fundamentalist sect to spring up, drawing people who are ready to kill in the name of that idea. It is as if everything capable of flight were to freeze in midair. So it is with ideas. As soon as they spring up, they acquire a monstrous materiality. Or, in other cases, a ridiculous materiality."

The high representative of the Congregation once more burst out laughing. "You tell me nothing new, beloved friend in the Lord. What I ought to ask you, of course, if I do not make too bold, is whether the Romanian Orthodox Church is not concerned about the welter of new alternative religious movements that have appeared overnight in Romania."

Here, the high Romanian prelate felt somewhat chafed. Thus, he answered boldly, "No, for our subjects, our beloved faithful, have an imagination much richer than other nations in this world, and some of the things dreamed up by their minds are not to be found else-where. Sometimes, they can be led like lambs of God from one square to another, under machine-gun fire and through choking smoke, sometimes they can all be seated obediently in front of the television and told what to do, for, yes, they are obedient, while at other times they can be found to do the most unexpected and impertinent things. Our best philosophers have speculated on this national trait."

"But, my friend, is this not a dangerous thing for society?"

"And what can the Orthodox Church do except to pray for them? However dangerous it might be, if people do not come to the Church, where can the Church go after them? Into the catacombs where they crawl to materialize their sinful ideas?"

With a highly serious air, Bishop Marianini, leafing through the file in front of him, said, "Here, for example, is the report I received last year. In it there is a story about a Romanian subject who declared he had been kidnapped by a UFO. He was driving in his car, and the spacecraft came to a stop above him, achieving the optimal technical conditions for interception. So he recounts. Well, this citizen claims that onboard the ship he was greeted by Our Lord Jesus Christ Him-self, Who transmitted to him precise orders for the salvation of man-kind. Such a report might pass unnoticed, as an anomaly, as a highly particular case. What is strange, however, is that, having 'returned' to earth, this man founded a sect. He was believed by other men, who followed him and began to interpret the Apocalypse of Saint John in their own terms. I found out about all this before they wrote a report addressed to the Pope, which the Apostolic Nuncio received exactly one year after the so-called abduction event."

"Ah, yes, that's nothing more than a trifle. We know all about that sect. There are fifty of them, and they are completely harmless. There are dozens of such groups in Romania, but, in general, they deflate after a few months. We are accustomed to not paying them any mind."

"Yes," said Bishop Marianini gravely, "but if they harm Holy Doc-trine, perhaps we ought to be more mindful of such things."

And on saying that, he clapped his hands together, in a gesture that might have meant anything. He added, "In times gone by, we would have solved such situations completely differently."

"Oh, yes," agreed Manoil of Snagov, who all of a sudden began to feel the skin of his scalp crawling strangely, for since the days of his youth he had had a certain allergy to papists. But he did not betray this in any way, as is fitting in diplomacy.

"Another sect that has emerged recently in Romania," went on Bishop Marianini, "is that of the so-called Son of the Archangel Michael. I think it is superfluous for me to tell you, beloved brother in Christ, that, from the doctrinal point of view, this sect is purely demonic in nature. We have clear reports about the angelic apparitions seen by declaredly Orthodox eyewitnesses. The problem should be treated with the utmost seriousness, not left in the hands of country priests, whose training is sometimes below the exceptional level of the superb tradition of the Romanian Orthodox Church."

Here, Manoil of Snagov said nothing, because it seemed to him that the worthy guest was telling him what to do. The discussion had gone too far. In his mind, he said to himself that, for some thousand years, things had been going differently in Romania. He joined his hands together in prayer in front of his face, simulating that he was listening mindfully. The bishop went on in the same tone. "Of course, we have reliable reports on these heresies, as well as on others. But what is very different as far as Vespasian Moisa is concerned is the fact that he has produced documented miracles."

Here, Manoil of Snagov pretended to laugh. "Miracles? What miracles?"

With that, so it seemed to him, he had caught out the high Roman prelate. Where had he come up with proof of miracles worked by a down-and-out from Bucharest? He had seen him with his own eyes and hadn't been impressed. He wasn't even capable of argumentation. How was he supposed to perform miracles, then?

"Here," said the Italian bishop, and produced a videocassette. "We have here a recording of a miracle that Moisa performed in Lahovary Square. Beneath the eyes of hundreds of people, he changed the form of some water. The incident was filmed by an observer from the Holy See who happened to be there on the spot."

Manoil of Snagov was left dumbstruck in amazement. He did not have a video player handy, and even if he had had one, it would not have been of any use, given that he did not know how to operate such a contraption. He had seen other people using them, but now was not the moment. He did not know anything about this. He had had no idea. No one had said anything to him about miracles. This, of course, changed the nature of things. Could it be true? It must be, otherwise the Vatican would not have sent an emissary. The distinguished guest said, "This man is either a conjurer or a genius, or someone we should be mindful of. And I tell you this with all my friendship. This is the message with which the Holy Father entrusted me."

"I understand," said the Romanian bishop. "So it's true . . ."

Then, as if shaking off a bad dream, Manoil of Snagov confessed, "Unfortunately, however, yesterday evening an unexpected incident occurred. This mysterious character, this Vespasian Moisa, vanished."

"What?" said the Italian bishop in surprise. For an instant he recalled Aldo Moro, and broke into a sweat.

"It seems he was abducted by a commando of his rivals," said Manoil, gazing at the floor. "In Bucharest there are all kinds of people in the world of the shadows. Some of them took him off to an unknown destination."

"How? Why? Where did they take him?" asked Bishop Marianini.

With a broad smile, Manoil of Snagov said, "The Lord alone knows. The police are working on elucidating the case. All we can do is pray for this Christian soul."

"A very strange occurrence," said Bishop Marianini pensively. "It seems like unclean work. On the very eve of my arrival . . ."

"The Lord works in mysterious ways," said the other, making the sign of the cross with his fingers in the air.

"I would have very much wished to meet him."

"The Lord will bring him back to light, if such is His will," said Manoil of Snagov, brushing dust from his cassock.

■ □ ■ □ ■

CHAPTER TWENTY

"COMMANDANT, SIR, PLEASE TURN ON THE TELEVISION SET," SAID THE
secretary, entering unannounced the office where Filip Pop was catching up on the files of the most recent investigations.

"What is it?" he asked. "Give me the remote. Where's the remote?"

The secretary switched on the television and placed the remote on
the desk in front of him.

On the national news there was a live broadcast from the first floor
of the Hotel Bucharest. In the foreground there was a table with a
floral arrangement such as the Bucharest had never seen before. It
was an ikebana of blue petunias combined with wildflowers, symbol-
izing purity. Behind the flowers, Filip Pop recognized the determined
faces of those from the Tidings of the Lord: Dr. Apolodor Arghir,
Maximilian, Julius, and Pavel, the former secret services officer. They
were all wearing suits and neckties, and looked like the representatives of a company presenting some new model of washing machine.
It was a press conference of the Tidings of the Lord, which, it would
seem, had access to the financial resources required to hold such a
lavish event. Something in them had changed. In the first place, they
had given up that beggarly and impoverished air. Then—and this
seemed very curious to the commandant—who had ever heard of a
sect which proclaimed itself to be an Orthodox order but which was
not even officially registered as a foundation? And they were holding
their conference in the Hotel Bucharest! Crazy . . .

"Damn it," muttered Filip Pop. "Who gave them access to the mass media? Why weren't we told anything?"

"If they were holding a press conference, how could we have stopped them?" said the secretary. "The television cameras went as a matter of course. All the channels are there."

When the lieutenant colonel turned toward the secretary, he had the look of a wounded lion. She felt embarrassed, and so she lowered her eyes and withdrew to the anteroom.

Filip Pop had missed the beginning of the press conference. He turned the volume up and heard Dr. Arghir explain, *The canonic notation of Byzantine ecclesiastical music is the best representation we have to date of the description of man's road to God. Between man and God there is a wall, through which the voice cannot pass. A wall of porous stone, crisscrossed by labyrinthine capillaries, many of them blocked up. The hymns of old notate only the inflections of the voice, not the musical notes. The voice must either rise or fall, this is all the musical notation tells us, as if it were guiding us through a labyrinth, a labyrinth of vibrations, a labyrinth tried and tested by the Church Fathers. This is what we do when listening to a hymn more than one thousand years old, which every Sunday, for century after century, has borne prayers from man to God through this porous wall made from our deeds. The Doctrine of Vibrations, which I have had the honor to present to you, is nothing new, but has been known and accepted for centuries by the Romanian Orthodox Church. We rejoice in having the opportunity to urge you to pray: pray ceaselessly, with heart and with mind, pray and chant, for only thus will you reach the vibration from the beginning of the world!*

He cleared his throat, sipped some water, and went on:

—This is, of course, an unusual press conference. Where in the world have you heard such advice given at a press conference? But do not forget that Bucharest is a chosen city. The city called upon to play the role of the second Jerusalem, a place of blessing and redemption. Oh! What an opportunity we have! We, Romanians, the bearers of a seven-thousand-year-old language, a language which, even in its most wretched oaths, codifies the profoundest mysteries of the universe! A lucky language, like the combination to a bank vault, an encrypted, unprecedented secret, initiatory, astounding language! We, Romanians, are its keepers!

Listening to him, Lieutenant Colonel Pop drummed his fingers on the desk in boredom. He had already gone through a sheaf of reports about this raving lunacy, and he was bored to death of it. They all repeated themselves; it was the same burbling verbal diarrhea ad nauseam. All of a sudden, he remembered that he had heard the same things at officer training school and thought that maybe this was why it bored him so much.

—In conclusion, ladies and gentlemen, for me it is an honor to announce that I have accepted the proposal of the party that has invited us here today and will be standing as a candidate for Bucharest in the parliamentary elections. It will be an honor for me to represent in the next government the choices of my brothers in the Tidings of the Lord, in a perfect conjuncture of destiny with this young, but nonetheless historic, party that has invited me here today. We appreciate that the evolution of ideas of extraordinary transparency and modernity in the Romanian political spectrum today allows the unproblematic incorporation of a natural, spiritual movement within a political party of profound national tradition. We love this party and are honored to find ourselves among its ranks today. Our sole policy is that of the Romanian nation and it is for this nation that we are here today, ready for sacrifice!

A question from the auditorium, probably from a journalist:

—What are your objectives in the future parliament? As a member of parliament what goals will you pursue, if the Bucharest electorate grants you its trust?

—Thank you for your question. I like questions, and I love the press. My principal aim is to free from captivity Vespasian Moisa, this peacetime hero of the Romanian people. (Applause.) *Then, we will provide political support for the construction of an Orthodox cathedral in University Square—a daring design that will leave even the boldest architects breathless!* (Applause.) *And last but not least, over the long term, what we will pursue is a higher standard of living for our entire nation!* (Prolonged applause.)

Here, Filip Pop heard from the television set swelling applause, followed by shouts of joy, as if the whole of the Hotel Bucharest were filled only with followers of the Tidings of the Lord. In fact, he had no way of knowing that the doctor had taken the money of the Emir of Salibaar from its keeping place and, after the disaster at the villa in Lahovary Square, had moved the entire Tidings of the Lord movement to the hotel, thus mingling its devotees with the parliamentarians, barmen, footballers, fashion models, functionaries, courtesans, heroin traffickers, and diplomats that also frequented it. For the first time in his life, Filip Pop had the feeling that things were so out of control that he no longer had any objective to study, anyone to report to, any reason to gather information about anything, and that the entire battle was being waged on a scale and at a speed he could no longer catch up with, however hard he strove, however hard he toiled. And so, to shake off the vanity of vanities, he took the remote control and hurled it at the television set with such fury that it exploded and filled the room with suffocating black smoke. Filip Pop cursed and opened the door, to escape from that ill-fated room in which he received only ill tidings. The black fumes poured from the television set and swathed him as though in a smoke screen. In the doorway he bumped into his secretary, whose forehead dealt an uppercut to his chin. Then silence fell.

■ □ ■ □ ■

As evening fell, Bishop Marianini wrapped himself in lay garb and left the mission of the Holy See in Bucharest by the back door, which gave onto a passageway leading into one of the deserted streets around Icon Gardens. He looked behind him, wondering whether anyone might recognize him. The way he was dressed, he looked like a disgruntled rocker. He knew from reliable sources that in Bucharest you could be shadowed by anyone, from the secret services to agents faithful to the Patriarchate. However, he did not wish to give rise to a diplomatic incident: in the course of the morning, he had mentioned to the Orthodox bishop that he would be leaving Bucharest on the first flight to Rome. Something had made the Romanian believe that the truth was other than what he had been told, however.

Once he reached Lahovary Square, he recognized it from the video-cassettes he had seen. He recognized the place where Vespasian Moisa had performed the miracle of changing the form of the water, but he did not recognize the building. He was walking over rubble and dust. There was still a smell of burning in the air. But where was the building onto whose balcony Vespasian emerged? The bishop withdrew to one side, next to a wall. So, it was true: the building was completely destroyed. What could have happened here?

He saw the remains of the villa's reinforced concrete structure and descried the traces of the courtyard. Contorted iron poked from the ash and rubble. There was no one to be seen in the vicinity.

All of a sudden, he heard a whispered voice from somewhere among the remains of the building.

"Your Excellency! How happy I am to see you again!"

The bishop took a step back, with the air of one who realizes everything is lost. He had been recognized. But by whom? Something nonetheless held him back. The warmth of that voice made an impression on him. Could it be some friend? Could it be someone from the Vatican, on a mission to the ruins?

"Who is there?"

"Your Excellency does not know me. I am Lieutenant Trăistaru. I was assigned to shadow you on your first visit to Bucharest, in 1990."

"I remember," said the bishop, without any trace of irony in his voice. "One night, I found one of your secret service men asleep under the Nuncio car."

"Are you looking for Vespasian Moisa?"

The bishop took a step closer to where the voice was coming from. It seemed to him that the voice was coming from the remains of the building, from beneath a broken doorframe, which looked like a bullet-riddled Ionic column. But no one was there.

"Yes, I would like to talk to him."

"I know what you want from him. You want to find out how he performed those miracles."

"The matter is more complex than that," said the bishop, making an impatient gesture. "Where are you, Lieutenant? I can't see you."

"I'm here, close by, but the nature of my mission means I must remain hidden."

"Oh, I understand," said Bishop Marianini. "You are on a mission."

"Yes, and I know where Moisa is."

"Would you be prepared to communicate this information to me? It is, as I am sure you realize, of the greatest importance to me. I would remain profoundly in your debt."

From behind the Ionic column there was heard a titter.

"You're not going to believe this. Vespasian Moisa has been abducted by a rival sect, tried, with the knowledge of Bishop Manoil, and found incapable of working miracles, incapable of being a prophet, incapable of being the Son of God."

"Impossible," said Bishop Marianini, in total disbelief. "How do you know this?"

"I had access to information," the voice said.

"What rival sect? And why did Manoil not tell me?"

"Oh, Your Excellency, you know very well why. Manoil does not obey His Holiness the Pope. On the contrary, he has all kinds of aversions. Beneath his air of bonhomie hides a man very ill adjusted to reality, if I can put it like that. He has his career in mind. He's staking a lot on it."

"What do you mean to say?"

"He's the most deranged of our bishops, Your Excellency. He is so eccentric that some would like him packed off to a monastery. And he gets involved in all kinds of things, he dabbles in politics and is in cahoots with all kinds of ne'er-do-wells. You don't even know how much he loves life and how hard it would be to post him somewhere outside Bucharest."

"What can you tell me about Moisa?"

"I could take you to him. In fact, he could even use some help. I came here to find someone trustworthy, someone to help him, in the predicament he finds himself in."

"In what situation does he find himself?"

"Without exaggerating, he is a prisoner and his future is not at all rosy."

"I understand. And what can I do for him? Please, do not lose sight of the fact that I am here on a diplomatic mission, and any involvement on my part in Romanian domestic political matters is out of the question."

"Yes, but the man is in dire straits, and it would be well for someone to rescue him. Those weirdos are violent and capable of anything. I've seen them myself. It's not good at all."

"All right," said Bishop Marianini. "I shall go with you to Vespasian, and I beg you to tell me what I need to do to rescue him from there. I ask but one thing of you in return. Please assure me that I shall be able to examine him afterward, that I shall be able to draw up my report based on information of the highest quality."

"Of course, Your Excellency," said the voice. "But I too need some assistance. A mere courtesy, rather, a connection, a good word, a token of understanding. In the old days, when our secret service officers opted to remain in Rome, you did many things to help them. We know this, and, without flattering you, I assure you that you are better loved in Bucharest than in Rome. This is why I permit myself to make this request to you . . . My request is of a diplomatic nature. I would appreciate it if you could recommend me to a certain superior officer in the Romanian Intelligence Services who has difficulty accepting" (here the voice hesitated) "my present appearance."

"Agreed," said the bishop, then, after only a moment, "How is that? How is it, I mean, that one of your superior officers does not accept your appearance? Have you put on excessive weight for an officer in your field? I assure you that if this is the case, I do not know what I can do. Even the Holy Father, as you of course know, chose to replace the Bishop of Boston this spring after he reached the incredible weight of 280 kilos. The Holy Father is convinced that the image of the Holy See is crucial nowadays. But in espionage it is the same: when you shadow someone you need to be faceless, when you go and have a coffee in a bar you need to be anonymous-looking."

"Nothing of the sort, Your Excellency. It's much more complicated in my case," said the voice, with infinite sadness. "I was disfigured in the line of duty."

"Oh, how dreadful!" said the bishop, genuinely moved by this unexpected situation. "Who did it to you?"

"The KGB, Uzbek division."

"Oh, yes, I recognize their style," said the bishop, placing his hand on the remnants of a wall.

"I am afraid, however, that Your Excellency will be struck by my appearance, and I would like to assure myself that your reaction will not be inappropriate."

"My son, I have heard the confessions of people in the Peruvian-Ecuadorian conflict. I have been on the front line and have seen men mutilated."

"Not like me."

"Believe me, I have heard many things in my life."

"Very well, Your Excellency. I have trust in you, because I know you are a man of integrity."

CHAPTER TWENTY

The bishop looked around him and saw nothing behind the Ionic column except a fragment of burned tire. A little further away there was an iron without its electrical cable. The corner of a mirror poked up from the rubble. From the spot there emerged a ginger tomcat.

"I do not see you, Lieutenant."

"Here I am," the voice seemed to come from the tomcat.

"Where?" said the bishop, his eyes boggling.

"Here," said the tomcat, and the bishop realized that it was the animal that had spoken.

Then the bishop recalled the teachings of Saint Bonaventura and the twenty-two descriptions of the devil, and he recognized before him an example of the thirteenth. He saw himself snatched away by the devil, dragged through the backstreets of an inimical Bucharest, where the Church would not lift a finger to help him, while the devil impaled him on his trident and subjected him to tortures. He lifted his hand to his brow, trying to recover his former advantage over reality, and thought that he ought not to have left his room that evening. He thought that only prayer could save him, that when confronted with delusions this was the sole solution. And so he began to pray in Latin, invoking a procedure for driving away the devil that had been patented by the Vatican in centuries past.

In front of him, the tomcat stood motionlessly, listening to him pray aloud. Lieutenant Trăistaru had attended courses on scientific atheism in the old days. The image of Bishop Marianini praying struck him as depressing. Instead of a partner in dialogue, instead of assistance, this is what he got. Such obscurantism! What a disappointment! He had not been expecting something of the sort on the part of a high emissary of the Holy See.

The bishop saw the tomcat suddenly turn his back on him and go away. Before the high emissary of the Holy See had a chance to say another word, the tomcat leaped over the fence and vanished.

■ □ ■ □ ■

CHAPTER TWENTY-ONE

TELEVISION SETS WERE INVADED BY AN AURORA BOREALIS. IN EVERY living room in the country the television screen vibrated bluish, a sign of the concord and conviviality that rule everywhere over this world which man strives to make better, ever better. That evening, His Holiness the Patriarch gave a televised interview from the Chancellery of the Patriarchate:

—Dearly beloved, for the rest of mankind, of course, it would not be possible to say whether Vespasian Moisa was a fraud whose theory did nothing more than to trouble reality or whether he was not somehow the second Messiah whom, for a second time, out of confusion, violence, acerbity, and ignorance, we have crucified, and after whose second coming there is nothing more to be expected than the long night of time, as if we had all been swallowed up by the viscera of a gigantic beast that had ingurgitated the whole earth. Thinking about his disappearance, for no one now knows anything of his whereabouts, all that remains is for us to pray. Our Father, that art in heaven, help, O Lord, Thy servant Vespasian, and bring him back unharmed to us. For we shall never know whether Thou knew or whether in all this time we were alone and Thou put us to the test, for the judgment at the end of days. Because here, on this earth, we bear ourselves as if we were alone, and, in fact, we ought to look after ourselves, just as children in the crèche ought to look after themselves, when the nurse turns her back. Thou let us dream of a world in which cancer and baldness and other maladies might be cured, and theories and

working hypotheses might be simultaneously true and all meanings might coherently interpenetrate, within a fabric as perfect as a sphere, permitted for Thy greater glory. Thou let us dream, Lord, of a world in which each and every sentence is true. This is what we are now undergoing.

Having reached this point, the evening broadcast was interrupted for almost half a minute by white noise, and the image of the Patriarch was obscured by strange colors. When the broadcast returned to normal, the happy viewers were able to hear the Patriarch's blessing:

—May the Lord preserve and keep you!

But his voice was altered, profoundly baritone, as if this world had been superimposed, at least in the televisual spectrum, with some other world.

■ □ ■ □ ■

Around twenty Stephenists, all that had remained of the army which a few days previously had tried to conquer Bucharest, gathered on the Hill of the Patriarchate at midnight, in front of the very building that had once housed the Chamber of Deputies. It was a beautiful moonlit night in late June. Torrid summer had not yet descended upon the city. The air, pure and free of dust, recalled the evenings of long ago, when *voievods* used to ponder dynastic matters here with manly wisdom. On those evenings of nobler times, their hands never wavered when certain territorial matters demanded urgent solution.

Vespasian Moisa, bruised and bloodied, was lying on the cobbles. He could barely see. They had beaten him the whole evening.

Darius was waiting. Not even he knew what he was waiting for. It was as if he had not expected things to come this far. It was as if he wished that someone would leap from the shadows and say, "No!" But this did not happen. Suddenly, he said, "They lied to us. They said that they would demonstrate and demand the release of Stephen from the police station. They didn't do it. We have a prisoner here who has been proven to be a false prophet and a sorcerer. What else can we do except execute the sentence? What other course do we have except to rise to the lofty heights of the historic mission the nation and all its history now call upon us to fulfill?"

"Yes," agreed some two disgusted and weary voices.

It had been a hard week for them all.

Darius approached Vespasian Moisa, who was lying inert on the ground, and whispered, "They say that a man becomes himself only before his death. Tell me, prophet, now do you know who you are?"

"Where the hell did you come up with that one?" asked Negru, taking Darius by the shoulder.

Vespasian opened his eyes and saw their black boots and studded trousers, the chains they were wielding, and their black overcoats. From somewhere the hoot of an owl was heard.

Wings beat through the night air.

"Is the stake ready?" someone asked.

Then, Vespasian Moisa saw as if in a mist three silhouettes, dragging behind them an enormous stake, with an A-shaped stand. The others stood aside, leaving Vespasian lying bound on the cobbles. He remained motionless. Then he lifted his head. From his right, one of them propped him upright and cut the cords that bound his legs. Vespasian Moisa saw the well-polished point of the stake and, in a flash of light, saw the tip. They slid it between his legs and, before he realized what was happening, five or six of them pinned him to the ground, holding his arms. One of them said, "I could hardly wait to see this. I've read so much about it, but there was nowhere I could have seen it with my own eyes."

In a solemn voice, Darius declaimed, "In the name of the Romanian people and as a consequence of the teachings handed down to us by our ancestors, who return to us this noble evening, for the treason and mockery you have made of them through your beliefs and deeds, Vespasian Moisa, you are hereby condemned to death."

Then he stepped back and allowed the others to approach.

"It's no longer important to execute him," said Negru.

"What are you talking about?" said Darius, as if he were acting a part in a play.

"We've won already. Look at him: what kind of prophet is this? Is there anything left of him? There's nothing left, because we've humiliated him. That is our victory."

"But no one sees us."

"He knows. He knows."

Indeed, there was nothing much left of Vespasian Moisa. After the humiliations of the past night, would Bucharest have believed that anything remained of the prophet?

CHAPTER TWENTY-ONE

185

"It's pointless impaling him on the stake," said Negru. "Let's piss on him."

A strong wind whipped up, causing a whole army of shadows to rustle.

"That's it," agreed Darius, as if illumined, seeming to glimpse a way out. "Let's piss on him!"

They gathered around his body. They were all looking at him, as if they were expecting some miracle. He seemed insensate, like a vegetable. Then, Darius looked more closely and saw that the famed Vespasian Moisa was nothing more than a man stooped from birth, who bore on the skin of his chest a hideous scar, like a burn, an ugly welt made of crests and shadows, which in the dim streetlights looked like the skin of a fig. He took aim and began to relieve himself on him. The steam rose from the skin of the prone man. Someone began to laugh. A second jet of urine was heard. Then a third. Soon, there was no longer any room around the supine body.

"Is it true that you can hear with your chest?" asked Darius. "Can you still hear now?"

Someone laughed. And then there was silence.

"We'd be better off going back and watching the football match," said one of them.

Darius looked at the face of Vespasian Moisa. The other looked back. It was no longer the look of a beaten man, prone on the cobbles. Darius spat and asked, "What match?"

"Galatasaray Istanbul are playing in the Champions' League tonight. We can't miss Mircea Lucescu, the scourge of the Ottomans!"

"That's right! Glory to him! Glory to the one who has got the Turks on the run!"

A murmur of approval passed over the lips of all. "How could we forget?" murmured Darius. "Mircea Lucescu. Our man. Damned good trainer." Then they started talking among themselves. Someone said, "We're wasting our time here. Let's get out the Galatasaray banners and raise the Turkish flag over the government building like that time when they beat Arsenal, so as to mark that government of bandits with the sign of the enemy. We're wasting our time with this loser. Let's go." Someone else said, "Let's impale him on the stake and prop it against the wall of the Patriarchate. Or better still, up against the Patriarch's balcony, so that he'll wake up tomorrow with the corpse hanging over the balustrade. As it is, he said he loves him on television."

"When did he say that?"

"This evening."

"He didn't say anything of the kind."

"Oh yes he did."

"Oh no he didn't."

"Quiet," said Darius. "Have you all gone mad? The sentence has already been executed. Our problem is a political one. We're dealing with an influential enemy, someone who's been visited by politicians, the person to whom the whole of Bucharest came, whom everyone took seriously. Who can take him seriously now, after he's spent all these nights with us? You realize, don't you?"

And he laughed, as if he knew a secret. Then, Negru said, "The risk of handing them a martyr on a plate is too great. Right here on the Hill of the Patriarchate, this urban Golgotha. Have we all gone mad? What are we, amateurs? Aren't we capable of a cunning plan? We pissed on him. That was the cunning plan. That was the political coup we were looking for. It's over."

And on saying that, he prodded Vespasian Moisa's mouth with the tip of his shoe.

"It's over," he said once more.

There followed a moment of silence. Vespasian closed his eyes. He could still feel the point of the stake between his legs. All of a sudden, he sensed the figures moving away from him. Their footfalls sounded on the cobbles. One of them shouted like a madman, "Cim Bom Bom! Come on, Galata! Let's get out of here."

"Right."

"It's over," said Darius. "We've ended it."

Then Vespasian heard footfalls once more. Had they left or had it only seemed so? What difference is there between an impression and a memory, when you are aching all over, when every thought is bound and led away by interminable pains, pains that follow upon one another, pains that annihilate organs, senses, the body, because they make you feel everything much closer, when your heart is beating everywhere and every heartbeat is pain?

Vespasian Moisa remained on the cobblestones. He no longer had anything of the triumphant air of the prophet.

CHAPTER TWENTY-ONE

187

▾

He was breathing with difficulty, and it was hard for him to gather his thoughts. He felt an acute pain in his back, between his shoulder blades, and his arms, knees, and stomach ached from the blows he had received. Every movement caused him pain.

Then a ginger tomcat approached, which rested his whiskers against his cheek and said, in a distinct Bucharest accent, "Mr. Moisa, I saw what you went through. What horror. What methods. What suffering you have gone through."

Vespasian opened his eyes and could not believe it: could it be another temptation from the devil? Then, it seemed to him that he had seen this tomcat somewhere before, but he could not remember where. His eyes were too clouded. The tomcat seemed friendly, sympathetic, familiar. He would have liked to smile, but could not.

"I have followed your entire career," went on the tomcat, "and— why hide the fact—I am deeply impressed. Your public presence is more impressive than that of the president. You are a man of genuine charisma. I think that you ought to work with us. In our line of work, which involves management of the contemporary flow of information, the way in which this information is presented to the public is a matter of the utmost importance. If you like, I can tell you more. I would be happy to talk to you about this proposal. For now, I will limit myself to assuring you of the genuineness of my offer. Your talent is absolutely remarkable, and I would be glad to place you in contact with someone who will know how to appreciate and nurture it. It is very hard to succeed in a career. I understand this very well. Even in the career of prophet, if we may say so . . . We will be able to help you, to support you. And to be honest, I think that you need us, too. Think about how many things you could do for Romania, with the money that the Tidings of the Lord has now, if you also enjoyed our discreet support . . . I would be glad to serve such a cause as a liaison man, or rather liaison tomcat. Ultimately, what we will ask of you is only a minor thing, a few pieces of information, in exchange for the boundless support we will offer you . . ."

But Vespasian Moisa no longer heard him. Shaken by fever, he rolled over. The tomcat looked at him with wide eyes and sniffed him. Could he have fainted? So it would seem. Ugh, what an unpleasant situation. Just as the subject matter was so appropriate to recruitment. It was a classic textbook situation. How could he blow the whole

recruitment just as he was so close! And when such a spectacular recruitment would have saved his skin, too, since he had fallen into
disgrace and lost his contact officer in the division . . . What a knife-
edge moment! Hey, sniff, sniff, wake up . . .

Then, two figures emerged from the gloom.

The Troubadour approached and chased away the cat. He bent over
the body of Vespasian and lifted his head from the cobblestones.

"Lord, what a fever he has! I've never seen anyone burn like this."

"Have they gone?"

"Yes, they're somewhere far off now," said Barbie.

Somewhere in Unification Square a choir of drunken voices could
be heard intoning the national anthem. Or some patriotic hymn or
other.

"You're right. That's them. What a stench of onions they left behind them!"

"What have they done to him? God, what a stink," said Barbie.

Vespasian's eyes were half-closed, and he was barely breathing. His
right arm hung limply, and he could probably not move it.

Then Barbie told the Troubadour, "*He's finished.*"

He turned toward her. She was standing, blocking the glow of
the only streetlamp in the little square in front of the Patriarchate.
Somewhere nearby a dog could be heard barking and then a cat hiss-
ing. The cat streaked past them with the dog hot on its heels. Toni
gave a start.

"It would have been better if they'd killed him."

She shouldn't have said that, thought the Troubadour. Although,
as he held Vespasian in his arms, he knew it was so. No one would
have followed him after a night like this. After so much humiliation.
After the last few days. It was rumored that he had been raped, that he
had been tortured, that they had defiled him. Who had been spread-
ing these rumors? On the way here he had heard so many things.
What a political assassination these enemies from the shadows had
committed!

And if she were right? What if it were better for him to have been
killed?

Then he heard her say, "Shall we finish what they were about
to do?"

He laid Vespasian on the ground and moved away from him, as

CHAPTER TWENTY-ONE

189
▼

if his body had burned him. He pressed his brow against the wall of the church, and he saw himself as if for real raising Vespasian in the noose, then taking the news to those who loved him and believed in him. He saw them all coming to weep for him, saying that he was the Son of God, that the Son of God was slain by Satan, that mankind could no longer save itself because Satan was too powerful. He struck his brow against the wall, for he saw all these things, he saw them for real, they were real, palpable, achievable, necessary. His mind had formed them, and the thought now pained him. For a moment he felt that it was necessary, that he must do it. Barbie was right. They had to raise him in the noose. And everybody would think that the followers of Stephen did it. Only thus would Vespasian's humiliation and defeat be transformed into a victory.

"We don't have much time," she said. "Come on, let's do it. I'll help you."

They went up to him and dragged him by the legs. Vespasian hung inertly. She brought from the other sidewalk a rope the others had abandoned. She looked at it and realized she did not know what kind of knot to make.

The Troubadour was leaning against the wall, his face frozen, as if he had already killed the Teacher. He realized that if he did it, the legend of Vespasian Moisa would live forever. The most beautiful legend Bucharest had ever given birth to. All the more beautiful given that it might be true. True? What was He? Was He the Son of God? And then, how to kill Him? He tried to chase this thought from his mind, shaking from every limb. O, Lord! Was this not an abominable crime, one that might imperil the salvation of all mankind?

"Hold the rope," she said, after the knot was ready.

It was also she who placed the noose around Vespasian's neck and said, "You have to throw the noose over that beam in the porch of the church. Come on, you're taller. Quickly. Why are you looking at me?"

He obeyed her without hesitation. Trembling, he cast the rope where she had told him and pulled the end down.

Then, Vespasian sat up. He looked at them as if he saw right through them. He looked at them as if they were air and he were fire. He was sitting up, like a man who was coming round from drunkenness, and hunching his shoulders. He seemed to be gazing into space.

"Now, pull the rope," Barbie whispered to the Troubadour.

But the Troubadour remained motionless. He whispered, "But what if . . . what if he really is the Son of God, and this is His second coming, to redeem the whole of mankind?"

With slow movements, like those of a drug addict, Vespasian Moisa picked himself up from the ground, removed the noose from around his neck, and, without looking at them, took his first steps. His right arm was probably broken. It dangled lifeless. He was disfigured with pain. It was as if he were a different person. He turned to the man who had been close to him for so long and gazed into his eyes without saying anything. There was nothing more to say. They were beyond death, they were beyond murder, where there is no longer anything at all. Barbie took a step backward. It seemed to her that Vespasian was giving off a reddish mist. The Troubadour watched him melting into the night and, after a few steps, into the darkness, it seemed that his body split in two, like one shadow emerging from another, like a deceptive flame flickering in argon, like a Transylvanian shadow emerging from a Wallachian body, like a bat vanishing into a cave in the Apuseni Mountains, like matter splitting into its ultimate elementary forces, like an alchemical sublimation producing gold from lead. Thenceforth only rumors were to accompany him: that one of the shadows vanished into the heavens, that the other was flattened by a no. 32 tram or that it dissolved into the air, still living, breathing, and dragging its broken arm. That it disappeared like an uncertain fluid, which is to say its essence turned to air, that it became ether, because those that are made of two halves end up unmatched, at high temperatures, and dissipate into the atmosphere. And it was also said that one puff of smoke detached itself from the other, at pressures close to those of plasma, like an unrepeatable chemical distillation, if such a theory makes any sense. There were so many things said about that disappearance . . .

■ ☐ ■ ☐ ■

The next day, deacon Macarie tripped over a blood-soaked rope, not far from the steps of the Cathedral of the Patriarchate. He picked it up from the ground and made the sign of the cross with his tongue against the roof of his mouth. It is said that devils from Tartarus sometimes mislay ropes thereabouts when they come up into the world. He saw a puddle of urine not far away. He remained motionless for an instant, as if not able to believe his eyes, and then he fled at a run, returning with a broom and a bucket of water. He felt a need to cleanse not only the cobblestones but also the air, the sky and the stars whose gleam was fading in the bright red of a summer dawn, and the clouds with their unraveling feather dusters high above the earth. Let no one else see what shameful things stalk the Bucharest night, so near to the holy places, where the head of our Church is sleeping and where official delegations arrive from the Patriarchate in Constantinople and from the Vatican. So thought the deacon. When he had finished cleaning up, a cock was heard crowing. From the portico of the bishopric window, a large, ginger tomcat, with green eyes, like a devil's, was watching, as if disappointed, while deacon Macarie finished cleaning his corner of the world, at the beginning of a new day on the highest hill in Bucharest. Then, when the first rays of the sun lit the world with vestal gold, the tomcat sneezed, sadly.

CHAPTER TWENTY-TWO

GENERAL MIHALACHE OPENED THE DOOR TO THE MEETING ROOM AND saw anew the dispirited faces of the officers from the division which had lately been so overworked. Then he took a step back and bade the special guest to that meeting to enter. It was a priest in full regalia, dressed in red and gold, the glory colors of Byzantium after Byzantium, wielding a censer and followed by a chorister in a suit and tie, carrying two gigantic books. The priest sprinkled the room with holy water, and a few drops landed on the files on the desk. He blessed the assembly, after which the general said, "I decided the time had come to sanctify our division and to seek assistance in our efforts to defend the homeland from diversionary elements and groups with a dangerous social impact. Let us pray together before we start the meeting."

As if strengthening his words, the priest gave a throaty cough and then let rip with a baritone *Lord have mercy* before scattering the holy water once more.

The officers had risen to their feet and were standing up against the wall. Filip Pop looked on, his eyes beady in stupefaction.

All of a sudden, Major Baldovin released a high-pitched, feminine scream and jumped up onto the table. From there he pointed at the general and cried, "Ha!" as if to say that he knew what this was all about. "Ha! Ha!" he repeated, and then sprinted across the baize table, running in the opposite direction from the unit commander. To the general's amazement, when he reached the open window, he spread his arms wide and jumped. Commandant Pop immediately ran after him and poked his head through the window. Then he slumped over the sill, shaking his head. The priest's censer stopped shaking. The general clutched at his hair, and one of the officers began to sob loudly.

■ □ ■ □ ■

Stephen was released from prison on bail the next day. He was under investigation for disturbing the peace, organizing unauthorized demonstrations, and exploiting domestic animals without a permit in the central districts of the capital. Negru and Darius were waiting for him in front of the prison. They embraced him and whispered in his ear, "Welcome back, Your Majesty!"

"We shall recommence the fight as soon as possible! We shall conquer Bucharest together!"

"Glad to be back, warriors," he said, looking up at the azure summer sky above Bucharest.

His clothes were badly crumpled, and his blond beard had grown. He looked feverish. He had not been looking after himself inside. But not to worry—with a hot bath and a little pampering he would be as good as new, and then they could mount him once more on a white horse.

With a faraway look and an air of great nobility, Stephen told them, "They gave me medication in there, in the prison infirmary. Some of it was very strong, it made my head spin terribly . . . It was as if my muscles were chiming under my skin. That's what it felt like. It was like a tempest, and I remembered everything, as if it had been yesterday . . . It was as if my body clock had been turned back, as if it had taken me back hundreds of years. Good people, listen here, it is only now that I can see my true past and my true destiny . . . Believe me, it is only now . . . I have only had one previous life, but in that life I was Voievod Ion the Terrible . . ."

Darius and Negru jumped away as if electrocuted. What was this nonsense? How could he say something like that? Wasn't he Stephen? Hadn't it been established, following the oral examination by Neagu, who had studied all the history books? How could he now claim something so stupid? Negru raised his hand to his brow, dumbstruck.

Darius fell to his knees and bellowed at him from the bottom of his lungs, "What's this nonsense? What about all your memories from the battle you told us about?"

"They were from a different battle," said the blond man, with an awkward smile.

"You're nothing but a shyster," Negru flung at him, gnashing his teeth in fury and clenching his fists, prey to the syndrome of those shaken in their beliefs.

"Silence, pagan," said Stephen in a low but authoritarian voice, "or else I'll command that you be beaten on the soles of the feet with a bull's pizzle."

Suddenly, Darius leaped on the blond man and started punching him. The latter feinted him and tried to punch him in the stomach. As if nothing were happening next to him, Negru sat down on the curb.

■ □ ■ □ ■

An attentive observer would have been able to recognize Colonel Focşăneanu among those who were strolling on Schitu Magureanu Street, not far from Radio Broadcasting House. He was the same, except that his eyes were now more intense, his face harsher, his gestures more hurried, his steps zigzagging, and his arms seemingly longer than before. He was dressed rather too warmly for the weather outside, with his woolen scarf, ski mittens of an indeterminate blue, and a wide-brimmed black hat, with which he was wont to hide his face when the situation demanded discretion.

Our observer might have glimpsed how this man out for a stroll all of a sudden hurled himself onto the sidewalk, catching a cat by surprise. He murmured something in its ear, as if imparting a secret or as if it were a scene of tenderness. The cat tried to escape, to scratch him, but its claws embedded in the thick material of his gloves. For an instant, the intense gaze of the retired officer fastened on the cat's whiskers, as if he were waiting for it to say something, as if his life depended on it, as if the cat were irrefutable proof of his innocence. Then, without warning, he tossed the cat over the fence of the nearest house, gnashing his teeth loudly enough for passersby to hear. "Blasted Uzbeks!"

CHAPTER TWENTY-TWO

195
▾

Afterward, the observer might have seen him winding the scarf dozens of times around his neck, as his eyes continually scanned the nearby bushes for the answer to the question of his life.

■ □ ■ □ ■

The story goes that from two mists merging together on the lip of a rainbow above the mountain by the Buzăul Bend in the Carpathians was born Marian Tihomir, the young man of whom it had been lately said that he was a true prophet, perhaps even a Son of God, the indubitable savior of mankind, the man who would rescue the people of Bucharest from their provincial inertia and transform that beautiful city into the promised City of Light, the famed City of Light for which the hermits in the wilderness prayed, for which the 1848 revolutionaries returned from their Parisian studies, for which Greater Romania was created, and for which Romanians have endured in the most precarious conditions for two thousand years, waiting for this city to be transformed into the Second Jerusalem, into the city to fulfill our highest, choicest hopes. He entered Bucharest in the autumn of 1996, and the entire city was waiting for him. Everything had been readied for him, as if reality itself were a purple carpet laid at his feet and his footfalls resounded on that carpet like the music we were all longing to hear. He entered the city riding an ass, and the friendly populace of Bucharest greeted him with olive branches and laurels, with bread and salt, with youthful music and infinite hopes. The story goes that his first words in public were about Bucharest, and we listened to him and we breathed it all in, for there is nothing in this world we love more than the destiny of this city, the chosen place, the only place in the universe where past, present, and future meet, blending like Bantu percussion with motifs from Mozart mixed by a deejay of genius, for each of us is that deejay of genius. It is from this city that our salvation in the world to come and our happiness in the present world originates, from here that we draw our energy and reinvigorate our blood. And the words of Marian Tihomir seemed to be drawn from a poem: *Behold me, for now I have reached thy door.* It was thus he spoke! It was thus he spoke of his coming, of freedom and the unleashing of energy that his entry into Bucharest had provoked. He came from afar, from a lost world, from the off-key time of our wounded, heightened senses, he now came and he spoke to us of Romania in the 1930s, of glory and of freedom, of our triumph as a nation and our rights as individuals, of our salvation in the eyes of the Lord God. Oh, how beautifully he spoke to us about the salvation of each and every one of us . . . He spoke to us of all those ideas to which we are so sensitive, ideas on hearing which, as soon as we encounter them in someone's talk, we are ready to blossom. For we do not blossom when we come into money, when we eat or drink, but when we come upon ideas! Many prophets has the homeland known in recent times, but none was like him, none came with arguments so lucid, none performed such convincing miracles, and none shone so brightly among us, for everything resides in charisma, in style, and in the posture of the arms, where the angle of the shoulders allows room for the imperial light to filter under the armpits and strike the masses with billions of rays of stellar light . . . None had ever heard any other speak the way he did. He was better than the Son of the Archangel Michael or any of the other prophets that have come and whom we have already forgotten, prophets who have passed away forever. For many have been the prophets that Bucharest has known in all ages and in all reigns, but all have come from nowhere and back to nowhere have they returned. All have had something to say and of their sayings only dust and mockery have remained, regardless of what mixtures of unprecedented theories they might have concocted or what wise counselors they might have had. From nowhere back to nowhere, so it has been. But not so with Marian Tihomir. Upon him did we gamble on the roulette wheels of our lives, only upon him, upon his intuition, upon his word, for he was different. The story goes that he said, *With this nation of madmen you would not make any headway even if Christ Himself were to make His second coming, invested with the absolute power of the Lord God, Who in His great wisdom and omnipotence had nothing else to do except try to redeem the whole of mankind once again and had decided to start here. And it would not at all be certain whether He would succeed, for the starting point is everything in such enterprises.* This is what they say he said. Oh, how beautiful! Listen to me and believe, for the storyteller is I, and I truly heard it. He spoke to us of the City of Light, the city to which we bind all our hopes, whose uninterrupted growth was the sign of our vitality, the city through whose air could be heard the passage of moonbeams and whose stylized appearance had begun, for a time, to sprout from all our bodies, as if our epidermis were stamped with the stigma of this place, as we traverse the world, wracked by fevers, slaves to our profoundest obsessions, to the most terrible diseases of our times, those that are passed on through sneezes, kisses, handshakes, words, promises, contracts, memberships, conversations, lectures, and newspaper articles, which is to say through all those acts of togetherness that accrete the substance of ascension to the heavens at the judgment of nations, whither all countries arrive in their hour of glory, carrying on their shoulders their knapsacks of images and aspirations.

Nothing heralded what was to follow on that July morning of the first year after Tihomir. It was unexpected. It was an outbreak. It was something unforeseen by any political analyst, professional psychologist, religious observer, or military strategist. It was like an outpouring, like the explosion of a cosmic gas canister, like a bolt from the blue. At first, it was only a handful of people who had gathered in Sudului Square, carrying banners inscribed in Romanian with Slavonic characters, inspired by some flag or other from the Cantacuzino period. Then, a few hundred people gathered in Eroilor Square. Among them were itinerant coffee vendors, drug pushers plotting new formulas in defiance of the basic laws of biochemistry, new composers of ethno-rock music capable of turning a dirge into a whip and nuclear rockets into plowshares, artistes from the defunct State Circus juggling free of charge in honor of the homeland's new prophet, the splendid coquettes of our times redolent of Christian Dior and demonstrating in the street like French philosophers in their youth, former revolutionaries and future members of parliament, amateur rugby players and professional boxers—all of them joined together in the most motley multitude Bucharest had ever seen. One and all, they poured from Eroilor Square toward the other central squares of the capital, while all the television stations interrupted their programs to broadcast live the new prophet of Romania as he seized political, religious, and spiritual power, the prophet at whose feet lay a whole new world, exploding with the most variegated imagery of which homo sapiens has ever been capable. Filmed from a helicopter, the whole spectacle looked much like a Rio de Janeiro carnival, except that along the banks of the Dîmbovița River paraded not samba schools but schools of thought, each with its own dance and banner, each with its own exoticism and metaphors, each with its own allegorical float, on which subtle ikebana melded in a postmodern way with the funerary wreaths to the memory of our dead in the battles of Tapae, Posada, the High Bridge, Călugăreni, Mărăști, and so on. By midday, a million eccentric figures had blocked the whole of central Bucharest, each performing magic acts of the utmost uniqueness, each dedicating this act to forebears and descendents, each inspired in this new manifestation of freedom by the new prophet, yes, the new prophet, the one who had brought freedom, democracy, love, and, not least, progress. They danced and kept the rhythm by beating pots, pans, scrap metal, anything that came to hand, so that the whole of Bucharest was transformed into a single drum, which sent into space a constant, intense, and deafening vibration, unvarying and tuneless, like the Steaua football stadium to the power of one thousand, like a revolution under greenhouse conditions, like hacking into the central processor of the universe, like the epochal explosion of a pot of maize porridge. Television viewers were able to see at one point a young man perched on a lamppost, and those who still recalled the Tidings of the Lord could recognize him as Julius. He was still the same, his face more drawn, but seemingly more enthusiastic, genuinely elated at taking part in this new consecration, hanging above Magheru Boulevard at a considerable height, dangling above the universe. He was perched up on the lamppost and waving elatedly at the whole world, until the embarrassing moment when his shirt buttons burst and something resembling a book fell out. He tried to catch it, but it was too late. He dropped it. The television cameras caught it in close-up, revealing it to be a card index, which scattered in midair, showering kisses over the surging crowd. Then, around one o' clock in the afternoon, the ecstatic crowd began to chant the national anthem, softly at first, but then ever louder. A banner, stitched in gold against a green ground—a combination of colors formerly reserved for the nobility—was unfurled, and on it could be read in letters visible from outer space: *In every hollow could be found a god.* And no one stayed to listen to the old man whom in other times they used to call Saint Peter. Nodding his head and displaying a never-before-seen kind of facial tic, he gave an exclusive statement in front of the television cameras: "Like the sea at high tide, this is what happens when Nemesis nears the earth, it floods the world with a tide of ideas."

A few moments later, the camera toppled over and began transmitting images of the sky above, while across the television screens, in red, yellow, and blue, rolled the words LIVE BROADCAST.

1999–2004
East Lansing, MI;
Scottsdale, AZ;
Fullerton and Irvine,
CA

NOTES

Chapter One

5
born twice
The two births of Vespasian Moisa correspond to the two historical parts of Romania: the Old Kingdom and Transylvania. The historical principalities of Wallachia and Moldavia united to form the Old Kingdom in 1859. Transylvania, formerly a province of the Austro-Hungarian Empire, united with the Old Kingdom to form Greater Romania on December 1, 1918.

5
vehicle registration number 17-B-1504
The license plate prefix seventeen was reserved for ambulances. "B" stands for Bucharest. The year 1504 is when Prince Stephen the Great of Moldavia died.

7
George Coşbuc [1866–1918]
Romanian nationalist poet from Transylvania, who wrote during the time when the province was under Austro-Hungarian rule. Given their nationalistic ideological content, George Coşbuc's poems were part of the mandatory school curriculum during the Ceauşescu period (1965–89). See also the note regarding "We Want Land!" in chapter 15, below.

7
Octavian Goga [1881–1938]
Romanian poet and right-wing politician. His pre-1918 poems, written in Transylvania when the province was part of the Austro-Hungarian Empire, expressed Romanian aspirations toward national unity. Between 1937 and 1938, as leader of the anti-Semitic National Christian Party, he served as prime minister of the national unity government. His early-twentieth-century poetry was part of the mandatory school curriculum under Ceauşescu.

7
texts written in Slavonic script
The Romanian language was written using Cyrillic letters up until the 1860s, after the unification of Wallachia and Moldavia, when Romanian culture became more Western oriented.

8
plentiful listening to the radio and watching television
During that period, there was only one television channel, broadcasting for two hours on weekdays, from 8:00 P.M. to 10:00 P.M., and five hours on Saturdays and Sundays, from 2:00 P.M. to 4:00 P.M. and from 7:00 P.M. to 10:00 P.M. The content of television broadcasts consisted almost entirely of speeches by Nicolae Ceauşescu and the official propaganda of the isolationist communist system. Likewise, the three national radio channels were mostly ideological in content. Emanuel is thus saturated with the propaganda of Romanian communist nationalism.

8
Flame Cenacle
"Cenaclul Flacăra" was a cultural mass movement during the Romanian communist period, initiated by Adrian Păunescu (1943–2010) and involving rallies, with popular music, poetry readings, etc. It was eventually banned by the authorities in 1985, who saw its popularity, which often reached the pitch of mass hysteria, as a potential rival to the cult of personality surrounding the dictator.

8
The First of December Unites Us
A line from a poem by Adrian Păunescu. December 1, 1918, was the date on which Transylvania, formerly a province of the Austro-Hungarian Em-

pire, was unified with the Kingdom of Romania, comprising the provinces of Wallachia and Moldavia.

8

And nonetheless a love exists, / And nonetheless a curse exists
Lines from a poem by Adrian Păunescu (see note above).

8

"Pe mine mie redă-mă" ("render me unto myself")
A line from "Odă (în metru antic)" [Ode (in ancient meter)] by Mihai Eminescu (1850–89), Romania's "national poet."

9

Samuil Micu [1745–1806]
Theologian and philologist. He was responsible for the second translation of the Bible into Romanian, in 1795. The first Romanian translation of the Bible—the *Bucharest* or *Cantacuzino Bible*—dates from 1688.

9

Vasile Alecsandri [1821–90]
A poet and folklorist.

10

Costinești
A Black Sea resort. It was here that the Union of Communist Youth organized music and cultural festivals in the 1980s.

Chapter Two

13

Ferentari
An ill-famed slum district of Bucharest.

13

Phoenix
A Romanian rock band formed in Timișoara in 1962. Their music blends rock and blues with Romanian ethnic and folk music influences.

13

"Andrii Popa"
A ballad about the legendary *haidouk* of the same name. Now a standard Romanian street musicians' number.

14
a patrol of gendarmes
In Romania, the gendarmes are a separate force from the police. The *Jandarmerie* is a military structure whose duties include maintaining public order, crowd control, guarding important public buildings, and so on.

14
wing beating next to wing
Here, as well as throughout the book, the narrator alludes to the work of Nichita Stănescu. In this case, *"aripă lîngă aripă bătînd"* ("wing beating next to wing") is a misquotation of the lines *"Din punctul de vedere-al aerului, / soarele-i o aer plin de păsări, / aripă în aripă zbătînd."* ("From the point of view of the air, / the sun is a bird-filled air, / wing jerking on wing") from one of Stănescu's most famous poems, "Lauda Omului" ("Praise of Man") from the volume *A Vision of the Sentiments* (1964). The narrator confuses *"bate"* (beat) and *"zbate"* (jerk).

15
President Ion Iliescu
Leader of the National Salvation Front during the Romanian Revolution of December 1989. President of Romania 1990–96, 2000–2004.

Chapter Three

23
Maria Tănase [1913–63]
Romania's greatest singer of traditional folk music.

Chapter Four

27
Nichita Stănescu [1933–83]
A major Romanian poet, with a mass popular following in the 1970s and '80s. Folk singer Nicu Alifantis set many of Stănescu's poems to music, and his recordings became hits. These are collected in two albums, *Piața Romană nr. 9* (1988) and *Nichita* (1996). In Romania it is widely felt that Stănescu's premature death, at the age of fifty, robbed Romanian literature of a potential Nobel laureate.

27
"Autumn Feeling"
Autumn has come, cover my heart somehow,
with the shadow of a tree or better still with your shadow.

I fear that I am no longer to see you, at times,
that from me pointed wings will sprout up to the sky,
that you will hide in an unfamiliar eye,
and it will shut with a wormwood leaf.

And then I befriend stones and fall silent,
I take the words and drown them in the sea.
I whistle the moon and raise it and mould it
into a love that is vast.

Published in the volume *O viziune a sentimentelor* [*A Vision of the Sentiments*] (1964).

28
he kissed his heel
An allusion to the following quatrain by Nichita Stănescu, also published
in *O viziune a sentimentelor:*

Tell me, if I were to catch you one day
and kiss the sole of your foot,
would you not limp a little, thereafter,
for fear you might crush my kiss?

28
Ploieşti
The city of Nichita Stănescu's birth, north of Bucharest.

29
Mihai Eminescu, as he appears in the Prague photograph
There are only four photographs of Mihai Eminescu in existence. The
Prague portrait, made by Jan Tomas in 1869, shows him as a romantic young
man. In Romanian nationalist ideology—both the fascist nationalism of
the Iron Guard and the communist nationalism of the Ceauşescu period—
the photograph becomes an iconic image of the "perfect man of Romanian
culture." The later photographs show an Eminescu who is older and marked
by the ravages of illness.

31
On Angels
This is the title of a best-selling book by Romanian art historian and thinker Andrei Pleșu, published in 2003.

31
House of the Spark
"Casa Scînteii," a large building complex in northern Bucharest, built, in the style of the Lomonosov University in Moscow, during the communist period to house centralized press and publishing offices. Now called the House of the Free Press. The building is situated near Herăstrău Park, the largest green space in Bucharest.

33
[Saint Constantine] Brîncoveanu [1654–1714]
The ruler of Wallachia from 1688. The Brîncoveanu period witnessed an important cultural and artistic renaissance. Brîncoveanu was martyred by the Turks and subsequently canonized by the Orthodox Church in 1992.

33
Galatzi
A port town on the Danube.

Chapter Five

38
In every hollow could be found a god
Nichita Stănescu, from "The Second Elegy, The Gaetic," published in *11 Elegii* (1966).

47
boiled wheat and honey
Romanian *colivă* (Greek *kollyba*), eaten at Orthodox funerals and services to commemorate the souls of the dead.

Chapter Six

50
the absolute man of Romanian culture was the poet Eminescu
Romanian philosopher Constantin Noica (1909–87), much of whose work argues for the ontological uniqueness of the Romanian language, wrote

a book entitled *Eminescu, or Thoughts About the Absolute Man of Romanian Culture* (1975).

53
getting ready to build some blocks on the site
In the 1980s, the Ceaușescu regime demolished vast swaths of old Bucharest to make way for monotonous apartment blocks.

53
Knjaz
East-European medieval rank of nobility (Russian *knjaz'*, Romanian *cneaz*, Hungarian *kenéz*, etc., from Old High German *Kuningaz*).

Chapter Seven

55–56
His Holiness Father Teoctist
Toader Arăpașu (1915–2007). Teoctist was the name he chose on receiving the tonsure. He was Patriarch of the Romanian Orthodox Church from 1986 until his death.

59
Saint Andrew the Apostle
The patron saint of Romania and the Romanian Army.

61
Călărași
A town south of Bucharest, on the Danube.

61
Spiru Haret [1851–1912]
Romanian mathematician and politician.

Chapter Eight

71
întru
A Romanian preposition meaning, approximately, "within." There is an allusion here to the philosophy of Constantin Noica (see note above), in which this preposition becomes a unique ontological vehicle, a culminating stage in the history of the spirit, whereby Being uniquely articulates

itself through the Romanian language. Cf. *Devenirea întru ființă* [*Becoming Within Being*] (Bucharest: Editura Științífică și Enciclopedică, 1981, pp. 200–203), in a chapter entitled "The Meaning of an Ontological Closure": "What is astonishing in this preposition is the fact that it expresses a spatiality that is not at the same time fixity; and that, given that it is thus, it can take up within itself, as if within a matrix, almost all the other prepositions, with all their spatiality. In 'întru' is not just captured 'in'; likewise there is room for 'de la' (from), 'din' (out of), 'spre' (toward), 'sub' (beneath) and 'peste' (over), 'cu' (with) and 'fără' (without), 'lîngă' (next to), 'în jurul' (around) and 'prin' (through). What other languages are forced to express indirectly, in terms of prepositionality, is here expressed directly, with a preposition that takes up within it all the closures of the others, in order to bring them into opening. 'Întru' is thus the paradigm of the closure that opens. Ontological particles, such as the prepositions, converge within an ontological operator, which is 'întru.'" See Constantin Noica, *The Becoming Within Being*, trans. Alistair Ian Blyth, Milwaukee: Marquette University Press, 2009.

Chapter Nine

81
Isaia Faur
Real person. In 2000, Isaia Faur made the news when he broke through a security cordon and squirted ink over President Emil Constantinescu's beard.

Chapter Ten

86
Chișinău [or "Kishinev" in Russian]
The capital of the Republic of Moldova, formerly the Soviet Socialist Republic of Moldova, formerly the province of Bessarabia, part of Greater Romania until Soviet annexation during the Second World War.

88
Pastor Tőkés
The Hungarian pastor in Timișoara who triggered the protests that escalated into the 1989 Revolution.

89
the Fourteenth Army
The Fourteenth Army is stationed in the breakaway Republic of Transnistria/Pridnestrovie, which lies along the eastern border of the Republic of Moldova.

Chapter Eleven

95
like a linden flower within an abstract thought
A line from Nichita Stănescu's final volume of poems, *Noduri şi semne* [*Nodes and Signs*] (1982).

96
ideas current in sixteenth-century Transylvania
In Sibiu/Hermannstadt, Transylvania, in the sixteenth century, Conrad Haas (1509–76) built what seems to have been a three-stage rocket, to judge from the surviving manuscript evidence.

Chapter Twelve

103
Stand quietly in your places!
Staţi liniştiţi la locurile voastre! Ceauşescu's famous last words in his speech from the balcony of the Central Committee in Bucharest on December 21, 1989, shortly before his escape by helicopter, capture, and execution.

112
Professor Radu Pirgu
Gore Pirgu is a character in the novel *Craii de Curtea Veche* (1929; *The Rakes of the Old Court*) by Mateiu Caragiale (1885–1936). Pirgu is an unusual surname in Romanian. See the epigraph at the beginning of this novel.

118
Ciprian Porumbescu [1853–83]
A celebrated Romanian composer of Romantic and patriotic music. The national anthem of the Socialist Republic of Romania, in official use between 1977 and 1989, was set to the music from Porumbescu's song "Trei culori" ("Three Colors"). After the 1989 Revolution, "Trei culori" was felt to have been tainted by its communist associations and was replaced.

Chapter Thirteen

123
Anghel Saligny [1854–1925]
A Romanian engineer, a pioneer of reinforced concrete.

Chapter Fourteen

127
Petrache Lupu [1907–94]
A shepherd from the village of Maglavit who claimed to have spoken with God.

129
twenty-three million
The population of Romania in the 1990s.

Chapter Fifteen

136
House of the People
In the 1980s, Ceaușescu demolished an entire district of Bucharest to clear land for the pharaonic House of the People (now the Palace of Parliament). The gargantuan structure is the second largest building in the world, after the Pentagon.

137
The years have passed like clouds over the plain / And never will they come again
From a poem by Mihai Eminescu.

137
Let not God by His holy hand / Make us demand blood, not land! / When we shall no longer endure, / When hunger to revolt does lure, / Were you Christs, still will you be damned / Even in the grave!
From the poem "We Want Land!" by George Coșbuc. In his speeches, Ceaușescu frequently used to quote from poems by Coșbuc.

138
who strengthened Stephen the Great at Baia and the High Bridge, who gave succor to Brîncoveanu

Both Stephen the Great and Constantin Brîncoveanu (reigned 1688–1714) were sanctified by the Romanian Orthodox Church in 1992, during an upsurge in religious national feeling. Baia and High Bridge were two famous victories for Stephen the Great, against the Hungarians and the Ottoman Turks, respectively.

139
[Lucian] Blaga [1895–1961]
A major Romanian philosopher whose work was banned by the communists until after his death. Blaga translated Goethe's *Faust* into Romanian. He defended his Ph.D. thesis, in German, at the University of Vienna. Along with George Bacovia, Ion Barbu, and Tudor Arghezi, Lucian Blaga is one of the four most important modernist poets in Romanian.

141
unredeemed skeptic of a world in agony
These were the words Romanian philosopher Emil Cioran (1911–95) famously used to describe himself.

142
Revolution and Reform
A book by Ion Iliescu, published in 1993.

Chapter Sixteen

153
Saint Filofteia
A local saint of the Romanian Orthodox Church, whose relics are displayed in the church at Curtea de Argeş.

160
Stephen, Stephen, the great prince . . .
From a folk ballad collected and edited by Vasile Alecsandri (1821–90).

Chapter Eighteen

168
Hill of the Patriarchate
In central Bucharest, the highest point in the surrounding area.

Chapter Nineteen

174
Aldo Moro [1916–78]
Italian Prime Minister from 1963 to 1968 and from 1974 to 1976. He was kidnapped by the Red Brigades and murdered after one and a half months of captivity.

Chapter Twenty-one

184
The air, pure and free of dust . . .
Allusion to a nostalgic passage in *Rakes of the Old Court* by Mateiu Caragiale.

Chapter Twenty-two

193
Byzantium after Byzantium
The title of a book by historian Nicolae Iorga (1871–1940), who saw the Romanian-speaking lands as continuing the traditions of the Byzantine Empire after it fell to the Turks.

194
Voievod Ion the Terrible
Ion the Terrible (Ioan III or Ion the Armenian), *voievod* of Moldavia, 1572–74.

196
Behold me, for now I have reached thy door.
From a poem by George Topîrceanu (1886–1937) parodying the poetic manner of Tudor Arghezi's "Psalms" (1880–1967). The opening lines of the poem are as follows: *Behold me, for now I have reached thy door. / Hard flint, aloft, from the peak did I soar, / Thence, 'mid the obdurate rocks, did I thrust / Myself, with ankle bloodied, from the dust.*

■ □ ■ □ ■

WRITINGS FROM AN UNBOUND EUROPE

For a complete list of titles, see the Writings from an Unbound Europe website at www.unboundeurope.com/ue.

green
press
INITIATIVE

Northwestern University Press is committed to preserving ancient forests and natural resources. We elected to print this title on 30% post consumer recycled paper, processed chlorine free. As a result, for this printing, we have saved:

3 Trees (40' tall and 6-8" diameter)
1,386 Gallons of Wastewater
1 Million BTUs of Total Energy
84 Pounds of Solid Waste
288 Pounds of Greenhouse Gases

Northwestern University Press made this paper choice because our printer, Thomson-Shore, Inc., is a member of Green Press Initiative, a nonprofit program dedicated to supporting authors, publishers, and suppliers in their efforts to reduce their use of fiber obtained from endangered forests.

For more information, visit www.greenpressinitiative.org

Environmental impact estimates were made using the Environmental Defense Paper Calculator. For more information visit: www.papercalculator.org.